To my Angus Girls: Els, Luce and Georgie.
For all our adventures in the northern wilderness.

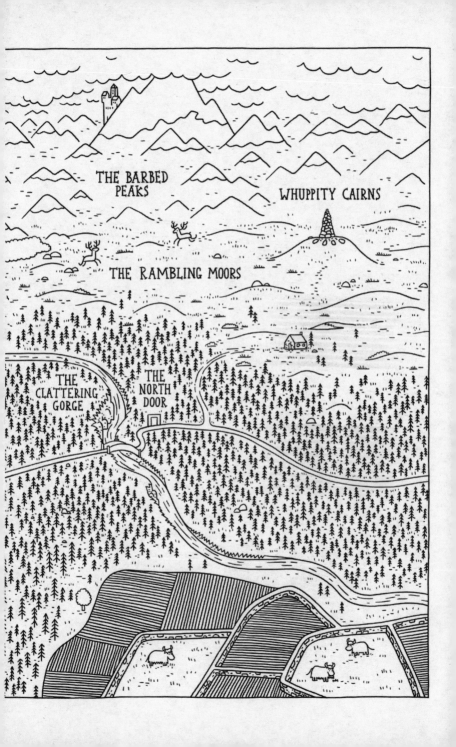

Prologue
The Rookery

Few remember the monastery. Carved into the face of a towering mountain, it perches above the surrounding peaks, its forgotten turrets twisting into the clouds. The Rookery, the people of the north call it. Once, monks were said to have passed through the courtyard into the cold, stone chambers. But the monks have long since gone and now only the rooks remain, huddled on crumbling ledges. Sometimes the birds launch off, circling the turrets like scraps of the night, and crying to each other with lonely *kaahs*. But mostly they are silent and still, turned inwards on the ledges, watching and waiting, because they know something the people don't. There is still somebody left inside.

In a dark room a figure sits on a stool before a spinning wheel, his robes silhouetted in the candlelight, his face half hidden by shadow. It is night outside the turret, but Wormhook has no intention of sleeping. Extending a hand towards the spindle, he lifts it from the wheel, then sifts through the strands of glittering black hair that have gathered

1

there. He glances at a rook watching from the open window.

'Hair belonging to the Guardians of the Oracle Bones,' Wormhook mutters. 'Spun with spider silk and a thousand nightmares from the depths of the Underworld to form the thread I need.'

The feathers on the rook's neck rise and shiver apart, but Wormhook only smiles. His face is covered by a mask of tattered sack with the eyeholes cut away, a slice for the mouth and straw straggling down instead of hair. He cradles the thread and, from inside an old wardrobe at the far end of the room, a hollow pummelling sounds. Placing his thread on the stool, Wormhook crosses the room.

'I am ready for you now,' he whispers, and he lifts the plank of wood that holds the wardrobe doors closed.

At first nothing happens and then slowly, quietly, two shadows slip out. They hang in the air like clouds of soot and the turret darkens. Then Wormhook walks back to the spinning wheel, sits on the stool and, with his thread in his lap, he summons the shadows closer.

They obey, gliding soundlessly across the room, while Wormhook plucks a needle from a sewing box at his feet and slips the thread through it. The shadows are suspended in front of him now, side by side, and he sets his needle through the first, then pulls it across to the second. His fingers rise and fall through the darkness, binding the two shadows together to form a jet-black quilt that shimmers silver in the middle where the stitches show.

Wormhook tucks the last of the thread into the quilt and

as it shifts up and down in a regular, trembling rhythm, he blinks coolly in the knowledge that his creation is now a living, breathing thing. He closes his eyes and listens. There are sounds coming from the quilt now, muffled and distant, but they are there, as he knew they would be, locked inside the thread: sobs, screams, gasps – echoes of nightmares snatched from the Underworld. Wormhook looks up and walks over to the window which sends the curious rook skittering into the sky.

'The girl and the beast may have destroyed four Shadowmasks and broken our Soul Splinter,' he says, and the eyeholes in his mask narrow at the stars above the clouds, 'but there are still two of us witch doctors left – two Shadowmasks armed with deadly curses – and, on top of that, we now have a weapon more powerful than anything that has come before.' Wormhook turns his back on the night and raises his hands. 'Behold the Veil!' he cries.

The quilt rises and Wormhook throws back his head and laughs. Then his voice drops to a purr.

'You, my precious Veil, will travel across the land, from the northern wilderness to the southern seas, spreading evil wherever you go. You will fill souls and minds with fear; you will break the spirits of the people so that they are ready to obey the Shadowmasks' rule when it comes.' He pauses. 'And once Orbrot has stolen Molly Pecksniff's impossible dream you will kill her and her wildcat! Then your power will be absolute and the dark magic will rise in all its glory.'

Wormhook points at the window and the Veil floats

through it before hanging in the darkness as it waits for its next command. The witch doctor places a hand on the turret wall and the rooks still gathered on the ledges outside spring into the sky, wheeling above the monastery in frenzied circles.

A crooked smile breaks across Wormhook's face and he leans out over the Veil. 'I can feel your hunger awakening,' he whispers, 'but you will need a rider – someone to lead you until you are powerful enough to lead yourself.'

The Veil shivers with delight and then it follows the witch doctor back inside the turret, on through the winding passageways.

Chapter 1
Eavesdropping

That same night, many miles south of the Rookery, a group of gypsies had gathered round a campfire deep inside Tanglefern Forest. Lanterns dangled from the branches of the oaks that lined the clearing, throwing light on a ring of colourful wagons and picking out the good luck charms scattered along their ledges: lemon peel, shards of mirror, fox teeth, iron nails.

The night was hushed and still. Clouds swallowed the moon and stars, foxes sat tight in their dens and even the owls were unusually quiet. Only the Elders of the camp broke the silence, a dozen of them huddled round the flames on upturned logs, with voices folded into whispers. Theirs was a conversation too dark for the children tucked up inside the wagons, but for the girl crouched just out of their sight on a branch overhanging the clearing, this muffled talk was most frustrating.

Moll scampered along the branch, straining her ears towards the murmurs, and behind her a wildcat followed with silent paws. They stopped halfway along the bough, two sets of green eyes blinking in the dark, while down below, Oak, the leader of the camp, took a sip of rosehip tea, then stoked the fire.

'We're running out of ideas,' he muttered. 'Moll can't throw the Oracle Bones to find the last amulet – everyone knows a Guardian only has one chance at that ... And Cinderella Bull, you say you've searched your crystal ball for answers without any luck?'

Across the fire, a very old woman nodded and, as she did so, the coins lining her red shawl tinkled. 'I've tried the orb again and again, and looked for clues in the tea leaves, but something's preventing me from reaching the old magic.' She paused. 'I think it's the Shadowmasks' curses; they're trying to stop us from finding this final amulet.'

The darkness around the camp seemed to inch closer and Moll shrank inside her duffle coat. It had been three days since they'd found the second amulet in a secret cave down by the sea and then fought off the Shadowmasks in a terrifying battle in the sky, but, every time anyone mentioned the witch doctors, Moll's skin crawled with dread.

'We need to wait for a sign from the old magic,' Cinderella Bull said eventually, 'here in the forest where our ancestors first heard the tree spirits and the water spirits stir.' The coins on the fortune-teller's shawl glinted in the firelight. 'The old magic will find us, even if I do not have the strength to find it.'

Oak took off his wide-brimmed hat and turned it over in his hands, then after a while he nodded. 'We'll wait for two days, but we can't afford to delay any longer. The Shadowmasks may have lost their Soul Splinter—'

Again Moll shuddered as she thought of the deadly shard of ice the witch doctors had used to kill her parents ten years ago.

'—and that might buy us some time,' Oak continued, 'but it won't be long before the last two witch doctors come for Moll. We need to cast a powerful protection charm to keep her safe.'

There were nods from the Elders and murmurings about spells involving hedgehog bristles, acorns and moonstones, but Moll wasn't thinking about her safety. Talk of the Soul Splinter had stirred unwanted memories inside her, thoughts so raw she felt her chest tighten. She had spent almost a month living as an outlaw in a seaside cave with her best friends, Alfie and Sid, and a few other members of the camp as they searched for the second amulet. But not everybody who'd set out on that journey had come back.

Moll tried to blink her thoughts away, but Alfie's final moments came crashing back to her: the giant eagle they'd ridden out over the sea together after they'd found the second amulet; Alfie destroying two of the Shadowmasks – Ashtongue and Darkebite – *and* their Soul Splinter so that she, Gryff and Sid could go on with their quest; and then Moll watching, powerless to help, as Alfie faded to a wisp in front of her before disappearing completely.

Moll closed her eyes. Alfie hadn't even been part of her camp at the beginning. He'd been living under the

Shadowmasks' command, a neglected orphan snatched into the folds of their dark and terrible magic. The witch doctors had used his tears in the making of their Soul Splinter and in doing so they had broken something deep inside Alfie that meant he could only be seen by those who believed in the old magic. To others, he was invisible, as if he wasn't even *real*. But he had torn free from the witchdoctors' clutches, he had helped Moll escape from a Shadowmask's lair and he had journeyed with her and Sid to find the first two amulets.

Moll sighed. She had come to regard Alfie as a part of Oak's camp, as someone whose loyalty could be counted on in the very darkest of times, and, though it had been a friendship forged in the unlikeliest of situations, it had been a friendship that mattered, one that had stamped a mark deep upon Moll's soul.

The wildcat beside Moll nuzzled into her side, as if he could sense her thoughts, and Moll tried her best to focus on what was happening down in the clearing.

Oak was standing and the Elders, a jumble of patterned headscarves, neckerchiefs, caps and tin cups, were looking up at him expectantly. 'All those in favour of waiting for a sign from the old magic, raise your hand.'

One by one, the men and women round the fire lifted their hands.

Moll turned an indignant face to the wildcat. 'We're not waiting, Gryff,' she whispered. 'Alfie's gone and I'm not just going to sit back and do *nothing*!' She spat the last word out with such force that she lurched forward on the branch and several Elders glanced up at the trees. Gryff shot a paw out to steady Moll, then he curled his black-and-white striped tail round her as the Elders turned back to their meeting.

'The old magic has never let us down before,' Oak said. 'We have to keep faith now.' He looked at the others. 'Does anyone have anything to add?'

Moll felt the unsaid words rise up inside her and without thinking she scrambled further down the branch.

'Yes!' she shouted, raising her body to full height. 'I have a lot to add!'

The Elders were on their feet at once.

'Moll?' Oak spluttered as his gaze fixed upon her. He turned to the woman beside him whose round face was framed with a spotted headscarf and two large hoop earrings. 'You said she was asleep, Mooshie!'

Mooshie blinked. 'I thought she was!' She narrowed her eyes through the dark at Moll. 'Do *not* jump from that tree, young lady!'

Moll lowered her body on to the branch then, with her arms and legs clinging tight, she swivelled beneath it before dropping like a furious raindrop into the clearing. She landed in a crouch just beyond the fire and, a second later, Gryff leapt down beside her and then slunk towards her wagon. Despite the bond he shared with Moll, the wildcat was a solitary creature.

Mooshie seized Moll by the shoulders, then brushed the

9

bark from her coat. 'This is only your second night back in camp and you're already stealing out of bed and swinging from trees!'

Moll shrugged Mooshie off. 'Waiting around isn't going to bring Alfie back. Or help us find the last amulet.' She threw up her hands. 'I'm the Guardian of the Oracle Bones and the Bone Murmur doesn't talk about sitting tight until things just happen – it talks about me and Gryff fighting back against the dark magic!'

The Elders knew the words of the Bone Murmur, the ancient prophecy handed down through Moll's ancestors, almost better than anyone, but, before they could say anything, Moll was off again.

'The Shadowmasks know how to drag the darkest curses from the Underworld across our land. They rotted fields and tore apart cliffs and beaches when they searched for me all last month – so what if Tanglefern Forest, *our home*, is next? They don't care what happens to our world!' Moll shook her head. 'And they don't care what happens to our friends and our families either! The Shadowmasks have taken my parents *and* Alfie already, and we know they're making a quilt of darkness – a weapon more deadly than the Soul Splinter – so they'll use that to take me and Gryff soon.'

Mooshie flinched but Moll went on.

'And then afterwards? There won't be an old magic, the goodness at the heart of all things, that's for sure. This world will belong to the Shadowmasks and to all the cursed creatures they conjure from the Underworld. I don't know

10

what their new world is going to look like, but I'm not waiting to find out. I'm going to find the last amulet – and I'm going to find Alfie. Because I made a promise to him,' Moll said firmly. 'I swore that wherever he went and whatever the Shadowmasks had in store for us, I'd go after him.' She lowered her voice. 'And I promised that I'd make him real – so that *everyone* could see him.'

Mooshie squeezed Moll's hand. After saying goodnight to Moll the evening before, she had heard the young girl whisper her promise to Alfie before turning off her light. 'It's not your fault that he disappeared,' Mooshie said gently.

Moll could feel a lump rising in her throat. None of the camp had dared voice the possibility that Alfie might be gone for good – that his disappearance might have meant something else – but Mooshie, who had raised Moll like her own child, knew the girl inside out and she understood that behind the desperation to find Alfie there lay a fear that he had gone to a place where Moll could not follow.

Moll glanced around, suddenly aware of the Elders watching her. She was surprised to see Oak's youngest son, Domino, among the adults – he was only in his early twenties so wasn't usually involved in such discussions – but she kept her gaze low and scuffed the ground with her boot.

Oak reached behind him and drew up another log. 'You don't exactly qualify as an Elder yet—'

'Because my legs still work fine and I don't need afternoon naps?' Moll muttered.

Mooshie gave her a quick thwack across the back with

her tea towel while Oak went on, '—but take a seat just for tonight and we'll answer any questions you have before we all head off to bed.'

Moll settled herself down between Oak and Mooshie.

'At least Siddy's following orders and getting a good night's sleep,' Mooshie sighed.

There was a nervous cough from beneath a blue wagon decorated with gold stars, then a boy with a flat cap sunk low over dark brown curls emerged sheepishly.

'I was going to sit it out under the wagon,' he said, shaking the mud from his cap, 'but it's actually quite hard to listen in when you're face down in the soil.' He dipped his head towards Moll. 'Didn't realise you were up and about too.'

Moll grinned at her friend. Things always felt better when Sid was around. He approached the fire, wincing as he caught sight of his mother shaking off a blanket and placing two indignant fists on her hips.

'Sorry, Ma,' he mumbled. 'But I couldn't sleep knowing the last two Shadowmasks will be coming for us soon. We can't just wait it out . . .'

Moll nodded. 'People wait for water to boil and rain to stop. They don't wait for dark magic.'

'So what exactly do they do, Moll?' Mooshie asked wearily.

Moll budged up to make room on her log for Siddy. 'They pounce,' she replied tartly. 'And they—'

Her words were cut short by a gasp from across the fire.

'Look!' Cinderella Bull whispered. 'In the flames!'

Moll watched the flickers dance, but saw nothing unusual.

'Look closer,' Cinderella Bull urged, 'with believing eyes, because it's not only the tree spirits and the water spirits who dwell within Tanglefern Forest.'

Moll's skin prickled. Was the old magic stirring? She leant in towards the fire and let her eyes travel up from the blackened logs to the twisting flames and the sparks flitting up into the surrounding trees. But she saw no sign of magic. She watched the Elders, their faces aglow in the firelight, their eyes locked on to something just out of her sight. Then she slid a look to Siddy who was also scouring the flames with a crinkled brow and, just as Moll was thinking that perhaps the old magic was only going to show itself to the Elders, she and Siddy saw it too.

Deep within the fire, like a scene stolen from another world, shapes were moving. They were not fitful and darting, like the flames around them: these images moved to a different rhythm. Moll held her breath as large clouds drifted across the heart of the fire, then melted away, and a huddle of houses appeared, still like stone amid the crackling flames. They slipped from sight and in their place were two hands clasped in greeting, which fizzled away to reveal a row of jagged peaks. Moll narrowed her eyes, trying to understand, then there was a bang, like a gunshot, as the fire snuffed out and the gypsies were plunged into darkness.

Domino leapt up and grabbed a couple of lanterns from the surrounding trees which he placed in the middle of the Elders' circle and Moll saw in their flickering glow that Cinderella Bull was smiling.

'The fire spirits found a way through to us for a moment before the dark magic forced them away,' the fortune-teller said. She turned to Moll. 'The old magic listens for the sounds that our ears miss – the straining of our hearts and the fear in our blood – and it heard the pain beating inside you tonight, Moll. That's why the fire spirits came.'

Moll felt her cheeks redden. 'What was the old magic saying? I saw clouds and houses – and hands and mountains!'

Cinderella Bull's eyes glittered. 'Not clouds, my dear, but steam. You have a train journey ahead of you. And the clasped hands, houses and mountains – they signify a meeting with strangers in the last village before the land grows fully wild. The northern wilderness – that's where the next part of your quest will start. That's where you will begin your search for the final amulet.'

'A train journey!' Siddy cried. 'I've never been on a train before, only horses and wagons. What a way to kick things off!'

But Moll wasn't listening. 'The northern wilderness . . .' she murmured, looking over her shoulder to see Gryff watching from the steps of her wagon. None of the camp knew where the wildcat had come from – he had simply arrived in the forest to keep Moll safe the night the Shadowmasks killed her parents – and he had been by her side ever since. But there was talk that wildcats came from the north and Moll had always wondered whether the wilderness was where Gryff really belonged. She swallowed. What if this last adventure was a journey to lead him home?

Cinderella Bull leant forward. 'Now the old magic has sent a sign, you must leave at dawn.'

Mooshie shook her head. 'The children need more rest and—'

'There's no time to spare, Moosh,' Oak interrupted. 'It's a two-day walk to the train line from here. They have to leave tomorrow.'

'*They?*' Moll said quietly. 'You – you aren't coming with us?'

Oak turned to Moll and Siddy. 'The old magic might have saved me from the Shadowmasks' cursed owls – their wings, all sharpened like knives and coated in poison, couldn't kill me back on the cliff tops – but ever since that fight my legs have been slower. And you need to be led by someone strong, someone fast, someone who can keep you safe.'

Domino crossed the fire and crouched before them and Moll suddenly understood why he had been called to the Elders' meeting.

'You're coming with us, aren't you?'

Domino nodded. 'I promised my pa I'd protect you, Moll. You, Siddy and Gryff – and that I'd do everything in my power to find the last amulet.'

Moll tried to imagine a journey to the northern wilderness without Oak, without the man who had taught her how to climb trees and fire a catapult. But the old familiar structures that had once held up her world were gradually falling apart. Alfie was gone, Oak would be staying in the forest and she and Siddy would be on the move again, away from the safety of their camp.

Domino twisted the spiked rings on his fingers. 'For what it's worth, I don't believe Alfie's gone either, Moll. We've got no proof, of course, but sometimes a feeling deep in your gut is all you need to find someone.' He paused. 'I know I'm not the same as Pa, but I'll help you bring Alfie home, I promise.'

Everything Moll had ever learnt about speed in the wild – how to outswim the river's currents, how to track the swiftest deer and how to run with wild ponies out on the heath – had come from Domino. And as she thought about those times and looked at Domino's face, the same dark hair, olive skin and kind eyes as Oak's, suddenly the shift from father to son didn't seem quite so strange.

The Elders began to clear away their upturned logs and tin cups, but Oak, Mooshie and Domino stayed with Moll and Siddy. Beneath the silent trees, they spoke of the northern wilderness and all that might be waiting for them there. And, when the rest of the Elders had gone to bed and only they were left, they wrapped arms around each other and, in the fragile shell of lantern light, Mooshie called upon the old magic to keep them safe.

Chapter 2
Stowaways

They set off at first light, their quivers filled with arrows and their rucksacks stuffed with blankets, food and water. The whole camp had come out to the edge of the forest to see them off, but it was Oak's and Mooshie's tear-stained faces that Moll held in her mind as she followed Domino across the heath and then past numerous villages and rivers before they stopped to spend the night in an abandoned barn.

The next morning they were up again at sunrise as they headed on through the countryside, but it was only as twilight fell on the second day and they found themselves on a bridge above the railway line that Domino explained the exact nature of the rest of their journey north. And that conversation had meant a drastic rethink for Siddy, who had spent a large proportion of the walk chattering about polished train carriages and leather seats.

Moll gripped the leather strap of her quiver, crouched low on the bridge and trained her eyes on the wall in front of her. She tried to count the slabs of stone to take her mind off the task ahead, but still her heart drummed.

'How long before it comes?' she whispered.

Beside her, Siddy straightened his flat cap. 'I don't think this is a good idea.'

'It was Oak and Domino's *only* idea, Sid. The station will be buzzing with policemen and ticket officers; there's not a chance they'd let us three *and* a wildcat on to a train for free.'

Siddy swallowed. 'Still, jumping on to a freight train as it shoots out beneath a bridge – it's not exactly how I imagined the journey . . .'

Moll glanced at Domino who was hunkered down behind the wall beyond Siddy. His duffle coat was fastened right up to his neckerchief and Moll knew that inside the pockets he had a pistol and a knife – he wasn't taking any chances.

'How long, Domino?' Moll asked again.

'The train left Congalton station at six and it takes half an hour to get here.' Domino checked his pocket watch. 'We've got ten minutes.'

Moll glanced at Gryff beside her, his muscles tense under his fur, his ears swivelled towards the undergrowth before the bridge, to the tangle of blackthorn, willow and knapweed. Moll could see nothing beyond the autumn leaves and branches scattered with berries, but she knew Gryff could. He could see and hear things humans couldn't. A rabbit hopped out of the bushes, its nose twitching, and the wildcat bared its teeth and hissed. The creature bolted and Moll smiled as Gryff moved closer to her. The wildcat's reactions were often unpredictable, but to her he was fiercely loyal.

Siddy took a deep breath. 'And we're absolutely definitely sure there's no other way of getting north except for throwing ourselves on to a moving train?'

Moll nudged her plait over her shoulder and turned to him. 'Come on, Sid. We've faced Shadowmasks, cursed owls and deadly eels before. Leaping on to a train is nothing compared to all that.'

Siddy picked at the cuff of his coat. 'It's just that starting the trip off with a train jump makes me a bit nervous about what to expect next . . .'

Moll scowled. 'This is not a *trip*. It's a mission.'

Domino put a finger to his lips. 'Shhh. Listen.'

Behind them the tracks were humming and crackling. A train was drawing close.

'Keep down or the driver will see us,' Domino whispered. 'But, when you see the steam, climb up on to the wall – it means the train is passing under the bridge and it's time to jump.'

Moll smoothed the sweat from her hands on to her trousers and then she waited, clutching the tiny gold boxing fists that hung from a chain around her neck, her talisman to ward off evil. She tried to steady her mind by thinking of the blackthorn growing either side of the bridge, how Oak would have carved a walking stick from the wood and Mooshie would have picked the sloe berries to make jam. But Moll's heart was now thumping and her thoughts were skittish.

A rhythmic chuffing began behind them, distant at first and then louder, closer, until the roar of wheels against steel filled Moll's ears. A horn blared, the bridge beneath them seemed to tremble, and then clouds of billowing steam hissed and puffed around them.

'Now!' Domino roared.

They all scrambled up on to the wall. Gryff followed and Moll felt her toes curl inside her boots as she fought for balance and then there, shooting out from beneath the bridge, was the train – a blur of freight trucks half hidden by steam. Moll's eyes grew wide. It was the fastest thing she'd ever seen, a bullet charging through the tangled undergrowth.

'Jump!' Domino shouted, leaping from the bridge with Siddy's hand clutched in his.

A split second later and they were gone, lost in the steam and the speed. Moll's body froze, seized by panic, and the bridge beneath her seemed to sway. Then she felt Gryff's body lean into her own, drawing out her courage. She bent her knees, clenched her teeth, and they jumped.

Moll's feet slammed on to metal and the force juddered through her bones before she flattened herself to the roof of the truck, her fingertips gripping hard and her eyes shut tight against the rush of wind. She'd made it.

Moll opened her eyes a fraction to see Gryff crouched beside her, his fur and whiskers rippled back in the wind. They were beneath the trail of steam now and were charging through the countryside, the brambles, cow parsley and nettles either side of the tracks just a blur of undergrowth as they sped on past.

Moll lifted her head. Siddy was sprawled face down two trucks in front, but Domino was now scampering over the roof on all fours in her direction.

'Come towards me!' Domino shouted above the chugging and the hissing of the train.

Moll pressed her palms on to the roof, let the wind stream down her neck and began to crawl. Gryff prowled by her side, keeping low, and, though the truck jostled and juddered, they kept moving towards Domino – hands and knees inching over the metal. But, when Moll reached the edge of the truck she was on, she peered down and gulped. There was a metre gap between her and Domino – and a racing streak of gravel and tracks in between.

'Give me your hand!' he cried.

Moll loosened her hold on the truck roof and held out one shaking palm, then the train jerked and she stumbled forward, her body lurching into the gap. But, in that second, two strong hands grabbed her coat. Moll's legs clanged against the metal couplings connecting the trucks and her heart beat double time, but Domino's fists tightened and he hauled her up on to the next truck. A moment later, she was beside him, and Gryff was pawing at her chest.

Moll sat up and blew through her lips. 'Thank you,' she panted. 'That could've been a disaster.'

Domino winked. 'I said I'd look after you.' He gestured

further along the carriage. 'I've got him to sort out now though.'

Siddy was still lying face down on the truck roof, his curls flapping in the wind. Moll scrambled towards him with Domino and Gryff.

'I'm not moving,' Siddy groaned as they drew close. 'I'm travelling all five hundred miles to the northern wilderness right here.'

Moll poked him in the ribs. 'I nearly died back there, Sid! You could've at least come and watched.'

Siddy opened one eye. 'You nearly die most days, Moll. I can't be there every time.'

Domino put a hand on Siddy's shoulder. 'We've got to get down inside this truck before we're seen – it'll be dangerous if there are bridges ahead.'

Moll nodded. 'Other train jumpers might land on you when they leap, Sid.'

Siddy forced himself up on to his knees. 'There are no other train jumpers, Moll. We're it. We're the only ones mad enough to hurl ourselves on to moving metal.'

Domino looked at Moll. 'I was meaning it's dangerous because the bridges ahead might be lower than the one we jumped from and we could be crushed.'

Moll was silent for a moment. 'That, too, is dangerous.'

The undergrowth either side of them gave way to gravelled banks and fields full of cows and Moll's eyes streamed as she took in the hedgerows and sycamores, bright orange in the sunset. A month ago trees and heath had been her whole world, then the Shadowmasks had started coming for her and Gryff and she'd discovered secret caves and waterfalls, she'd met a smuggler kid and a lighthouse keeper, and now – as they sped on through the fading light – there would be the north.

Domino inched towards the edge of the truck, then pointed down. 'There's a door here; if I can slide it back, we can hide inside.'

He lay on his front, bent over the bolt and pushed against it with his fist until it slid back and the door clanked open a fraction. Domino manoeuvred himself over the edge before nudging the door back a bit further and disappearing inside.

Moll followed Gryff into the truck and eventually Siddy clattered down after them. Then Domino pulled the door to, shutting out the whir of fields, farmsteads and steam. The compartment was dark and musty and filled with sacks of grain, but it was quiet and safe and, as Gryff slipped off into a shadowy corner, Moll and Siddy lifted the quivers from their shoulders and flopped down on top of the sacks.

'Well, it's not exactly as I imagined,' Siddy mumbled, 'but at least we're on our way north.'

Domino shook his rucksack open and reached for a chunk of bread. 'Moll's lucky to have you, Sid. There's aren't many friends who would come on a journey like this.'

Moll laid down her quiver and bit into her bread. Sid had followed her through everything, right from the moment the first Shadowmask, Skull, had come after her, and although his was a quieter sort of courage than Moll's, slow to build and sometimes shaky, it was invincible when it really mattered.

'You take a while to get into adventures, Sid,' Moll acknowledged, 'but once you're in you're pretty nifty.'

They listened to the train chugging north for a while and Moll hoped with everything inside her that Alfie was alive and that they were moving closer towards him.

'By dawn we'll be in Glendrummie,' Domino said, 'the northernmost village on the line. We should get some rest.'

Siddy tugged a blanket from his rucksack, threw one end to Moll and tried to get comfortable beneath it. '*A meeting with strangers in the last village before the land grows fully wild.*' He shuddered. 'What happens when things get *fully wild*?'

Domino loosened his neckerchief and leant back on the sacks. 'Pa says that beyond the North Door – the gateway to the northern wilderness that lies just beyond Glendrummie – there are miles of moorland with peat bogs that suck you down whole and great lochs as deep as the mountains are high. There are ospreys, stags and highland cows too.' He paused. 'And selkies and giants, if you believe the old stories.'

Moll thought of everything the Shadowmasks had done, of the pain that they had caused. 'We can handle all that,' she muttered.

Siddy groaned and then rolled over. 'I'm going to sleep.'

Chapter 3
Sneaking into Glendrummie

Moll woke suddenly. The compartment was no longer jostling from side to side – it was absolutely still, the chug of wheels and steam drained to silence. Moll felt a brush of fur against her arm and sat up, blinking into the darkness. Gryff's eyes, burning green in the shadows, shone back at her and she placed a hand on his back.

'Have we arrived?' she whispered, nudging the others awake. 'Is this Glendrummie?'

Domino crawled over the sacks, pulled the door back a little and peered out. Moll and Siddy stood up behind him and squinted through the gap.

It was still night, but they had pulled into a station. *Millbury*, the sign above the waiting room said, only just visible in the light of the lantern the man on the platform held. He was some distance away from the truck that they were hiding in, but Moll could see that he was dressed in uniform – a peaked cap and a large overcoat with shining gold buttons – and he was talking to a woman dressed the same way.

'Train drivers,' Domino whispered, 'Looks like one's finishing a shift and the other's taking over.'

Siddy settled himself back down on the sacks. 'Well, I hope the new one's a better driver. That man had no idea how to take corners; I'm bruised all over.'

'Look!' Moll hissed. 'There are more people on the platform – *lots* more people . . .'

A large group emerged from the waiting room: elderly folk hobbling on sticks and little children clinging to their parents' hands. They shuffled towards the drivers, and Moll, Siddy and Domino strained their ears towards the conversation.

'Congalton?' one driver scoffed. 'That's five hours south of here. You'll have to wait until tomorrow afternoon for the next passenger train.'

There were hushed whispers, then a woman's voice rose up – desperate, pleading. '*Please*. There must be a train sooner. We've fled from our homes beyond the North Door and walked for two days to get here. We've nowhere to stay!'

More words were exchanged and a small child began to cry. Then a driver's voice came, loud and firm.

'This is madness, all this talk of evil stalking the northern wilderness and forcing you out.'

'It's not madness!' an old man within the group cried. 'There's something poisoning people's minds as they sleep and we've seen it! A blanket of darkness covered our houses and our farms, and people woke jabbering like madmen. Grown men reduced to wrecks, children with haunted eyes . . .'

Moll glanced at Siddy, wondering if he was thinking the same as her. When the Shadowmasks murdered Moll's parents, they shaved their heads and, for a long time, Moll had never known why. But the second amulet had held her ma's soul and she'd told Moll and Siddy that the hair had been taken to be used as thread. *And, with it, the Shadowmasks plan to weave a quilt of darkness* – those were the very words Moll's ma had used. What if the 'blanket' this man was talking about was the quilt?

But before they could listen to any more a whistle shrieked and the train lurched forward. Once again they were off, bound for the northern wilderness.

Moll, Domino and Siddy sat in the shadows and for a while no one said anything.

Then Siddy took a deep breath. 'Moll's ma told us about a quilt of darkness. It can't be a coincidence.'

Moll ran a hand down Gryff's throat. 'But the Shadowmasks' magic has only ever been directed at those connected to the Bone Murmur. The witch doctors have stayed out of dealings with other people.'

'Until now,' Domino said. 'We need to stop them – for the sake of the old magic *and* for all the people living here. Just a couple more hours and we can speak with the villagers up in Glendrummie and see what they know. We've got to trust the fire spirits' message.'

Goosebumps peppered Moll's neck as she recalled the words of the man on the platform: *Grown men reduced to wrecks, children with haunted eyes.*

'What if the last two Shadowmasks have already reached Glendrummie?' she said. 'What if we're too late?'

'We've got to try,' Domino replied.

They lapsed into silence again and listened to the wheels rattling on and on into the night, then Siddy gave a resigned sigh. 'The whole country moves south, away from the danger, and we move north. Right into it.'

Moll pulled back on the pouch of her catapult and forced her voice to be strong. 'I hate following what other people are doing.'

Siddy lay back down and looked at the roof of the compartment. 'I miss him,' he said after a while. 'It feels all wrong going after the amulet without Alfie. We were a Tribe before – we broke rules, built dens and got stuff done – but now . . .'

Moll tried to reply, but the words choked in her throat.

Domino fumbled in his rucksack for a box of matches, then he struck one and light danced about the compartment. His face shone beneath it, stubbled and tanned from years of outdoor living. 'We're going to do this. All of us together,' he said. 'We're going to find the final amulet, we're going to destroy the Shadowmasks and we're going to find Alfie.'

They were only words, but they were the ones that mattered and the confidence of them burned bright in the gloom.

Siddy pulled the blanket up to his chin. 'I wish Porridge the Second hadn't turned down the trip,' he mumbled. 'All that slithering out of my pocket and burying his head in the soil. I mean, I can see why Hermit wasn't keen, what with the train being so far away from the sea and everything. But I expected more from Porridge.'

Moll smiled. Siddy's latest pets, a terrified crab called Hermit and a depressed earthworm called Porridge the Second, hadn't joined them on the journey north, despite Siddy's best attempts at getting them fired up, so he had been forced to soldier on without them. But Siddy always knew when to lighten the mood and Moll was suddenly glad of the friends she had around her.

Eventually they drifted off to sleep again and, when they stirred hours later, they woke to a crisp slant of sunlight streaming through a crack in the compartment.

Domino pulled back the door and whistled. 'Take a look at this.'

Moll and Siddy huddled behind him and gasped. It was like a different country out there. Fields rushed by, but they were no longer filled with haystacks or closed in by hedgerows. The landscape here was rugged – sprawling fields and tumbled stone walls – and everything was coated in a silver-blue frost that glinted in the dawn. Gates were dusted white, wild grasses had been stiffened and whole woods sparkled. Moll looked towards a forest in the distance. Even from the train she could see it was bigger than the one she'd grown up in – bigger and wilder somehow.

She glanced down at Gryff whose eyes were fixed beyond the trees, to where the valleys rose and fell, then built up into moorland that stretched for as far as she could see. The beast *from lands full wild*, the Bone Murmur called him, and as Moll looked upon this strange land she found herself putting an arm around Gryff. She understood that wild animals didn't belong to anyone, but, even so, the thought of Gryff returning to the northern wilderness without her made her want to hold him tight and never let go.

They passed a field full of horned cows with shaggy orange coats which Domino pointed out were highland cows, then they turned back into the compartment and began packing blankets into rucksacks.

'We'll need to jump from the train before we arrive at the station if we want to avoid being seen,' Domino said.

Moll climbed over the sacks and swung her quiver on to her back. 'What time will we reach Glendrumm—'

The train horn blasted.

They looked at each other, wide-eyed, then hurried back to the door. The train bent round a corner suddenly and there, no more than five hundred metres away, was the station. Domino's eyes flicked between it and the bank of frosty grass whirring past beside them. Then he lowered himself into a crouch.

'Jump!'

Sid's jaw fell open. 'Now?'

Domino leapt from the train, Moll and Gryff followed and then, finally, Siddy hurled himself on to the bank after them. The train careered away and, as Siddy dusted the frost from his coat, the others picked their way towards him.

'Train jumping before sunrise,' he muttered. 'What'll we be doing by midday?'

Moll tugged on a moleskin flat cap and the leather gloves lined with sheepskin that Mooshie had made for her last winter, then they clambered up the bank and over the stone wall into the field. There were no highland cows or sheep around, just a rusted trough glazed with ice and a few scattered clumps of bracken.

Domino handed round the last of the bread and nuts, then he pointed towards the other end of the field. 'We'll head for that copse of woodland. It's just past the station so we're bound to stumble across the road to Glendrummie beyond it.'

Moll nodded. They'd found the first amulet by following an Oracle Bone clue that Moll's pa had left for her and they'd unearthed the second using the reading Moll had deciphered after throwing the Oracle Bones herself. But now they were on their own, with only the fire spirits' fleeting message to go on. Moll pulled the collar up on her coat and crunched over the frost after Domino.

'It's so quiet up here,' Siddy said as he drew level with Moll and Gryff.

She listened for the coos of the wood pigeons or a robin's trill, but she heard nothing. The landscape was mute and what had seemed almost magical before now made Moll's stomach churn. It was only autumn and yet the countryside around them was on the edge of winter.

She looked at Domino. 'I knew it was going to be colder in the north, but frosts in early autumn – that doesn't seem right . . .'

Domino nodded. 'I'd been thinking the same. Something's amiss.'

Siddy tightened his grip on the bow slung over his shoulder. 'When we were down by the sea, the Shadowmasks sucked whole woods and farmlands of life. What if this is the same?'

They glanced to their right to see the train pulled up into the station. Heads down, they carried on walking into the copse of fir trees, tall and dark around them, until they came across a dirt track. Moll placed one hand on her catapult, the other on her bow, and turned down it with Gryff by her side.

'Glendrummie,' Siddy murmured as they passed a sign on the side of the road with bold lettering stamped above a painting of a white plant with wiry brown stems.

'White heather,' Moll said. 'Mooshie told me you only get it up here in the north – it's meant to grant luck and protection, I think.'

Domino took a deep breath. 'Well, let's hope it does.'

Where the fir trees ended, the village began. Stone cottages with slate roofs and green doors lined a wide track and behind them frosted gardens glinted in the sun. Parked along the kerb were several carts and empty horse traps and, as the group walked on, they spotted narrow side streets leading to smaller roads fringed with cottages. They carried on walking, past a cluster of shop fronts with CLOSED signs hanging in the windows and striped awnings jutting out above: *Glendrummie Grocers, Bel's*

Butchers, The Tweed Tea Shop. There was a church too, further down the road, its steeple climbing high above the rest of the village. But there was one thing very obviously missing.

'Where are all the villagers?' Siddy whispered.

Moll scanned the cottages, but the windows were shuttered and every door was closed – some had even been barred with planks of wood – and a heavy silence hung over everything.

'It's like a ghost town,' Moll murmured, reaching a hand down to Gryff's back.

Domino twisted the rings on his fingers. 'They can't *all* have left. Can they?'

Moll gritted her teeth. 'The old magic told us to come here – it's the only lead we have.'

She glanced towards a cottage on her left, then frowned. There were no shutters on the upstairs windows and she could have sworn she glimpsed a movement behind the glass. Moll blinked and looked again, but there was nothing and so, shaking her head, she walked on.

They made their way through the village, the sound of their boots scuffing the track coarse against the silence. And then they heard a sound that made their blood run cold. It was quick and sharp, like silk being ripped. Only it wasn't silk. It was something much, much worse and Moll and Siddy had grown to fear that sound almost as much as the Shadowmasks themselves. The noise came again and Moll's spine pricked with sweat.

The air was tearing. Invisible thresholds were opening in

the sky all around them. Gryff snarled. He knew as much as Moll and Siddy what that meant.

In moments, the Shadowmasks' dark magic would pour in from the Underworld.

Chapter 4
Dark Skies

G ryff's hackles rose and Moll swung her bow down from her shoulder, grabbed an arrow from her quiver and nocked it to the string. Siddy did the same while Domino drew out his knife. Then they waited, braced for the owls or the wolves – whatever cursed creatures the Shadowmasks had conjured to kill them.

But what came was very different.

The weathervane on top of the church spire creaked, then a large cloud rolled over the sun and the village grew suddenly dark. Slowly, the arrow on the weathervane began to turn, grating round and round even though there was no wind.

'Wh – what's happening?' Siddy stammered.

The world turned darker still as more clouds pushed across the sky and the air closed in around them, brooding with an unspoken darkness.

Moll blinked back her fear. 'Whatever's out there, we can fight it.'

Gryff growled, pacing a circle around her.

There was a moan of thunder in the distance which,

seconds later, spilled through the village into rumbles so loud they burrowed inside Moll's bones. Then the sky opened and rain poured down.

Moll wiped the water from her eyes. 'Maybe – maybe it's just a storm,' she spluttered. 'And we've got to sit it out.'

Siddy shook his head. 'But the thresholds – we heard them opening. There'll be worse to come than this.'

The rain fell faster – harder – until what seemed like litres and litres of water were bucketing down from the sky. Moll stood against it, poised with her bow, but no creatures advanced towards them and no masked figures appeared. Only the rain clattered down, churning the track to mud, and with every breath Moll took she felt the water clawing its way in through her lips and snaking into her ears. The sky grew darker still and the thunder bellowed, but this time there was something sinister in its call – something intended just for Moll. She gripped her bow tighter as a single word groaned through the thunder: **MOLLY**.

Domino stepped in front of Moll, shielding her with his arms. 'The Shadowmasks have sent this storm because they know you're here. They can't be far away now.'

Moll's eyes darted around, but only the rain thrust down, smacking against her skin, needling through her coat.

Domino lowered his knife. 'Get under the shop awnings! We need to make a plan!'

They charged across the road, spraying mud and water up over their boots, then they crouched together in front of a shop, their clothes soaked through.

36

Moll narrowed her eyes. 'We can take them – whatever they bring. We—'

The wind came out of nowhere – sudden, wild and raging with menace. It slid beneath the shop's awning, buffeting them from every angle and shaking the glass in the windows.

'Hold on to each other!' Domino yelled.

The awning trembled, its metal poles clanked and Moll wrapped one arm round Siddy's waist and the other over Gryff's back. Shutters clanged, a pot plant crashed to the ground and the awning tore off into the sky.

Then, before anyone could react, the storm snatched Moll.

She screamed as the wind wrenched her backwards, sending her flying into the track. Sharp gusts followed, whipping her legs over her head and dragging her face down through the mud. Gryff charged through the water, then set his teeth into Moll's coat and yanked her over. Her face was smeared with dirt and she was gasping for air, but the wildcat steeled his body against the wind, shielding Moll from its force, until Domino and Siddy could pull her back up. Again the wind roared and the rain pelted down and Domino wrapped his arms round Moll, claiming her as his amid the gale.

'You can't beat me with a storm!' Moll shouted at the sky.

But even she knew this wasn't an ordinary storm; the Shadowmasks hadn't finished with them yet.

'The cart on the side of the road!' Siddy shouted. 'We can hold on to it!'

37

Heads down, they battled up the street towards the wooden cart. Gryff slid beneath it, out of the wind, and Moll and Siddy clung to the sides while Domino looked up and down the street. His eyes grew suddenly large.

'Look!' he yelled. 'In that cottage across the road! People!'

Sure enough, a family was peering out from a gap in the curtains framing an attic window. But, as Moll took in their pale faces and haunted eyes, she shivered. She had seen fear before – Siddy's expression in the face of the Shadowmasks' owls, Alfie's look when he discovered the truth about his past – but this was as if fear itself had crippled the villagers' bodies.

'There's – there's something not right about them,' Moll cried.

'Stay here and hold on to the cart just in case these people *are* mixed up in the Shadowmasks' magic,' Domino gasped, 'but my bet is that they're scared, just like us.'

He ran through the rain towards the cottage and hammered on the door. No answer. He yanked the knob, then pushed hard, but it wouldn't budge and, as Domino shouted and beat his fists against it, Moll and Siddy watched the people slip away from the window and draw the curtains across. Reeling backwards, Domino tried the next door, and the next – but every single one was locked. He looked back at Moll and Siddy.

'There are people hiding in this village!' he cried. 'Someone will let us in – surely?'

The storm seethed and Moll felt the wooden planks of

the cart burn into her fingers as the wind tried to yank her free.

'We need to help Domino look!' she panted.

Siddy bit his lip. 'You saw those people, Moll – all thin and hunched with eyes full of terror. Something dreadful's happened to them and they could be bound up in the Shadowmasks' magic for all we know.' He gripped the cart harder. 'I don't think we'll be any safer inside.'

Moll groaned. 'We can't just wait here until the witch doctors come for me!'

As if in response, a clap of thunder ground out Moll's name a second time and then the rain drummed down even harder and great balls of hail clattered down from the sky. They pounded against Moll's head and stabbed at her cheeks, but she clung to the cart and watched as Domino battled his way towards the church. He ducked beneath the porch, out of sight, then emerged a second later.

'Over here!' he roared. 'The church door's open!'

Moll and Siddy lunged into the hail, their arms wrapped tightly around each other's shoulders as they waded across the mud track with Gryff to the church. Domino bolted the door behind them, then they collapsed on to the wooden pews, clutching their hail-bruised faces. It was cool and still inside the church as if the mighty stone walls might be enough to hold the storm back.

'Are you OK?' Domino asked, wiping clumps of mud from Moll's trousers.

'The villagers,' Moll stammered. 'It's more than fear that's keeping them inside their homes. Sid and I saw it in their faces.'

Siddy brushed the hailstones from his hair. 'Something dark has happened here.'

Domino nodded. 'In the last cottage I tried I saw a couple rocking on the floor, their skin so white they could have been ghosts ... That's what made me turn back towards you both.'

The thunder pealed and Gryff stalked a circle around Moll's legs, his ears flattened to his head.

'We're not safe,' Moll muttered. 'Gryff can sense it. We need a hiding place.'

They staggered down the aisle, past the stained-glass windows lining the walls, right up to the altar at the far end. Outside the thunder boomed and the hail slammed down, then there was a flash and the whole church brightened for a second before plunging back into gloom.

'Lightning,' Moll whispered.

Siddy's shoulders bunched. 'There *must* be somewhere safe we can hide.'

Once more the church lit up and as Moll looked through the stained-glass windows she saw bolt after bolt carving up the sky.

'We need—'

An almighty crash drowned out her words as the two windows either side of them imploded, sending shards of glass hurtling inwards. The group charged back down the aisle, their arms folded across their eyes, as the next set of windows exploded in a shower of glass around them. But there was no time to check if everyone was OK. Window after window burst, as if the glass itself was chasing them back through the church. They ran faster, the sound of shattering glass ringing in their ears, until they threw back the bolt on the door and burst out of the building beneath a sky scarred with yellow.

They shrank back beneath the porch. Domino's hand was bleeding, Siddy's coat had been ripped and the fur on Gryff's leg was stained red. The lightning struck again, hitting the church and sending a chunk of stonework crunching down towards Moll. But Domino threw himself against her, knocking her out of the way, before leaping aside as the slab smashed to the ground. Gryff limped towards Moll who held him close.

'We can't fight the storm,' Moll panted. 'We can't run from it either. We need protection – somehow.'

The lightning crackled on.

'The last cottage on this side of the road that you didn't try.' Moll squinted through the hail and pointed to it. 'It has flowerpots outside it and it looks like they're filled with white heather.'

Domino frowned. 'Why does that mean we should trust the people inside or even that the door will be open?'

Moll forced her words out, the bare bones of a plan in the face of a howling storm. 'Mooshie said heather was a protection charm, remember? Maybe we'll get inside that cottage and – maybe – we'll be safe there.'

Siddy huddled closer to the group as another peal of thunder tore across the sky. 'It's our only option, isn't it?'

41

Domino braced his body. 'On three then.'

They gripped each other's hands, Gryff narrowed his eyes and they forced their way up the road. The wind hollered in Moll's ears, hail beat at her face and forks of lightning pierced the sky, but every muscle in Moll's body was steeled against the Shadowmasks' magic.

'Faster!' she cried.

They raced on towards the cottage, right up to the terracotta pots filled with heather lining the front wall. There were no shutters over the windows or boards across the door, but there was no sign of life from within either. Moll gripped the doorknob and hoped hard as she turned it. There was a click and Moll's heart leapt, then the door opened and the group charged inside before pushing the door shut against the pummelling hail.

The sudden quietness of the house surrounded them: the rocking chair on their left motionless by the fireplace and a clock ticking faintly above it. There was a threadbare rug in front of them and a rickety table to their right surrounded by copper pans and cooking utensils hanging from the walls. Moll breathed deeply. Perhaps the house was deserted. Perhaps this really was a haven from the Shadowmasks' menace and they'd be safe until the storm passed.

And then Siddy began to edge back towards the door. 'The table's set for four people . . .' he whispered to Moll.

It was at that moment the stairs beyond the rug creaked and Moll's stomach flipped as a man very unlike the villagers they had glimpsed came into view: broad about the shoulders, ginger-haired, dressed in tartan. And in his hands he held a shotgun. He clicked the safety catch back.

'Let's be having you, then,' he muttered.

~~ Chapter 5 ~~
An Unexpected Clue

Siddy dropped his bow to show that he meant no harm and Domino took a tentative step forward.

'We're—' he started.

Moll nudged Domino aside and pulled back on her catapult. 'Let's be having *you*,' she spat.

Siddy turned an appalled face to her. 'What are you *doing*?'

Moll blinked. She had no idea what she was doing. The catapult had just seemed like an obvious reply to the situation.

'We came in here for protection,' Siddy hissed. 'Not a fight!'

The man on the stairs stepped down on to the flagstones. He was small but stocky – two ginger-haired legs set firmly apart beneath his kilt, hands tight fists around his gun and hair so red and wild about his face it looked as if he had rusted a little at the edges. Moll gulped as she took him in properly. There were few things more worrying than small, angry people – and she would know.

'Who are you?' the man grunted. 'And why are you in my house?'

'We're from the south,' Domino said. 'We needed shelter from the storm and when we saw your protection charm – the white heather – we thought perhaps you could help us.'

The hail outside had eased off and the wind had dropped, but the man looking down the barrel of his gun wore all the fury of the gale in his eyes. 'Did you bring this evil with you?' he growled. 'The storms and the quilt and the madness it brings? This darkness has attacked our town for the last three days,' he took a stride towards them, 'but today I swore I'd keep my door open so that I could fight this menace once and for all.'

Siddy shook his head. 'We're here to fight it too.'

The man snorted, then curled a finger round the trigger of his gun.

'Please! We don't mean any harm,' Domino cried. Then he dipped his head and very quietly uttered a word that Moll had never heard before: 'Sìth.'

For a few moments, only the water dripping from the gypsies' clothes on to the flagstones filled the silence and then, to Moll's surprise, the man lowered his gun and, at the top of the stairs, a woman and two ginger-freckled children, a boy and a girl, appeared.

Moll frowned at Domino. 'What . . .'

'The northern word for peace,' Domino whispered. 'It's a promise you won't fight. Pa taught me – and it's a little friendlier than a catapult.'

45

The red-haired man placed his gun against the wall, but his expression was still guarded. 'How does a southerner like you know the rules of the north?'

'My pa spent some time working on a farm down south with a family who had come from up here,' Domino said. 'They taught him about their customs and my pa shared some of his . . .'

The red-haired man stiffened. 'His . . .?'

'We're gypsies,' Domino went on. 'And we come in peace.'

He raised his palm slowly and then folded it into a fist and crossed his chest. Moll and Siddy exchanged looks; the ways of the north were so different from the ways of their woodland world.

'And the wildcat?' the man asked warily.

Moll puffed out her chest. 'He's with us. And he also comes in peace.'

The man eyed the group for a few moments and then eventually he too lifted his palm and crossed his chest with his fist. 'I'm Angus MacDuff and this is my wife, Morag, and our twins. We haven't had newcomers to the village all month – more people leave than arrive with these dark goings-on. And then you stop by and we have the worst storm yet. What's all this about?'

Moll thought of the villagers she'd seen huddled in their houses and felt herself hovering between trust and watchfulness. But Angus and his family kept a protection charm outside their house and seemed bent on forcing the dark magic back, so surely they were people Moll could confide in? She thought back to Cinderella Bull's words: *a meeting with strangers in the last village before the land grows fully wild . . . that is where the next part of your quest will start.* Perhaps this was what she had meant. Moll's heart quickened. She knew she had to act fast because the Shadowmasks would be on to them now they knew she was in Glendrummie.

'It involves magic,' Moll said.

Angus threw up his hands. 'Well, of course it blinking well does! A figure slipping a quilt of darkness through bedroom windows at night and people waking up jabbering in fear about a Veil and someone called the Night Spinner!'

'The Night Spinner . . .' Moll's voice was barely more than a whisper as she glanced from Domino to Siddy. 'Do you think he's one of the last two Shadowmasks?'

Siddy twisted his flat cap in his hands and looked at Angus. 'Did – did anyone see the Night Spinner's face?'

Angus's eyes narrowed. 'Masked, they say.'

Moll stretched a hand down and felt for Gryff.

Domino took a deep breath. 'What else do people say?'

Angus shifted his weight from one foot to the other. 'That a masked man comes in the dead of night, riding a veil of darkness. They say it feeds on people's souls and leaves only fear behind.'

Morag shook her head. 'It's as if something inside each victim dies, as if they're locked in a dreadful curse. They won't eat; they barely drink. They'll be dead in days if we can't find a cure.' She paused. 'And they speak of worse to come – of an eternal darkness that we must all obey when the Night Spinner reaches his full power.' She looked at her husband. 'Our guess is that these storms are the start of something much, much worse. Neither the people nor the land are safe . . .'

Moll's shoulders crept higher. 'The last two Shadowmasks are working together,' she whispered. 'One commanding the Veil, the other conjuring storms. I'm sure of it.'

Angus started forward. 'Shadowmasks? What do you know about all this?' His voice rose. 'Tell us!'

Before Moll could answer, Morag took the twins' hands and led them down the stairs to stand level with her husband. 'Come, Angus – this doesn't sound like it's going to be talk for the children. They need to eat and if our visitors are here to fight this dark magic, as they say they are, they'll want warming up with some food, too.'

Angus puffed out his chest to show that he wasn't finished with his new guests yet, but Morag pushed past him.

'No need to pretend, Angus dear.' She hurried to the sink where she wet a cloth, then passed it to Domino to clean the blood from his hand. 'Once they know you spend your spare time baking scones and playing the church organ, they'll see through all the bravado.'

Angus's ginger eyebrows twitched and the twins giggled, then he walked towards the fire, his kilt swishing crossly around his knees. Before long, flames crackled in the hearth and Moll's, Siddy's and Domino's coats were laid out on the drying rack in front of it. The storm outside had passed and Morag assured the group that her heather charm would protect them from the dark magic for a while longer, but still Moll felt on edge.

Gryff slunk beneath the rocking chair, licking his bloodied fur clean before biting into the meat Morag tossed him from the larder and, as the twins watched the wildcat, wide-eyed, from beneath the window and Morag busied herself over the stove, Moll, Siddy and Domino sat down around the table with Angus.

Domino lowered his voice. 'The Shadowmasks are a group of six witch doctors bent on spreading evil and, from what you say, it sounds as if the final two are behind the Veil and the storms.' He paused. 'There was a prophecy years and years ago—'

'The Bone Murmur,' Angus cut in. 'I've heard talk of it before – from those beyond the North Door.'

Siddy nodded. 'It speaks of a girl and a beast fighting back to restore the ways of the old magic.'

Moll sat up straight. 'I'm the girl.'

Angus raised his eyebrows. 'After the catapult episode, I feared you might be.' He glanced towards the window. 'Past the North Door people have always believed in the old magic. Giants in the mountains and selkies by the sea . . . But this side of the door, many people have forgotten all about it. The recent storms have killed crops and flattened houses, and most have put it down to an early winter, but when talk from beyond the North Door reached us – of a dark magic stirring – a few began to believe once again in the Bone Murmur and the need to protect the old magic.'

Siddy leant forward. 'You believed, didn't you? That's what saved you from the Veil when it came!'

Angus ran a hand over his hair, then he nodded. 'Those who ignored the warnings from beyond the Door and refused to believe in the power of the old protection charms awoke after the Night Spinner's visits as frightened husks. But the storms keep raging and the Night Spinner keeps coming, as if it's searching for something just out of its reach.'

Moll swallowed. She knew exactly what the Shadowmasks were looking for . . .

'You say the Veil has the power to hold victims in a curse,' Domino said slowly. He looked at Moll beside him, then across the table at Siddy. 'The Shadowmasks trapped their own souls inside the Soul Splinter and used it to spread their evil before, but, now that weapon is gone, perhaps this Veil holds the last two witch doctor souls.'

Moll looked down. 'They'll try and use the Veil to kill me and Gryff. The storms are just a way to hold us here until the Night Spinner comes . . .'

Domino swung an arm round Moll's shoulder and held her close. 'I won't let anyone hurt you, Moll. I made a promise in the forest, remember?'

Morag bustled in between their chairs, offering everyone a plate of piping-hot potatoes, vegetables and a lump of something brown and grainy. The twins ran over, hands outstretched for their plates, but Moll eyed her portion nervously.

Morag rubbed her shoulder. 'Neeps, tatties and haggis. Proper northern food.' She sat down at the table with them. 'So, you say you're here to fight this dark magic?'

Moll nodded. 'We've already fought back four Shadowmasks and it sounds like we're up against this Night Spinner and whoever is conjuring up the storms now . . .'

'How did you get rid of the other Shadowmasks, then?' Angus asked.

'Amulets,' Siddy replied, his mouth full of food. 'We used two of them to help destroy the first four Shadowmasks.'

Morag looked at Angus. 'Just like the Bone Murmur foretold . . .'

Moll nodded. 'There's only one amulet left now, but I'm hoping we can use it to kill the last two witch doctors.'

Angus's face brightened. 'Where is the amulet?'

Domino leant back in his chair. 'We don't know. We came north looking for it.'

'Well, what do the amulets look like?' Morag asked.

Siddy shifted. 'The first one was a jewel that contained Moll's pa's soul. The second was a giant eagle.'

'It held my ma's soul and we freed it so that it could pass safely to rest in the Otherworld with my pa's.'

'So really the amulet could be anything at all?' Angus said slowly.

They carried on eating in silence for several minutes, then Gryff emerged from beneath the rocking chair. No one except Moll noticed, but the wildcat's whiskers were twitching and his eyes were fixed on the front door.

51

Moll's hands stalled over her plate. 'Gryff's seen something,' she whispered.

The group watched as the wildcat paced across the room and then leapt up on to the windowsill. The twins scurried back behind an armchair and Gryff looked out on to the street, his tail low to the ground. After a few minutes, he turned to Moll and dipped his head.

Domino stood up. 'What's he saying, Moll? Is there danger out there?'

Moll watched the wildcat intently as he slipped down from the sill and wound his way between her legs.

'No,' she breathed. 'But I think he's seen something important.'

Angus stood up. 'I'll take a look. I'd better see the damage out there anyway. There'll be folk needing stonework repaired and awnings mended even if they're too terrorised to know it . . .'

He walked over to the door and as he pulled it open Moll's insides stiffened. What if she'd misread Gryff's signs? What if the final Shadowmasks had already gathered on the road and the Night Spinner had come to finish her and Gryff off once and for all? But as Angus glanced up and down the track he didn't look alarmed. Instead, he bent down and picked something up and, frowning, turned back into the cottage.

'The track's churned up, the church spire is in pieces and there's damage to almost all of the cottages.' He paused and looked at Moll. 'But it turns out your wildcat did see something – because there's also this.' He held out a rolled-up piece of parchment bound with twine and Moll noticed that it bore her name in green, swirling ink. 'Looks like someone left something for you after the storm. Someone who knew you'd make your way here.'

Moll shrank back in her chair. 'What if it's from the Shadowmasks? It could be cursed!'

Siddy raised an eyebrow. 'If the Shadowmasks want to kill you, Moll, they're hardly going to write you a note first.'

Moll took the parchment, turned it over in her hands and then untied the twine. As the paper unfurled, a leaf slotted inside the folds fluttered loose and dropped to the floor. Long and thin with serrated edges, Moll recognised it immediately.

'Willow,' she murmured. Then she glanced at Siddy. 'You don't think . . .'

Moll's mind whirled. Could this be a letter from Willow, the Oracle Spirit who had helped them when they were searching for the second amulet? Moll looked down at the dozens of symbols on the parchment – triangles resting on squares and circles filled with stars – laid out as a border around the words. Gryff leant into her legs, willing her on to believe.

'Oracle Bone script,' Siddy gasped.

'It's a message from the old magic – from Willow, I think,' Moll said quietly.

Domino moved his chair closer to Moll's. 'Well, what does it say?'

Moll's eyes flitted from one line to the next, then she read the words aloud:

'My dear Moll,
I am sorry that I cannot be with you in person. The Shadowmasks are doing everything in their power to stop the old magic from communicating with you now. But I am sending this letter with the wind spirits in the hope that it reaches you.
The last two Shadowmasks will not rest until their Veil has broken the people's spirits and their storms have ravaged the land. Snow and ice will follow the rain soon and, if you fail to stop them, the Shadowmasks will take the sun, ruling over our world in an eternal night.'

There was a tremble in Moll's voice now as she thought of Morag's words about the victims who spoke of the eternal darkness to come, but she carried on reading:

'The next full moon, in just five days, will be the brightest one since the first Guardian threw the Oracle Bones many years ago – and as it sinks a New Order will be born. You must find the last amulet before then. Because, if your quest fails, the sun will not rise again and we will be plunged into the darkness of the Shadowmasks' reign.

To find the Amulet of Truth, I know only this: that you must **steal the last note of the witches' song, then take a feather from burning wings and you'll find what you need one hundred years deep.**

Those are the words the old magic is pressing upon my heart, Moll. So travel boldly and know that I am willing you on every step of the way.

Your friend,
Willow x'

Domino looked from Siddy to Moll and, despite the threats hanging over them, his eyes lit up. 'We're in with a chance now.'

Chapter 6
The North Door

Moll blinked at the words on the parchment. 'Steal the last note of the witches' song? Take a feather from burning wings? It doesn't make *any* sense.'

Siddy took the letter and read the clue aloud again, but Domino was looking at Angus. A glance, only a split second long, had passed between the ginger-haired man and his wife, but Domino had seen it.

'You know what Willow's clue means, don't you?' he said to them.

Angus walked over to the fire, placed another log from the wicker basket on to it and sat down in the rocking chair. He creaked back and forth, but said nothing and Moll noticed Morag was avoiding their eyes as she cleared the plates away.

'Please tell us,' Domino said. 'The Shadowmasks will know Moll and Gryff are here now and you heard what Willow said about the next full moon – we haven't got much time.'

Morag ushered the twins up the stairs then looked down at the others. 'I know nothing of burning feathers and what

56

you might find one hundred years deep, but Angus will tell you what we know about witches.'

She disappeared after the children and Angus looked into the fire. 'Beyond the North Door lies the Clattering Gorge,' he said, 'a river that winds down from the moors and runs through a silver birch forest before flowing past Glendrummie. We used to fish for salmon there and the twins climbed trees and built dens in the rhododendron bushes. But all that changed recently.'

'Go on,' Moll said.

'The witches appeared a few weeks ago when stories of the dark magic started circulating from those beyond the North Door,' Angus said. 'A family was fishing down by the river, but only the mother returned to Glendrummie. Heartbroken, she spoke of women emerging between the trees, beautiful young ladies who played music so enchanting it lulled her family to sleep. She awoke by chance – a mother's instincts perhaps – to find her family gone and these women, these witches, running away through the woods.'

Siddy's eyes widened. 'And we've got to *steal the last note of the witches' song*?!'

Moll clenched her fist round the parchment and thought of Alfie, of the villagers poisoned by the Veil, of *all* the people they needed to help. 'We should sneak out of Glendrummie now – while it's light – and before the Shadowmasks conjure another storm.'

Angus reached for a jar on the mantelpiece and drew out three sprigs of white heather. 'One each,' he said, handing them round. 'They'll keep you safe until the North Door at least – but, beyond that, it'll take more than heather to ward off the dark magic.' He tossed an extra sprig to Moll. 'For your wildcat, though he'll have to carry it between his teeth. Morag will fix you up some food and blankets and—'

There was a rap at the door and Moll jumped.

Domino darted to the window and looked through. 'People from your village, I think,' he whispered to Angus. 'A woman and two children.'

Moll craned her neck towards the window and gasped. The woman's face was full of life, but her children's were sucked of colour. Purple circles hung beneath eyes that bloomed with terror and Moll gulped as she took in the Veil's victims. But why had the woman been spared the Night Spinner's curse?

Angus joined her at the window and, on seeing the three figures, he hung his head. 'Fiona lives just up the road. She believes in the Bone Murmur and she tried to place pots of white heather around her house, but her husband didn't have time for the ways of the old magic and he threw them away. The Veil poisoned him and their children two nights ago. Fiona was spared because of the sprig of heather she kept beneath her pillow, but her family won't eat or drink or speak any sense, so Fiona can only hope we'll find a cure . . .'

Moll turned to Domino as Angus went to open the door. 'I know I said we should get going, but we can't just up and leave these people,' she whispered. 'They need our help!'

They watched the children on the doorstep muttering under their breath, their voices strangled by gasps. 'The Veil is hungry,' they chorused, 'and it will be back. Soon all will bow down to the Night Spinner's eternal darkness.'

Fiona clutched Angus's hands. 'We have to find a cure – somehow – before my children lose their minds completely.'

Moll looked from Siddy to Domino. 'One of us needs to stay,' she said. 'The Shadowmasks sent the storm that destroyed this village because they knew me and Gryff were here. If we hadn't come, maybe these folk would still have their homes to hide in.'

Domino paced by the fire. 'I could stay and help rebuild the cottages. Perhaps, together, Angus and I could find a cure to help those poisoned by the Veil.' He paused and turned to Moll. 'But I can't let you face the witches alone – I swore to my parents that I'd protect you, that I'd look after you like an older brother should.'

The kindness of Domino's words cradled Moll and, although the sense of belonging, the force of family, made imagining leaving Domino almost impossible, Moll could feel Fiona's pain and hear the desperation in her heart, and she knew what had to be done.

'You should stay, Domino,' she said. 'I've got Sid and Gryff and a whole quiverful of arrows.'

Domino placed his hands on Moll's shoulders. 'But what if something were to happen to you? Or to Siddy? I couldn't bear it, Moll.' He shook his head. 'Pa wouldn't want me to leave you alone.'

Siddy stepped forward. 'The fire spirits told us our quest would start here.' He nodded towards Angus who was hugging Fiona. 'Well, our quest isn't just about us now. We need to look out for others too, and finding this last amulet is just as important as Domino helping these villagers.'

For a moment, Moll felt her heart wobble. She didn't want to leave Domino – it had been hard enough saying goodbye to Oak and Mooshie – but there was something growing in Siddy's voice and it made her feel bolder.

'Plans change,' Siddy went on, 'but our promise to fight this dark magic doesn't. So we keep going – we fight from all sides now – because that is our new plan and it's the right thing to do.'

Domino watched Fiona's children shivering outside the cottage, then he turned to Moll and Siddy, taking in their mud-streaked faces. 'These people need me,' he said. 'But, the moment I've helped rebuild their homes and done all I can to search for a cure, I'm coming after you.' His eyes met Gryff's wild stare. 'All of you.'

And Moll knew that those words were a promise, one made with all the love and loyalty of an older brother.

Hands curled round sprigs of white heather, they walked out of the ruined village together. Sycamore branches lay strewn across the track, hacked from trees by the storm, and shadows fell over the frosted fields either side of them as the sun dropped behind a forest. Occasionally a pheasant croaked from a thicket and a woodcock stirred, startled by

Gryff prowling through the bracken to the side of the track, but otherwise the countryside was quiet. The hail and rain had stopped, no carts trundled past and not a soul stirred from the cottages scattered along their way.

'*The last note of the witches' song* . . .' Moll whispered to Siddy as Domino discussed plans with Angus ahead. 'We don't even know what we're looking for, not really.'

Siddy straightened his flat cap. 'No, but I don't think many people do at the start of the journey. They sort of find out halfway through.'

Moll pulled her scarf tighter around her neck and thought of the clue they'd unravelled to find the second amulet. It had been just as scrambled and yet somehow, together, they'd managed to work it out.

She carried on walking as a skein of geese honked above her, a V-shape gliding on against the darkening sky, until eventually Angus stopped on a humpback bridge. A large river gushed beneath it, browned by peat from the moors and boxed in by steep slopes of rock that led up to woodland on either side.

'The Clattering Gorge,' Angus said.

Moll watched the water rush over jutting stones and froth beneath waterfalls. *Even the rivers are wilder up here*, she thought.

Angus walked over the bridge to the stone wall on the left-hand side of the track which ran alongside the road and masked the Clattering Gorge from sight. The others followed and then stopped behind him as he paused before a large wooden door set into the wall. Animals had been carved into it – stags and eagles mostly – but there was a wildcat too, and on seeing it Moll glanced down at Gryff. Another reminder that he belonged beside remote rivers and icy fields, not at the side of a girl in a forest hundreds of miles south.

'The North Door,' Angus said. 'The gateway to the northern wilderness.'

Domino handed Siddy a satchel that Morag had filled with food, water and a blanket, then he put an arm around Moll and Siddy's shoulders as Gryff stalked behind Moll's legs.

'This is where the next part of our journey begins,' Domino said. 'And, although things aren't as we expected them to be, we're still a team and we'll fight, on both sides of the North Door, to force this dark magic back.' He squeezed Moll's and Siddy's shoulders. 'However frightened you are or however desperate things seem, remember that you have beaten Shadowmasks before. You have fought against the creatures of the Underworld – and won. So, stick together at all times, at all costs – and, as you fight alongside each other, know that not so far away I'll be fighting too.'

Siddy swallowed and Moll ran a hand over Gryff's back.

'You're braver than you believe and stronger than you know,' Domino said. 'And, if I had to pick two people in the world to force this darkness back, I would choose you two.'

Moll tried to reply, but words couldn't hold in all that Domino, Oak and Mooshie meant to her. She hugged him fiercely, proudly, and with a hope that in that embrace Domino would feel the love that her heart struggled to voice.

'Once you have the last note of the witches' song,' Angus said, 'follow the path that runs above the gorge right out on to the Rambling Moors. You'll come to a bowl in the hills where you'll find a bothy – a cottage – and when you get there ask for Aira MacDuff. Aira's my sister and she's in charge of the Highland Watch, a group of people from Glendrummie – believers in the old magic – who swore to try and safeguard the north and force any dark magic back after the witches appeared last month.'

Moll stretched out a hand and turned the knob, but the door didn't budge.

Angus smiled. 'We use a blessing for safe passage to open the North Door.' Then he lowered his voice to a whisper and said:

> 'Young and old, wealthy and poor,
> Keep them safe, past the North Door.'

At Angus's words, the handle turned of its own accord and the door opened, scraping back on rusted hinges. Before them lay a narrow path, a dark snake winding beside silver birch trees on the right and rocky banks that plunged down to the river many metres below on the left. Moonlight filtered through the branches, dusting the scene in a cool pale light and, as Gryff looked through the door, he let the heather Moll had insisted he carry between his teeth drop to the ground. Moll tucked her sprig into her pocket and rested her hand on the bow slung over her shoulder. As Angus had said, they'd need more than protection charms beyond the North door.

Gryff stepped up to the threshold, ears pricked, whiskers twitching, then he looked back at Moll, dipped his head and slunk inside. Moll followed with Siddy, then she glanced over her shoulder at Domino one last time. She held the memory of him tight, of his large brown eyes willing her on, then the North Door clicked shut behind them and she turned to face the Clattering Gorge.

Chapter 7
The Witches of
Clattering Gorge

Moll strained her eyes into the trees as they walked. Long, thin trunks wrapped in silver bark, they gave nothing away, no sign that anyone might be lurking between them. Their roots sprawled down to the path where woodrush and moss began, and beyond that the river roared, a dark churn beneath the moonlight. Moll watched as a salmon leapt upstream, its flimsy body nosing through the water. She closed her eyes for a moment and tried to read the wind's spirit, like Cinderella Bull had taught her, but it sounded different here – hollow, like air blown through the top of a bottle. Every now and again, Gryff stopped, ears cocked, muscles taut, but the forest around them seemed empty. If there were witches here, they were keeping themselves hidden.

They walked on and on and the further along the path they went, the brighter the trees seemed to shine. Leaves sparkled like crystals against the darkness and, on the far side of the gorge, the birches looked as if they were coated in frost. Moll stretched out a hand and touched a leaf. It felt cool beneath her fingers – and stiff.

'Sid,' she said slowly. 'The trees ... they're not ordinary birches. They're not even made of wood. They're *silver*.'

Siddy ran his palm down a trunk and gasped. Moll was right. The bark was cold and hard, like a marble pillar. 'That's why the wind sounds different here,' he murmured. 'Because it's slipping between metal not leaves ...'

Moll adjusted the quiver on her back. The forest was beautiful – like a world frozen by moonlight – but trees made of silver meant there was an enchantment involved and if the witches were near it was bound to mean dark magic.

Moll dropped her voice until it was barely a whisper. 'Keep your eyes open, Sid. The witches could be close.'

They walked over a bridge covered in lichen that crossed a stream leading down to the river and, though Moll tried to focus her mind on the dangers that could be hiding in the Clattering Gorge, she found herself thinking of Alfie. Where had he gone when the Soul Splinter shattered? Down into the Underworld, forever a prisoner of the dark magic? Or was he here, somewhere in her world? Something inside Moll, perhaps just the feeling deep in her gut that Domino had spoken of back in the forest, made her feel as if Alfie was still here – that somewhere his heart was still beating and his thoughts were turning – but would finding the amulet mean undoing all the curses the Shadowmasks had conjured? Would it mean bringing Alfie back to life as someone who could be seen by everyone, not just by those who believed in the Bone Murmur?

Moll tried to hold her friend's face up in her mind, tried to remember his blue eyes and scruffy fair hair, his jay feather earring and old leather boots, but with each day that passed the image seemed to fade and with it a rising sense of panic trembled inside Moll.

'Look at those nests!' Siddy murmured as they stepped off the bridge back on to the path. 'They're *huge* . . .'

Moll pulled herself free from her thoughts and glanced up to where Siddy was pointing. Within the branches of the birch trees were large bundles of sticks. Like the rest of the forest they were silver, but they were bigger than any nest Moll had ever seen – bigger than a crow's or a buzzard's, bigger even than an eagle's eyrie.

'What kind of bird would live in a nest like that?' Moll asked.

Siddy shivered. 'I'm not sure I want to find out. Let's keep walking.'

The path wound on beside the gorge and, at first, Moll thought it was just the wind that she could hear, rustling through the metal trees. But, when Gryff stopped and growled, she strained her ears past the roar of water and the thudding of her heart, and then she heard it too. There was another sound in the forest, one not made by the river or the wind or the trees.

Moll grabbed Siddy's arm. 'Listen.'

They stood still on the path and, after a moment, they heard it more clearly. Music. Chords that started low and soft, like wind sighing in the hollows of a valley, then they faded and in their place notes rippled and slid.

Siddy bit his lip. 'Is that the witches' song?'

'It must be. But,' Moll's eyes flitted between the birch trunks, 'I can't see anyone.'

The music swelled and softened around them and with every note Moll felt a strange sleepiness close in, a fog inside her mind that seemed to swallow all her thoughts. She shook her head, remembering Angus' words about the family who had been lulled by the witches' music and then taken.

'Don't listen to the music, Sid.' Moll raised her hands to cover her ears. 'Keep walking and be ready to grab your bow.'

Moll concentrated hard on her impossible dream, on the only thought powerful enough to unlock the Oracle Spirit inside her arrows. *To make Alfie real*, that was her dream, and Moll knew she'd need to believe in it with every fibre in her body to bring the Shadowmasks' magic down.

Gryff stopped abruptly, his tail low to the ground. He'd seen something. Moll lifted her bow from her shoulder and, trying to ignore the music, she fitted an arrow to the string and looked into the trees. Set back from the path, beyond a cluster of birches laden with large silver nests, was a folly, a half-ruined temple of stones entwined with ivy. There were walls still, and long, rectangular holes where windows might once have been, but the roof had long since fallen in. The music was louder here – a crystal-clear melody that reminded Moll of water trickling – and it whispered to her that there was nothing to fear. She blinked again and again to keep herself awake and beside her Siddy yawned and even Gryff moved slowly, almost clumsily, through the trees.

'We've got to follow this music,' Moll said firmly, 'without getting trapped under its spell. And then we need to . . .' Her voice trailed off.

'Steal it,' Siddy finished for her.

It sounded ridiculous out loud – impossible even – but they had to try. Gryff shook himself, then prowled into the bracken and, with their bows raised, Moll and Siddy followed.

The music grew louder, throbbing in their ears and rolling through the silver birches. Every note seemed to soothe Moll's nerves and more than once she found herself yawning, but she swallowed the tiredness and pressed on between the trees until they were all outside the folly together, crouched beneath a window.

With an arrow still set to her bow, Moll lifted her head above the stonework. There were no witches huddled inside, singing; there were no people at all. Instead, in the middle of the folly, there was a grand piano with its lid propped open. Nettles grew around it, ivy twisted up the legs and moss clung to the strings splayed out under the lid. But the strangest thing about this piano was that *the instrument was playing by itself.*

Siddy peered over Moll's shoulder, his eyes wide. 'Where are the witches?'

'I don't know,' Moll whispered.

But she knew enough of dark magic to realise that just because the witches couldn't be seen didn't mean that they weren't there. The two children watched the piano notes rise and fall.

'How do we steal their song if they're not even here?' Siddy hissed. 'We can't just make off with a piano!'

Gryff growled behind them, a low, throaty sound that rose with the fur on his back. Moll and Siddy whirled round and the music grew louder and more discordant, the notes jarring and clashing before rising into a hideous roar that stamped out Moll, Sid and Gryff's drowsiness in an instant. But then, from the nests in the trees around them, shapes began to stir. Orange talons curled over the sticks and feathered legs crawled out, long and thin and black.

'B – birds?' Siddy stammered.

Dark hair followed the legs, spilling all the way down to the ground, and then female faces appeared, together with more talons where hands should have been, and porcelain skin with lips as red as rowan berries.

'Witches,' Moll breathed and her body tightened with fear.

Chapter 8
The Last Note of the
Witches' Song

Siddy backed up against the folly wall and fumbled with his bow, but Moll's instincts were quicker and she pulled on the string, thought of Alfie and her promise to make him real – then fired at the closest nest.

The arrow struck the silver twigs and the Oracle Spirit burst out from its tip, a cocoon of white that swelled around the nest and sent it hurtling to the ground. But the witch had moved fast and was now in Moll's sights, gliding down towards them, a cloak of crow feathers trailing behind her.

'Fire, Sid!' Moll yelled as she placed another arrow to her bow.

The witch slid nearer, her body slick with feathers, her talons outstretched towards Moll's face. The piano music grew louder and wilder, but Siddy mustered up his impossible dream just in time, sending an arrow straight into the witch's chest. She screeched as the Oracle Spirit ballooned around her, but all about the folly more and more witches emerged, floating through the trees towards them, their long black hair hanging down like oiled nooses.

'They're not armed; they've just got talons!' Moll cried, pulling back on her bow again. 'We can beat them!'

Gryff leapt forward, digging his claws into a witch's cloak and dragging her down, then Moll let an arrow thrum from her bow to finish the creature off, but still more witches advanced. Back to back, Moll and Siddy let their arrows loose while Gryff lashed out with his claws to give them time to reload.

Three witches landed between the trees in front of them and prowled closer, their feather cloaks rustling through the leaves, their lips split into terrible smiles.

'One each,' Moll muttered, closing an eye against her bow.

Siddy fired at the first, Gryff leapt towards the second and then Moll took down the third, but no one noticed the fourth witch crawling over the wall behind them.

Until Moll screamed.

Talons sank into her shoulders, then she was yanked upwards into the air.

'Moll!' Siddy roared.

Moll writhed and kicked, but the witch's talons gripped hard and together they lurched through the trees, back towards the path. Heaving against the claws, Moll blinked terrified eyes into the forest. She couldn't see Siddy or Gryff any more and, as the witch flew on over the path, Moll realised where she was being taken. A birch tree leant out from the path right over the gorge and perched among its highest branches, hanging some fifty metres above the river, was the biggest nest Moll had seen yet. She twisted and jerked, but the talons only wedged deeper into her shoulders, tugging off her scarf before letting it drop helplessly into the water.

The witch landed in the upper branches of the tree before hurling her prisoner down into the nest. Moll felt the metal twigs grate into her spine, but she struggled up, heart pounding. The sides of the nest surrounded her like the bars of a cage and even on tiptoe Moll couldn't see over them. She tried to ignore the remains of half-chewed bones scattered at her feet and the witch crouched by the side of the nest, running her tongue over crimson lips.

I can climb out, Moll thought, *and find Gryff and Sid.*

Her eyes flitted to the gaps between the silver twigs. She could make out the river – just – but it was raging far below. One wrong move and she'd be plunging to her death.

'Thinking of going somewhere?' the witch crooned.

Her voice was slippery, as if her words had been coated in grease, and as she spoke she ran her talons through the bundle of hair in her lap. Moll started backwards as she suddenly realised why her scarf had been hurled into the gorge, but in the flick of a wrist a noose of black hair unravelled towards her and closed firmly round her neck. The witch snickered as she reeled the hair in, dragging her victim across the nest until Moll was left gasping beneath her talons. Still the piano blared out into the Clattering Gorge and Moll ripped at the hair, her nails scrabbling to free herself. But, every time she moved, the noose tightened.

The witch sniggered. 'It's no use trying to fight, girl, because even if you do break free from my nest you can't beat us all. You're outnumbered and, so long as the piano plays, we witches will descend from our nests.'

Moll stood still, panic rooting her to the spot, and that's when she saw Gryff – a blur of black-and-white stripes between the gaps in the nest – moving down the birch branch towards the witch.

There were shrieks from somewhere nearby – high-pitched, strangled laughs – and Moll glanced through the twigs to see the rest of the witches gathered on the path.

'The beast is giving himself up to you, sister!' one squealed. 'See how he walks right into your hands.'

But Moll knew Gryff: he would have no intention of giving himself up to the witch's power. Gryff had a plan and Moll needed to work out what it was ... She scoured the twigs and then her eyes fixed on something glinting among the bracken set back from the path. It was the tip of an arrow poised on a bow and when Moll saw it her heart leapt. Siddy. *That* was the plan. While Gryff caused a distraction, Siddy was going to bring down the witch. The only reason he hadn't done so already was because he was waiting for Moll to see him – so that she had time to find a way to cling on to the tree when the nest plummeted into the gorge. Moll eyed the branch that the witch had settled on. Somehow she needed to grab hold of it.

The witch rocked back and forth above her. 'Come along, beast, there's more than enough room for you in my nest too.'

Moll watched as Gryff stopped on a branch a few metres from the witch, his eyes green slits against the darkness.

'Scared, are you?' the witch laughed, but, as she lifted one talon off her bundle of hair to beckon the wildcat closer, the noose around her victim's neck slackened and Moll seized her chance.

Bucking backwards out of the loop of hair, Moll scrambled up the side of the nest. Siddy's arrow sailed through the air, just as Moll jumped towards the branch and grabbed hold, then the Oracle Spirit hit its target, sending the witch and her nest crashing down into the gorge – and leaving Moll clinging on to the tree.

Moll's heart thundered as she took in the river frothing and churning below, then she clamped her arms and legs round the branch, as Domino had taught her, and hauled herself towards Gryff. As soon as she reached the wildcat, she held him tight, whispered a *thank you* into his fur and, though her neck was throbbing with pain, together they hurried down the tree.

The witches on the path launched themselves into the air and again and again Siddy fired to keep them at bay. But Moll knew what she had to do now, knew the one thing that would stop the witches coming.

'They're controlled by the music!' she yelled as she charged through the bracken towards Siddy. 'That's why we have to steal the last note of the witches' song! As long as the piano plays, the witches will crawl down from their nests!'

With Gryff at their side, Siddy and Moll raced through

the trees, sending arrows out at every angle to clear a path back to the folly. Moll tried her best to ignore the pounding in her neck as they ran – whatever the witch's noose had been made of, it hadn't been ordinary hair – but there was no time to worry about that now. They burst into the folly with the witches on their tail, clawing through the windows and climbing over the roof.

'Sid, you and Gryff hold them back!' Moll shouted. 'I'll deal with the music!'

But even as she said the words she had no idea how to stop the piano from playing. She watched the keys rise and fall as the music boomed around them and then, heart hammering, she pressed her hands down on the keyboard to try and smother the song. But still the piano played. The music grew louder, angrier, almost as if it could tell that someone was trying to force it back.

'Quick, Moll!' Siddy cried as he slotted yet another arrow to his bow and Gryff pounced on a talon that clawed through the window. 'We can't hold them back much longer!'

'There must be a way,' Moll panted to herself.

She skirted round the side of the piano and looked inside. Dozens of thin steel strings stretched the length of the instrument and little hammers struck each one as a note was played.

'Steal the last note of the witches' song . . .' Moll murmured. She thought of Alfie suddenly, of how he always thought clearly, carefully, even under pressure. She needed him now and the longing inside her beat wildly, but Moll's thoughts were reeling and it was instinct alone that made her dig inside her coat and draw out a knife, the one her pa had left her, from the belt around her waist. Bracing her body against the din and the shooting pains in her neck, Moll hacked at the silver strings. One by one they snapped and with every chord that was cut the music dimmed.

'Keep going!' Siddy yelled. 'It's working! The witches are disappearing!'

Moll looked up and sure enough there were fewer witches clawing at the folly now. She brought her knife down again and again until there was just one witch circling the wall and just one chord, the very lowest note, left inside the piano. Moll thought back to Willow's letter. *Steal the last note*, it had said – not hack it to pieces – and, as it thronged deep and strong like the first rumblings of thunder, Moll bent over the open piano and snicked her knife carefully through both ends of the string.

The music stopped and the witch climbing over the wall let out a blood-curdling shriek and then faded into nothing. Moll glanced from Gryff to Siddy and for a moment all three of them just stood, panting, unnerved by the sudden silence.

And then, eventually, Siddy lowered his bow. 'You did it!' he gasped, looking at the strand of shining silver in Moll's hand.

Moll leant against the piano and rubbed her neck. 'No, *we* did it. You and Gryff saved me in that nest – the witch almost finished me.'

They staggered out of the folly to find that the trees were

no longer silver. They were ordinary birches now that the enchantment had been broken, but the Shadowmasks' magic had rotted them through: bark peeled back in dead flakes and branches bulged with fungus.

Moll looked down at the piano string in her hand and her stomach lurched. There was nothing there. The last note of the witches' song had disappeared, along with the forest enchantment.

The battle had been for nothing.

Chapter 9
The Cursed Noose

'But – but I had it,' Moll stammered. 'The string was right here in my hand!'

Gryff hissed and scanned the nearby trees, but Siddy bent closer to Moll's palm. Her fingers were unfurled with nothing inside them, but still Siddy squinted, turning his head this way and that.

'It's still there,' he said quietly. 'When the moonlight catches it, I can see it – but only just.'

Moll brought her hand up to her chin. Her neck still ached, but she forced the pain down and tilted her head – and there it was, a long thread, as fine as spider's silk and almost completely invisible to the naked eye. As she moved her palm behind a birch trunk, out of the moonlight, the string disappeared, but, now that she knew it was there, Moll could just feel it brushing against her fingers.

'That piano string's magical and for some reason Willow meant for us to have it,' Siddy said, stooping to pick up an arrow from the ground. 'Keep it safe, Moll – I've got a feeling

79

we'll be needing it to find the amulet, even if it doesn't make much sense to us now.'

Very carefully, Moll wound the string round her fingers, but, as she did so, she realised something. The string just went on and on, encircling her hand as if there was an infinite length of it being conjured out of thin air.

She gasped. 'Sid, it's – it's *endless*!'

They huddled together in the moonlight and Siddy watched as Moll twisted more and more of the thread into a ball.

'It comes out of nowhere . . .' Siddy whispered.

Moll stopped winding and the string stayed at its new length, a small shining reel, then she tucked it into her coat pocket and buttoned it up tight.

'It's magical all right,' she said.

Siddy smiled. 'Now we need to follow the next part of Willow's clue: find the *feather from burning wings*.'

Moll bent down to pick up the rest of her arrows, but, every time she moved, the pain in her neck stung. It wasn't the kind of ache you might get from a bruise: this was sharper. It had bite. She sat down on a tree stump, wincing as she touched her skin, and Gryff leant into her, rubbing his head in circles against her knees.

'Are you OK?' Siddy asked.

'I'll be fine.' Moll turned away. She knew Siddy was only trying to help, but Moll didn't like fuss or attention or having to admit that she was hurt. She pointed back towards the path. 'We need to head on to find Angus' sister, Aira – she'll be able to help us find this feather.'

But Siddy knew his friend inside out and he walked round to face Moll. His eyes widened. 'Your neck!' he cried. 'It's covered in blisters! Why didn't you tell me?'

Moll buried her head in Gryff's fur. 'It'll be fine,' she mumbled. 'Probably.'

Siddy shook his head. 'Remember Oak's leg? It just looked like an ordinary cut at first, but the owl wings were cursed – that's what made it so much worse.' He bit his lip. 'What if it's the same thing with the witches' hair? They were conjured from the dark magic too, Moll.'

He drew out a flask of water from his satchel, dampened a handkerchief, then passed it to Moll. She raised it to her neck and tried not to flinch as the moisture seeped into her skin.

'Any better?' Siddy asked.

Moll clenched her jaw and Siddy knew that she was still in pain, but was too proud to admit it.

He crouched in front of her. 'Before we left Tanglefern Forest, Ma told me about a few of the remedies they use up in the northern wilderness that might help us on our journey. Now, what was it she said . . .?' He thought for a moment. 'Eating a mouse cures bed-wetting; victims of whooping cough should be passed beneath the belly of a horse . . .'

Moll threw up her hands. She was tired and in pain and Siddy was only making things worse.

He prattled on, desperately trying to remember. 'If you cut the fingernails of a baby before they're one year old, they'll be a thief; if—'

'Enough, Sid!' Moll snapped. 'None of that's going to help!'

She kicked out at a twig, suddenly cross with the world and everyone in it. 'If Domino was here, he'd know what to do. Or Alfie. They'd have listened properly and not been useless like you.' The words escaped Moll's lips before she could wind them in and instantly she regretted them.

Siddy's face reddened; he pulled himself up and then, to Moll's surprise, he stormed off into the trees.

Moll went to call out to get him to come back, but then she felt a familiar hardness close up inside her. 'Fine!' she shouted. 'I'll just sit here and wait for you to shake off your stupid mood. That's fine. Just *fine*. It's not as if we have anything *important* to do! Like halting an eternal night or anything!' She wound her hair into a knot as Siddy disappeared between the silver birches, then she turned to Gryff. 'He's such a child sometimes.'

But the way the wildcat looked at her, his head cocked to one side, his eyes wide against the night, made Moll feel guilty instead of cross. She forced the feelings away and rocked back and forth; the pain in her neck was worsening. Minutes drifted by and she hunched her shoulders against the cold and glanced around for Siddy. But he was nowhere to be seen. The night belonged to the animals now: the shriek of a tawny owl and a fox pushing through the briars.

Moll thought of the last two Shadowmasks somewhere beyond the forest. They'd be on to her now the witches had been beaten and she was alone in the trees because Siddy had wandered off. She began to plan what she'd say to him when he returned – how she'd list her complaints on her fingers so that he could see *exactly* why she was mad at him. But, as more time passed and still Siddy didn't return, Moll's heart quickened. What if he'd walked all the way back to the North Door to find Domino? What if he was in trouble?

Moll took off her moleskin cap and turned it anxiously in her hands as she remembered Domino's words: '*Stick together at all times, at all costs . . .*' She bit her lip as the night crept closer around her.

Chapter 10
Secret Cures

The sound of sticks snapping made Moll whirl round. Gryff snarled and rose to all fours, but then Siddy emerged through the bracken, soil streaked down his trousers and scratches criss-crossing his face.

'Oh, it's you,' Moll said, trying to hide her relief.

Siddy nodded. 'Yes. It's me.'

Moll got ready to rattle off her speech, but then Siddy thumped down beside her on the tree trunk and held up his hand. 'I don't care what you have to say, Moll. I really don't.'

Moll drew breath to argue, but Siddy forced his words out over hers.

'I may not be as nifty as Domino or as quick-thinking as Alfie or as brave as you, but I'm the one left fighting alongside you. And when you're angry or you're in pain you've got to remember that. You can't just fling words about without thinking. OK? We *have* to stick together.'

Moll plucked at the cuff of her coat. 'But you just wandered off and left me.'

Siddy shook his head and from his pockets he drew out a handful of long, square stems fringed with oval leaves, and a clump of dripping moss. 'Figwort,' he said, 'and sphagnum moss. They grow near water so when I finally remembered what Ma said – that together they can be used as a dressing to draw out poison – I went down to the river to pick them.'

Moll hung her head. She'd seen how steep the gorge was; she knew how dangerous it would have been to scramble down there – and Sid had the scratches to prove it – but he'd done it for her while she'd been seething in the trees.

Moll shifted on the tree stump. 'I thought you were just being cross.'

Siddy wrapped the moss and leaves inside his handkerchief. 'I was collecting herbs *and* being cross.'

He raised the poultice to Moll's neck and normally she would have shoved him away and told him that she could manage herself. But as soon as the plants touched her skin Moll felt the pain ease.

She looked at her friend. 'I'm sorry, Sid.'

Siddy dabbed the dressing around her neck and Moll blinked as the water from the moss seeped through the handkerchief and down her neck.

'Do you hate me?' she mumbled.

Siddy considered. 'No. You just annoy me sometimes.' Moll's face dropped. 'But I think that's OK. Everyone has fallouts – maybe not about witches and moss and stuff – but I reckon if you can patch things up again afterwards then that's when you know you've got a good friend.'

Siddy drew the moss and figwort round to the back of Moll's neck and she sighed. 'You're quite wise, Sid. For a boy.'

He shrugged. 'I think a lot.'

Moll picked at her nails. 'I don't.'

'No. You're too busy catapulting people and being rude.'

Moll ran a hand down Gryff's throat. 'I'm sorry for being cross. It's just that sometimes I feel like we don't really stand a chance. You saw that storm back in Glendrummie and the way those witches laughed at us – what happens if we can't find the amulet before the full moon?'

For a moment, Siddy looked surprised – it wasn't like Moll to speak this way – then he shook his head. 'Nothing's bigger than us, Moll. We might not always get it right, but we've got the power of the old magic on our side. And we've got each other. We're still the Tribe.'

'Not without Alfie . . .' Moll said, her voice suddenly small and cracked.

Siddy lifted the poultice away and Moll touched her neck to find the blisters had completely vanished.

'Thank you, Sid,' she said. 'It doesn't even hurt any more.'

Siddy wiped the dirt from his hands. 'Alfie's out there somewhere, Moll, and, if we follow Willow's clues, I know we'll get him back. We'll be a Tribe again soon. You'll see.'

Gryff burrowed his head into Moll's chest and she tried to nod, but something inside her was niggling, whispering fresh fears into her mind.

'I saw a beech tree this side of the river with roots spilling down from the bank to the path,' Siddy said. 'I reckon there's enough space for us to sleep safely under them.'

Moll hauled herself up and the three of them walked back through the trees towards the path. The beech was large and gnarled and beneath the roots they shared out the bread and cheese Morag had packed for them. A while later, Siddy lifted out a blanket and Gryff scratched a hole into the bank beside Moll and curled up inside it. Siddy glanced at the wildcat and Moll could tell that though he joked about Hermit and Porridge the Second he missed having them by his side and sometimes she forgot just how lucky she was to have Gryff.

Siddy sighed and lay down, pulling the blanket over him and Moll. 'We're one step closer,' he said sleepily.

Moll snuggled deeper inside her coat, whispered her promise to Alfie – the one she had whispered every night since he had disappeared – and, with the river rushing in her ears, she drifted off to sleep.

But beyond the Clattering Gorge and up past the Rambling Moors, Wormhook paced back and forth across the courtyard of the monastery. His cloak rustled over the cobbles and beside him hung the Veil, breathing quietly into the darkness. Wormhook stopped in the far corner of the courtyard, under a flaming torch wedged inside a gargoyle's mouth, and the Veil halted beside him, its thread glittering beneath the light.

'They have beaten the witches,' Wormhook said, each word spat, like venom, from his sack mask.

He placed a hand on the Veil and it rippled beneath

his palm, but the Shadowmask wasn't talking to the quilt. There was another figure in the centre of the courtyard, sitting on the lip of a stone fountain. Her body was draped in dusty robes and instead of skin covering her face there were cobwebs, a shroud of grey stretched over her bald scalp and withered features.

'The Veil has visited almost every village in the north now and its poison has seeped into thousands of people's souls,' Wormhook muttered. 'Tonight it will go south to spread yet more fear.'

The figure dipped her cobwebbed face. 'I have opened more thresholds so that you can conjure the thickest mists and the deepest snows from the Underworld. A Night Spinner might as well use his gifts after all.' Her voice was stiff and musty, like something forgotten. 'Once you lay waste to these lands, the people will be crying out for someone to lead them – and the dark magic will step in.'

Wormhook's sack face tightened. 'You need to find the girl and the wildcat if we are to succeed, Orbrot. Without Molly Pecksniff's impossible dream crushed, the darkness cannot rise.'

Orbrot trailed a hand into the fountain. 'The girl will be heading to the moors if she is not there already and I have summoned hideous beasts from the Underworld to find her and her wildcat. When they do, I shall drain her impossible dream, then—'

Wormhook seized the torch from the gargoyle's mouth. 'I will come with the Veil to finish the deed off.' He strolled towards the fountain and the Veil followed. 'We are so nearly there, Orbrot, but I think a little bit of that mist you spoke of will slow the girl down so that she is easier to capture . . .'

His voice shrivelled to a hiss as he lowered the torch over the lip of the fountain and Orbrot smiled, but when the flames met the water they did not fizzle out. Instead, the fire spread in a circle of bright green flames. Wormhook withdrew the torch, but still the fire danced and in the centre the water began to spin faster and faster until it swirled upwards into a spiral of mist.

Orbrot stood up and, as she spoke, the film of cobwebs sucked in around her mouth. 'The girl doesn't stand a chance. All will bow down to our darkness soon – even the sun will hide and the stars will tremble.'

She swept from the courtyard, loose cobwebs trailing from her scalp, and, after her footsteps had died away on the steps down the mountain, Wormhook turned back to the fountain.

'Arise and wreak havoc,' he growled.

And, at his words, the mist curled up into the sky and slithered away from the monastery. Wormhook watched it bulge over the mountains, then, with a dark smile, he turned to the Veil.

'I hope you are ready for your rider again?'

M oll woke to someone tugging at her coat sleeve
and for a second she imagined she was back in
her wagon in Tanglefern Forest and that Mooshie
had come to get her up for morning chores. Then her eyes
flicked open to see Gryff pulling at her cuff with his teeth
and the beech roots curved over her head.

The forest was already awake: a woodpecker drummed at
a nearby tree and a red squirrel scampered along the path.
It was a cold grey morning and even beneath the shelter of
the roots Moll's feet were numb inside her boots. She dug a
hand inside her coat pocket and, on feeling the very slight
weight of the piano string against her fingertips, she leant
over to tickle Gryff's throat.

His greeting call rumbled in her ears. 'Brrroooooo.'

At the sound, Siddy opened his eyes and yawned.

'We need to head on and find Aira,' Moll whispered. 'We
shouldn't stay in this forest any longer than we need to.'

Gryff slipped out from the roots to hunt for food while
Moll shook the last of the nuts and berries from the

satchel and Siddy stooped to pick a handful of wood sorrel growing by the path. Then they followed the wildcat along the path above the river. Once or twice they saw the forest stir – a greenfinch flitting between branches, a roe deer picking its way through the ferns – but otherwise the place was quiet, a woodland scarred by the Shadowmasks' magic.

Eventually the oak, ash and beech trees thinned and the path dropped level with the river. The water ran more slowly here and Moll watched the reflection of overhanging branches break apart as a small fish jumped and a dipper bobbed down from a rock to follow it. They walked on, right out of the trees, and there, rolling across the landscape for as far as they could see, were the moors. Where one hill sloped down another rose up, a sprawling wilderness purpled by frosted heather.

Siddy stopped for a moment. 'The Rambling Moors.'

Moll blinked, unable to find words large enough to describe the emptiness before her. She'd been out on the heath beyond Tanglefern Forest many times with Domino – she'd raced into the open where the wild ponies roamed and relished the freedom of space – and somehow she'd imagined the landscape here to be like that. But Moll's thoughts hadn't been big enough to hold in what the moorland was. It didn't rise up into towering mountains; it didn't need to. The hills owned the landscape just by being there. Grazing sheep were reduced to white dots, streams shrank to wrinkles and the path ahead of them was almost lost amid the heather. The moors swallowed everything and, facing them now, Moll gulped.

'How are we going to find *a feather from burning wings* out here?' she said.

Gryff stalked along the path, out on to the moors.

Siddy straightened his flat cap. 'By following him. By putting one foot in front of the other until we find Aira MacDuff and that bothy.'

Moll watched the wildcat's shoulders rise and fall, his paws silent on the rocky track, and she felt stronger somehow, and, with Siddy by her side, she followed. The river quietened into a stream and ran west, away from them, but they continued on the path as it wound on to the moors. Moll could see the distant hills were scattered with snow and from the hollows a mist was rising – but she had darker things than the weather on her mind. Out here on the open moors, she was easy prey for the Shadowmasks . . .

A covey of grouse sprang from the heather and Moll jumped as Gryff tore off after them. Her eyes widened as the wildcat bounded further and further away, then the birds flew out of his reach and he sloped back to join the others. Moll ran a hand over his back because, for a fleeting second, it had felt as if he might keep running into the wilderness without her. Here on the Rambling Moors she could feel a different kind of freedom rising from him, a slice of the wild only matched by the landscape around them. *This*, a small voice within her said, *this is where he really belongs.*

It was after they'd been walking for an hour that they

clambered over a gate set within a fence and Siddy noticed the highland cow – a lone male grazing further down the hill.

He looked at it longingly. 'Just think what we could do with a highland cow at our side. He could carry our bows and supplies and we could ride him when we got tired.'

Moll glanced at the cow's horns. 'It wouldn't end happily, Sid.' She paused. 'Once all this is over, I'll go hunting for a pet with you – something a bit bigger than Hermit, perhaps, and a bit less slimy than Porridge the Second.' She nodded down the path. 'Right now though we've got to keep going.'

'Can't we just rest for a moment?' Siddy asked.

Moll shook her head. 'We haven't got time.'

They walked on and, while Moll hastened to keep up with Gryff, Siddy began to lag behind, whistling every now and again to try and attract the attention of the other highland cows they passed.

'Come on, Sid!' Moll called without looking back.

She knew Sid was tired and sore after the climb into the gorge the night before and that he was missing Porridge and Hermit, but worrying about all that wouldn't help them now. Moll tried to ignore the ache in her own legs and focus on placing one foot in front of the other, and it was only when she looked up that she noticed how much the weather had closed in. Great bands of mist hung where the moors ahead had been and all around her tendrils of fog crept closer. Moll watched as the mist inched over the heather like a living thing. She spun round to look for Siddy, but the path behind her was empty.

'Sid!' she called. 'Where are you?'

She waited a few moments, but nobody emerged through the haze. Insides turning, she careered back down the track with Gryff.

'Sid!' she cried. 'Sid!'

She rounded the bend in the track to where she assumed her friend would be, but there was only a screen of mist.

'Sid!' Moll shouted again.

Her voice echoed across the moor, caught in the hanging fog, but Siddy didn't reply. Moll stumbled into the heather with Gryff and ran blindly, her face wet with sweat. She'd been impatient again, and charged off, even though she knew Siddy was tired and had only wanted a little rest.

Moll turned blindly, this way and that. 'Sid!' she called. 'Sid!'

Gryff brushed against her legs, but whichever way she turned Siddy was nowhere to be seen. Moll's mind whirred with images of her friend at the bottom of a ravine, of him gored by a highland cow or, worse, snatched by a Shadowmask. She blundered on, shouting his name.

The path had vanished and Moll could barely see Gryff's black-and-white stripes, even though he was just by her side. And then suddenly the ground gave way beneath Moll and she fell forward, landing with a slap on something soft and muddy.

'No,' she breathed, panic rising in her throat as she remembered Domino's words on the train – of peat bogs that could suck you down whole . . .

Frantically, she reached out her arms towards Gryff, but the peat sucked hard, dragging her feet then her legs and then her waist into the cold, wet earth.

'Help!' she yelled as Gryff clawed at her coat.

Then Moll's eyes widened as two shadowy hands in the depths of the bog wrapped round her shins before heaving at her legs and forcing her down. Moll heard Gryff growl as he tried to pull her from the creature, but whatever was lurking in the bog wasn't letting go. Its hands clamped tighter round Moll's legs and little by little she felt her body slip from Gryff's hold until the mud was slopping around her neck.

'No!' she gasped, her lungs snatching at the air. 'No!'

Moll's eyes locked on to Gryff's as the mud rose above her chin. She sealed her lips tight, forcing the breath out through her nose, then there was a loud belch as her whole face was wrenched beneath the surface. The earth closed round Moll and she thought of Siddy out on the moor without her, of Gryff struggling above the surface and of the Shadowmasks waiting to conjure their eternal night.

She bucked and twisted, but the hands kept pulling and Moll felt her mind shutting down and her limbs growing weak as she was hauled deeper and deeper into the blackness of the bog.

Chapter 12
Inside Fillie Crankie

Moll forced her eyes open and almost immediately she tensed. She was no longer out on the moors but inside, sitting in an armchair lined with sheepskin. In front of her was a fire pit and flames crackled inside the circle of stones. Nine other armchairs surrounded the pit, each lined with a sheepskin just like hers, and smoke drifted upwards into the chimney hanging down from above.

Moll kept still, trying to work out how she had come to be here when the last thing she remembered was being swallowed by the peat bog ... Her eyes darted about the room, taking in the flagstone floor and the tartan curtains, and then they came to rest on an armchair on the other side of the fire in which a young woman sat. She was in her twenties perhaps, with cropped red hair, and a shawl was draped over her blouse and tartan skirt.

She hadn't noticed Moll was awake yet and Moll wanted to keep it that way for two reasons: the woman was reading a book entitled *How to Stab Adders and Skin Hares* and a crossbow rested on her lap. Moll would have been impressed by the weapon normally – its owner had carved a hare's head into the tiller and used what looked like a twisted mulberry root for the string – but her mind was on Gryff and Siddy. Where *were* they? Where was *she*?

Moll's eyes slid to a wooden ladder behind the woman that seemed to lead up to another floor, then to the windows on either side of the walls. It was darker now, but Moll could see that the mist outside had pulled back a little and she was in a cottage in the middle of the moors. Pulse racing, Moll tried to think. Her quiver was gone and, as she straightened her back, she realised her knife was no longer pressing into the belt around her waist.

Catapult, Moll thought. But as she glanced at the woman opposite she found herself remembering what had happened in Angus' house, how she had reached for her catapult while Domino had reached for words. *Think first, speak second and fight later*, a voice inside her seemed to be saying.

And very, very slowly Moll moved a hand down her coat to check that the piano string was still there – but the movement had been enough to rouse the attention of the woman opposite. She dropped the book, seized her crossbow and walked round the fire pit towards Moll.

'I made a decision out on the moors that you could be trusted,' the woman said. 'But there's dark magic brewing left, right and centre so, before I do any more trusting and helping, you need to give me some answers. Who are you?'

Moll shrank back in the chair. 'I – I . . .'

It was then that she noticed a dark shape slink up on to

97

the windowsill behind the woman. Gryff was outside the cottage, crouched on the stone ledge as he squeezed himself through the gap in the window. Moll's heart surged at the sight of the wildcat.

'I said, who are—'

Before Moll could reassure Gryff that perhaps the woman could be trusted, he leapt from the windowsill on to the woman's back and she shrieked and stumbled backwards, flinging the wildcat to the floor. Gryff was up on his feet in seconds, mouth wide in a snarl. The woman's blue eyes flashed as she slipped a foot into the stirrup of her crossbow, pulled the string back on to the lock and slotted in a bolt. She aimed the weapon at Gryff and Moll screamed as the wildcat shot backwards and the bolt thwunked into a table leg at the far end of the room. The woman reloaded and Gryff raced across the room towards Moll, ripping through a sheepskin rug and sending an armchair crashing to the ground. Then Moll was on her feet too, a pebble slotted to the pouch of the catapult.

'If you fire your crossbow at him one more time, I'll blow your brains out!' Moll winced. Things weren't quite going to plan, but then she hadn't anticipated crossbows being fired at Gryff.

A huge man – all kilt and beard and knuckles – burst through the door. 'What the blazes is going on, Aira?'

'Aira?' Moll panted.

And, as the woman closed one eye over the sights of her crossbow, Moll dropped her catapult and raised her hands. 'Wait! We know your brother – Angus MacDuff,' she spluttered.

Aira paused for a second, then her face lit up and she let the crossbow hang down by her side. 'Ach,' she said, wiping the sweat from her brow. 'Why didn't you just say so?'

Moll looked at the bolt jammed in the table leg. 'Your crossbow put me off.'

Aira set her weapon down on the floor and the man in the doorway took a step towards them. His beard spilled out beneath his chin, finishing in five little plaits knotted with twine, his boots were so large they filled an entire flagstone and below his rolled-up shirt sleeves Moll glimpsed arms stamped with tattoos.

'Everything OK?' he asked. His voice was low and gruff, as if he'd swallowed one of Gryff's growls.

Aira nodded. 'I was just getting acquainted with the girl and her . . .' She looked at Gryff who was now thumping his paws on to the ground in front of the crossbow, '. . . cat.'

'*Wild*cat,' Moll corrected, her chin raised.

Aira looked at the man. 'I'll take it from here, Spud, but if you're able to fix us some heather tea, that'd be braw.'

Spud raised one ginger eyebrow and then, to Moll's surprise, he mumbled, 'I'm allowed back in the kitchen again?'

Aira nodded. 'So long as you don't snack *on anything*.'

'Wouldn't dream of it,' protested Spud as he left the room.

Aira sighed. 'Got to keep an eye on Spud. He's the best fighter in the Highland Watch, but his appetite is out

99

of control. Once he ate a whole chocolate cake before breakfast – and last week the youngest lad here woke up to find Spud nibbling on his toe in his sleep.'

Moll was silent. She couldn't decide who was worse: the woman with the crossbow or the chocolate-cake-eating cannibal.

Aira folded her arms. 'So, how on *earth* did you come by a wildcat, lass?'

Again Moll stayed quiet. How she wished Domino and Sid were by her side; they'd know what to say. She scuffed her boot against the flagstones and, beside her, Gryff snarled.

Aira nodded towards the wildcat. '*The only animal you can't tame*, we say around here. And yet you have one right by your side willing to fight your battles.'

Moll held her stare. 'Gryff isn't tamed,' she said sternly. 'He bites hard when he wants to and sometimes he even scratches people's eyes out.' It was a lie – the wildcat had never scratched anyone's eyes out – but Moll was still wary of the crossbow.

Aira took a deep breath and Moll wondered whether her first attempts at conversation might have been better without the mention of biting and scratching. She pressed on nonetheless.

'Have you seen my pal Siddy? He's a bit taller than me, with dark, curly hair, and he often wears a flat cap. We were out on the moors together, then the mist came in and . . .' She couldn't bear to finish the sentence, to say that she'd rushed off and left Siddy behind.

Aira sat down in an armchair and motioned for Moll to do the same. Moll stayed where she was and Aira shrugged.

'The Highland Watch rescued you from a peatbogger,' she said, 'just as it was about to drown you.'

Moll frowned. 'A peatbogger?'

'Nasty creatures that live inside the bogs,' Aira explained, picking a clump of dirt out from under her fingernails. 'They've got bodies of mud and heather and they surfaced a month ago, when the witches first appeared. We've had quite a job holding all the dark magic on this side of the North Door ...' She paused. 'Luckily, when you stumbled into a peatbogger, Spud and I were patrolling the moor behind our bothy so we heard the commotion and rode out to rescue you.'

Moll could sense that now was the right time to say thank you, but she was worried sick about Siddy.

'But there was only you,' Aira said. 'Your wildcat must have hidden in the heather as we approached because just now was the first time I've seen him.' She shook her head. 'You have to stick with your pals on the moors. The weather comes in fast up here – even more so since the dark magic began to stir. We've had storms that have lasted for days and mists so thick you can't see your hands in front of you – it's a dangerous place when you're on your own.'

Moll felt her knees grow suddenly weak and she reached for the back of an armchair and sat down. Losing Siddy wasn't a possibility she could bear. She swallowed again and again to force the lump in her throat down while Gryff scratched a paw against her boot.

It's OK, he seemed to be saying. *It's going to be OK.*

But as Moll sat in her mud-stained clothes she knew things were far from OK. She'd lost another friend and she'd never find the last amulet on her own, not in time. She reached into her coat pocket and breathed a sigh of relief as she felt her fingertips brush against the piano string. But it didn't make her feel any better about Sid and she hung her head, too afraid to meet Aira's eyes in case the guilt and sadness spilled out.

Aira twisted her head round towards the kitchen. 'Spud, could you send a few more men out? There's a young lad still lost on the moors.'

There was a shuffling in the kitchen, then Spud emerged looking incredibly guilty. 'Aye,' he nodded, walking towards them with two mugs of steaming tea. 'Will do.'

Moll raised glassy eyes. 'Thank you,' she said. 'He's called Siddy.'

Aira took the tea and passed one mug to Moll, then she looked Spud up and down. He puffed out his chest and she narrowed her eyes.

'Scones,' she hissed. 'You've been munching on the scones, haven't you?'

'No,' Spud replied. 'Definitely no.' His beard twitched and he flexed his tattooed arms, then he threw his hands up in the air. 'Ach, Aira, I'm sorry. I couldn't help it. They were just sitting there all buttery and plump—'

'Which, incidentally, is what *you* will be if you carry on snacking,' Aira cut in. She brushed the crumbs from his beard. 'We need this lad back here before the sun goes down. I'm counting on the Highland Watch, OK?'

Spud nodded and, in a whirl of kilt, beard and crumbs, he left.

Aira smiled at Moll. 'Welcome to Fillie Crankie, home of the Highland Watch. We joined together last month to fight the dark beasts that have been cropping up in the northern wilderness: witches, peatboggers, trolls.'

After the peatbogger, Moll didn't have the stomach to ask about trolls.

'Spud and the lads are a good bunch,' Aira went on, 'madly fond of fighting, high-spirited and quick to battle, but otherwise they're fairly straightforward.'

'Are you the only girl?' Moll asked.

Aira grinned. 'Aye. The folk back in Glendrummie said fighting dark magic was a man's business. But I'm up here to prove them wrong and, since the lads are useless at making decisions and getting things done, I seem to be the one in charge.' She paused. 'So, what's your name?'

Moll ran a hand across Gryff's back. Revealing her name had got her into trouble in the past. Skull had used it to control her mind back in Tanglefern Forest and the Shadowmasks down by the sea had used it to stop her from moving. But Aira was fighting against the Shadowmasks' dark magic and tucked inside the bothy Moll felt safer than she had in the Clattering Gorge. 'I'm Moll,' she said eventually. 'And this is Gryff.'

The wildcat curled back his lips and slid a tongue over

his teeth – he hadn't quite forgotten about the episode with the crossbow yet.

'So, how did you come across Angus, young Moll?' Aira asked.

Moll took a deep breath and then she told Aira about her journey as a stowaway on the train north, about the storm and meeting Angus, and about her role in the Bone Murmur and her quest for the last amulet. She drew out the parchment Willow had left for her and, though it was smudged with mud, the words were still clear.

'Me, Sid and Gryff fought our way past the witches by stealing the last note of their song,' Moll explained, 'and—'

'You silenced the witches in the Clattering Gorge?' Aira interrupted.

Moll sniffed. 'I'm quite handy when I'm not being drowned by peatboggers.'

'That's impressive, lass.'

Moll looked down. 'I had Sid to help me then. He was the one who patched up my neck after a witch chucked a noose of poisoned hair around it.'

'You need cleaning up,' Aira said. 'You'll catch a cold if we don't wash that mud off soon.'

Moll shrugged. 'I can't be bothered to be clean – not when I need to find the feather from Willow's clue before the Shadowmasks find me.'

Aira gazed into the fire for a while and watched the flames dance, then she looked back at Moll. 'I can help you try to find this feather,' she said quietly. 'Anything to force the Night Spinner and his Veil back and to make the north safe again.' She paused. 'I promise you we'll leave at first light, but I'm not letting you go anywhere until you've had a bath.'

Chapter 13
The Highland Watch

After trying, unsuccessfully, to coax Gryff into the kitchen for food, Moll had given up and let him wander outside into the heather. She knew he wouldn't stray far from her, that after finding a grouse or a rabbit to eat he'd slink back inside, so she followed Aira up the wooden stairs to the loft, past bunk beds laden with blankets, to a small room with a single bed and an old bath that stood on a stag's hide. But, even as Moll undressed and slipped beneath the warm water, she couldn't stop thinking about Siddy. It was getting dark outside and he was somewhere on the moors, at the mercy of the peatboggers and the Shadowmasks' magic.

Moll jumped. Down below, footsteps were traipsing into the bothy. She listened as the Highland Watch slumped down into their armchairs.

'We couldn't find him, Aira.' Moll recognised Spud's voice right away. 'Only a leather satchel with a blanket and a flask of water inside.'

The words hung in Moll's ears.

'Couldn't find him?' Aira said. 'You're the Highland flipping Watch! There's not an animal you lot can't track and you're telling me you can't bring a wee lad home?'

Spud's voice came, low and grave. 'We couldn't find him because he isn't on the moors around here . . . not any more. We located his tracks on the path, then they stopped – cut clean off.' He paused. 'We reckon he's been kidnapped. Taken by the dark magic.'

Moll climbed out of the bath and wrapped a towel around herself, then she sat on the bed, shivering. She hugged her knees up to her chest and stared at the floorboards. If she'd just waited with Sid while he caught his breath, perhaps none of this would have happened. What would Domino say? And Oak? Her thoughts were broken by footsteps climbing the stairs and then Aira stepped into the room.

'I'm so sorry, Moll, but the lads couldn't find Siddy.'

Aira sat down on the bed and clutched Moll's hand, but she flinched and shuffled away. She wasn't ready to let a stranger in; the hurt that beat inside her was something she felt alone, something that couldn't be fixed with kind words or hands held.

Aira looked at Moll. 'We *will* find him,' she said. 'You and me. We'll go after the feather at dawn and we'll find Siddy – wherever the dark magic might have taken him.'

Moll tried to summon up the energy to believe Aira, to will on the improbable as she did every time she fired an arrow from her bow. But it was getting harder to believe the impossible could happen. Alfie was gone. Siddy was missing.

And now it was just her and Gryff against the Shadowmasks' magic.

From downstairs there came a droning noise, loud and solemn, that filled the whole bothy and stirred something deep inside Moll's soul: the loss she felt for her parents and for her Tribe, and for adventures gone wrong and tasks unfulfilled.

'What's that?' Moll asked.

Aira smiled. 'It's Spud. He plays the bagpipes every evening when the sun goes down because the music keeps away the peatboggers who creep out of their bogs at midnight.' She paused and placed a hand over her heart. 'But it touches something in here too, doesn't it?'

Moll listened to the straining notes. They plucked at her heart, bruised and broken as it was, and she gazed out of the window. The tune rose and fell, flooding through her body and drawing out her yearning, and she wondered in that moment whether Siddy and Alfie could hear the music too, whether they were missing her under the same night sky. She flopped back on the bed, eyes closed.

'Here,' Aira said. 'I thought you could do with some fresh clothes for the journey ahead. They were things I was making for my god-daughter back in Glendrummie, but she won't mind, under the circumstances, if they arrive a little muddy.'

The journey ahead. Just thinking about going on without Sid made Moll's heart heavy. She hauled herself up, took the trousers, tartan shirt and thick, woolly jumper and changed into them. Then she slipped her catapult into the trouser pocket and turned to Aira.

'A catapult at the dinner table?' Aira said.

Moll wedged her hands in her pockets. 'You read with a crossbow on your lap.'

Aira grinned. 'I think you and I are going to get along quite well.'

They walked down the stairs to find the Highland Watch in the armchairs around the fire pit, drinking whisky – a huddle of ginger beards, tartan bonnets and freckled skin. Spud stood by the front door, playing his pipes, his large cheeks swelling like balloons, but when Aira clapped her hands he lowered the instrument and took a seat.

'Lads,' Aira said. 'This is Moll.'

Moll felt her face redden, then she caught sight of Gryff's tail poking out from behind the log pile and felt a tiny bit stronger.

'I'm going to need you to guard the moors close tonight and tomorrow because Moll and I are going to Whuppity Cairns.'

The Highland Watch exchanged nervous glances and a few began to whisper to each other. Moll frowned. Was Whuppity Cairns where Aira thought the feather was? Or perhaps even Siddy?

Spud looked at Aira. 'You can't just march off to Whuppity Cairns! That goblin there's a trickster. Only a handful of the people who have visited him have actually come back!' He nodded at Moll. 'And she's just a wee scrap – she won't stand a chance against him.'

Aira clipped Spud on the back of the head and drew herself up tall. 'This girl has beaten her way past the witches of Clattering Gorge, she's armed with a catapult, a quiver of arrows *and* a wildcat – and, to top it all off, she's the child from the Bone Murmur that the legends speak of. So, don't let me hear *any* of you calling her *just a wee scrap.*'

The Highland Watch looked at Moll, their eyes wide.

Aira carried on. 'Moll has been sent a message from the old magic with clues on how to crush all this evil. We need to find a feather from burning wings and you know as well as I do that Whuppity Cairns is the best place to search for it.' She budged one of the men out of his chair so that Moll could sit down. 'So, you great pack of jessies, I suggest you lot get acquainted with Moll while I go fix us up some neeps and tatties.'

Spud raised a hand. 'Any chance of you making us some clootie dumplings, Aira?' He twizzled his beard.

Aira nodded. 'Fine, but the next time you flutter your eyelashes like that at me, Spud, you'll feel the back of my hand.'

Spud reddened and pretended to be extremely interested in his tattoos as Aira marched off into the kitchen. Then, one by one, the Highland Watch turned to look at Moll. She lifted her catapult out of her trouser pocket and turned it over in her hands, embarrassed at the attention.

Spud cleared his throat and leant forward. 'Most of the girls I knew back in Glendrummie played with dolls not catapults. But that's a fine-looking thing you've got there.'

Moll looked up. 'There was a girl back in my camp in the forest who had a doll. I used it as target practice when I was learning to fire my catapult.'

The rest of the Highland Watch sniggered and Spud gave up with the small talk and picked up Aira's crossbow. 'Ever fired one of these?'

Moll shook her head.

'Well, I think we've got our evening's entertainment sorted then,' he replied.

The next morning, frost clung to the moors, stiffening the heather and juniper, and any dips in the track were sealed with ice. Moll blew into the sheepskin lining of her gloves while Gryff prowled restlessly up and down the path and Aira saddled the two highland ponies in front of the bothy. They were nothing like Jinx, Moll's cob back home. He was a palomino – small, nifty and soft to touch – but these horses were larger, with coarse coats and untrimmed manes.

Aira fastened the toggles on her thick green cape, then adjusted the girth beneath the dappled pony. 'This is Salt,' she said. 'I've been riding her since I was a wee lass.' She ran a hand over the mare's tousled white mane, then turned to the pony on her other side; its coat was dark grey like a smudge of smoke. 'You'll be riding Pepper – Salt's brother.'

Moll glanced at the black mane trailing over the pony's eyes. 'His mane's so long he won't be able to see where he's going,' she mumbled.

Aira hauled a saddle up on to Pepper's back. 'Highland

ponies *always* know where they're going. They're the hardiest animals on the moors and wherever you find yourself – on a hillside of scree, at the top of a crag or halfway down a bog – they'll get you safely home. The only time you've got to watch them is if they leave the moors because they get spooked by carts and cottages.'

Moll ran a hand down Pepper's neck and noticed that his mane was plaited with tiny silver bells.

'For luck,' Aira said. 'And it means we can hear them if they wander off.' She shortened the stirrups on Pepper's saddle. 'When they canter, the bells chime and rustle and I like to think that if a whole constellation of stars fell to earth it might sound something like our highland ponies galloping.'

She handed Moll Pepper's reins and walked back to her own mare. Moll looked out over the horse's saddle and watched the pale sun rising above the moors, brushing the sky pink. *I'm coming for you, Sid,* she said to herself. But just thinking the words in the face of the wilderness before her made Moll feel suddenly small.

Since losing Alfie, she was used to sadness, used to the grief that rocked inside her every time she thought about her friend, but this morning she'd awoken with a new feeling: a heavy guilt that sat in the pit of her stomach and made her want to curl up into a ball and forget that not only had she failed Alfie but she had lost Sid too. Moll was a fighter and she had pushed back at every threat that had come her way since learning about the Bone Murmur, but as soon as she had set foot in the northern wilderness she'd felt something inside her shift.

Gryff had been able to tell that things weren't right. He had refused to sleep upstairs in the bothy – the chatter and the snores of the Highland Watch were too noisy for him – and so he and Moll had cuddled up in an armchair by the fire, and, as they lay together beneath the sheepskin rugs, the wildcat had felt the sadness and the guilt brooding inside the girl. He had curled his tail around her and nuzzled her cheek, but both he and Moll knew that these were wounds not easily fixed.

Gryff blinked at Moll from the path and she tucked the tartan scarf Aira had lent her down into her duffle coat, adjusted the quiver on her back, then hoisted herself up on to Pepper. Aira mounted her mare and the Highland Watch gathered around the door of Fillie Crankie.

'You'll be careful, won't you?' Spud said, twisting his beard.

Aira slotted her crossbow into the holder on her back, then pulled the hood of her cape up over her hair. Her blue eyes sparkled against the rabbit-fur trim. 'You just keep an eye on the moors.' She kicked her mare on across the heather to the path. 'I'm relying on you.'

Moll dipped her head at the Highland Watch. 'If you find Sid, tell him ... tell him I'm sorry for leaving him. And that I'll be back once I've got the feather.'

Spud nodded. 'We will, lass. We will.' Although, in his eyes, Moll couldn't see much hope.

She tugged on the reins and followed Aira up the track

that led out on to the moors. Pepper's stride was unlike Jinx's and Moll was used to riding bareback rather than sitting in a saddle, but, even so, there was something reassuring in the pony's broad shoulders and the steadiness of his hooves as they clopped up the path and cracked through iced puddles.

For a while, they rode in silence, cantering side by side, while Gryff bounded over the heather in front of them. Moll listened to the moors – to a lark calling, to the grouse wings whirring over the heather and to the tiny bells jingling from within Pepper's mane – and with every sound she heard she prayed for Siddy's voice. But it never came. Once or twice she glimpsed a bog set back from the path, a dark pit surrounded by heather, but no creatures stirred from within them and the highland ponies sped by, on and on over the Rambling Moors.

As they approached a fence running across the hillside, Aira finally drew Salt back to a walk. 'The goblin at Whuppity Cairns,' she said as she unhooked the gate and pulled it open, 'apparently he's dreadful.'

Moll kicked Pepper through. 'Did the Shadowmasks bring him through the thresholds to the moors?'

Aira nodded. 'The north has always had its quirks: selkies and krakens down by the sea and the odd monster in the lochs. But the goblin is the Shadowmasks' doing and, from what I've heard, he's a crooked old trickster.' She closed the gate and they carried on walking, across a bridge of felled pines that ran over a burn and back on to the path. 'Kittlerumpit, they call him.'

'Sounds like a dodgy vegetable,' Moll replied. 'And why do people visit him if they know he's a trickster?'

Aira smiled. 'He collects things. Rare, magical things apparently and people have come from all over the northern wilderness to trade with him. But, as Spud said, not many come back.'

Moll gripped tighter on Pepper's reins.

Aira shrugged. 'Ach! But we're not most people, are we, Moll? *We'll* come back and with any luck we'll be carrying that feather you need.'

Moll's breath misted into a cloud in front of her and, when she looked up at the moors ahead, she saw that they were cloaked in white and the sky around them was heavy with snow.

'It's arrived,' Aira said quietly. 'The first snow of winter.'

And as Aira, Moll and Gryff made their way further across the moors a muffled whiteness stirred above them. Tiny flakes began to fall and Moll found herself pushing back her hood and letting them land, cold and wet, on her upturned face.

'It's never snowed this early up here,' Aira said, brushing the snowflakes from her cape, 'and, mark my words, it'll get a lot worse – the Shadowmasks will see to that. They're conjuring weather that's near impossible to live through ... It's the Highland Watch's guess that the witch doctors want to cripple this world – both its people and the land – so that when they do show themselves they have subjects so broken they'll be desperate to obey the dark magic.'

Moll's eyes were glued to the track. 'The Shadowmasks do

that. They destroy places and they take people, even though they've got no right.'

'We're going to find your friend,' Aira said.

Moll's gaze remained downward. 'They took my parents too. And Alfie – before I could even make him real.'

Aira frowned. 'Who's Alfie? And what do you mean, "make him real"?'

For a while, Moll said nothing, the pain of things too raw inside her, but then she told Aira Alfie's story.

'When Alfie and Sid were here, we were a Tribe and I felt like I could do anything,' Moll said. 'Whatever the Shadowmasks had in store for us I knew we'd be OK because we were all together.' She bit down on her lip. 'But I couldn't save Alfie – I didn't think quick enough ... and ... and it's all my fault Sid's gone too.'

Aira reached across and pulled on Pepper's reins. The pony stopped and Moll looked up at Aira.

'When you look at yourself in the mirror, what do you see?' Aira asked.

Moll sniffed. 'A muddy face that's always getting things wrong.'

Aira shook her head. 'You know what I see when I look at you?'

Moll said nothing.

'I see courage, lass.' Aira put a gloved hand over her chest. '*In here*. And your courage isn't just about bows and arrows and catapults. It goes deeper than that. There's a fight inside you, Moll, a toughness of the soul. And it refuses to give up, no matter what is thrown at it.' She paused. 'That fight isn't small – it's not something that always gets things wrong – it's fierce and loyal and, though I've no doubt it could bring down a mighty giant if it wanted to, sometimes it's strong just by being inside you.'

Moll swallowed. 'How do you know I've still got my fight? How do you know I'm not just going to give up because that's what I feel like doing now?'

'Because I can see it,' Aira replied. 'It's in your eyes and in your wildcat.'

Moll looked down at Gryff, his striped fur dark against the snow.

Aira kicked Salt on. 'Don't be too hard on yourself, Moll. You're allowed to mess up and fall apart – everyone does it – but know that however small, useless and full of doubt you feel, I believe in you. I see your fight.'

Moll heard Aira's words and she tried to let them in, but, like with Siddy's in the Clattering Gorge, something inside Moll pushed them back, as if, perhaps, there were darker forces playing with her heart. She clamped her legs round Pepper's flanks and the pony sprang forward into a canter until Moll was level with Salt.

Aira glanced across and smiled. 'Let's find this feather, then.'

Chapter 15
Peatboggers

They galloped over the moors with Gryff pounding beside them and, though somewhere the hills ended and the sky began, Moll couldn't see where because everything was blanketed white, like a world made new. But Moll thought only of the darkness lying at its core, of the eternal night just three days away. The ponies pressed on up a steep path towards the summit of a hill and then suddenly Gryff stopped. His tail slid to the ground and his ears swivelled towards the banks of snow-dusted heather on their left. Nothing stirred, but Gryff continued to stare at the same spot, a dip in the heather several metres away.

Then, without warning, the snow exploded, bursting into the air like scattered foam, and a dark, grimy hand ripped out of the ground. Pepper reared up and Moll clung to his mane, but Aira reached for her crossbow and swung it over her shoulder.

'Peatbogger!' she yelled.

The pit belched as a brown creature climbed out on to the snow. Moll fumbled for an arrow as it raised its body up to full height, a ragged torso of soil twisted with clumps of heather. It had no eyes or ears, just a dark hole for a mouth and arms that trailed to the ground.

Aira tucked her chin against the tiller of her crossbow, then fired and the bolt smashed straight into the creature. Its body collapsed into a heap of soil.

'Well done,' Moll panted.

But Aira wasn't smiling. 'Ride hard!' she shouted. 'I just bought us a bit of time, that's all!'

To Moll's horror, she watched the soil and heather rise up again, building itself back into a body until once more the peatbogger stood before them, beating earthy hands against its chest. It careered over the snow on all fours and Aira, Moll and Gryff raced further up the track. But, behind them, the peatbogger followed, a brown stain lumbering closer and closer. Moll squeezed her legs round Pepper's body, grabbed her bow and twisted back in her saddle. She closed one eye and tried to think of her impossible dream – *to make Alfie real* – but her promise seemed to belong to a world long gone. She fired – and her arrow fell short.

Gryff turned to face the peatbogger, lashing out with razored claws, but the creature merely lifted one large hand and batted the wildcat into the snow.

'Gryff!' Moll yelled.

He struggled up, charged again at the peatbogger and bit hard on its leg. A chunk of soil and heather fell away, but the creature only grunted, shunting the wildcat aside and blundering on after the ponies.

Moll tore another arrow from her quiver, but, even as she fired it, she knew she would miss. It careered into the snow and her insides clenched; where her fight had once been there was doubt. Moll leant into Pepper's strides and glanced nervously at Aira as the peatbogger growled behind them. 'Use your crossbow again!' she cried.

But Aira was fumbling for something else, something fixed to her saddle that Moll hadn't noticed before: a single stag antler. Yanking it free, she hurled it towards the peatbogger. It sank into the path just in front of the creature and then a remarkable thing happened. The antler began to grow, new points splitting through the bone, and Moll watched, open-mouthed, as it twisted up and around the peatbogger, trapping it inside a cage. It seized the antlers and shook them hard, but they remained firm, like prison bars, and behind them the creature thrashed its head from side to side.

'That'll hold it,' Aira panted. 'Peatboggers can only last for a few hours outside their bogs so with any luck the cage will be strong enough to contain it until it dies.'

Half dazed with shock, Moll kicked Pepper on, away from the howling creature and up on to the summit of the moors. An icy wind slid towards them and, though it chilled Moll's cheeks and Gryff had to dip his head against it, Moll didn't tighten her scarf or shiver. She felt numb inside. The old Moll would've crushed that peatbogger with a single arrow, but her impossible dream was fading, her fight – whatever Aira said – was dwindling inside her.

Aira didn't mention the arrows. 'The Highland Watch find

the only things that keeps those brutes away are stag antlers washed in the spring behind Fillie Crankie,' she said. 'It's surrounded by white heather and I think some of that magic must spill into the water and on to the antlers.' She sniffed. 'But I often chuck a crossbow at them first – gives me time to untie the antler.'

She slid from her horse and Moll noticed that heaped in front of them, on the highest point of the moors, was a circle of large, rectangular stones, flat against the snow and pointed inwards towards each other like the spokes of a wheel.

Aira pulled her hood up against the wind. 'Welcome to Whuppity Cairns.' She walked over to one of the large slabs and began pulling at the pile of stones built into a small pyramid in the middle. 'Should be in here somewhere,' she muttered.

Moll dismounted and, together with Gryff, she began hauling the stones back too. 'What are we looking for exactly?'

'An opening into the moor itself.' Aira drew back, hands on hips, and stood upright on one of the large, flat stones. 'I could've sworn the entrance was—'

Before she could finish her sentence, the slab beneath her crunched and then tilted back a fraction. Aira's eyes widened and then the stone see-sawed forward, shooting her down into a hole before clamping back into place.

Moll blinked. 'She's – she's *gone!*'

Gryff nudged at Moll's calves and she knew what that meant. *Follow Aira.*

She looked up to see Salt and Pepper grazing the heather. 'We'll be back up again for you soon,' she whispered.

Pepper whinnied softly as Moll placed a tentative foot on the slab and Gryff lifted one paw on after her. The stone held their weight and they moved the rest of their bodies on. Then Moll crouched low, clutched Gryff, and once again the stone crunched and rocked before sliding forward and propelling them both down into the heart of Whuppity Cairns.

Chapter 16
Inside Whuppity Cairns

They landed with a thud and Moll blinked into the darkness as the stone above them closed back into place, blocking out the moors. They were in an underground tunnel, lit by candles fixed inside iron brackets, which was several metres wide with earth walls that curved above them into a web of heather roots.

'Grand,' Aira said, brushing the soil from Moll's coat. 'No broken bones, I hope?'

Gryff picked himself up, then looked down the tunnel in front of them, his hackles raised.

Moll ran a hand over his back. 'I don't like being underground either,' she whispered to him.

'The feather's here though, I'm sure of it,' Aira said. 'And I've coins for any price Kittlerumpit names.'

Gryff growled into the tunnel and Moll could tell that he was still unsure of the place.

'I'll go first if your wildcat's feeling a bit nervous,' Aira added.

Gryff prowled past her, turning briefly to show his fangs, then stalked on ahead.

'Don't take it personally,' Moll said to Aira. 'His people skills aren't much good.'

Aira winked. 'You've got a lot in common, you two.'

Moll tried to smile, but ended up scowling. She walked abreast with Aira. 'How do you think we find Kittlerumpit?'

Aira shrugged. 'All I know is that he lives beneath Whuppity Cairns.' She placed a hand on her crossbow and kept it there. 'Keep your wits about you, lass. I'm not quite sure what to expect from a trickster goblin.'

Moll remembered how both her arrows had missed the peatbogger earlier and she fumbled inside her coat pocket for her catapult instead – perhaps she'd have more luck with that. But as the dimly lit passageway wound on into the heart of the moor, twisting this way and that, one thing became crystal clear: this was no tunnel. At every juncture there were three or four paths to choose from. It was a maze.

'Aira,' Moll said, casting her eyes upwards. 'We're back where we started . . .'

Aira cursed as she looked at the slab above them and then Moll had an idea. She dug a hand into her pocket and drew out the piano string. It was almost completely invisible in the tunnel, but now and again the light cast by the candles caught an edge and it glinted gold.

'This is the last note of the witches' song,' Moll said. 'It's what Willow told us to find first.'

Aira squinted at it. 'It's beautiful, but how's it going to help us?'

Moll tied the end to the candle bracket on the wall beside

her. 'The string is never-ending, just like the witches' song was. If we wind out the string as we walk, it'll show us where we've already been.'

Aira's face lit up. 'And it'll show us how to get back too; I don't much fancy being trapped down here.'

Moll nodded, then, with Gryff by her side, she walked on down the tunnel, threading the piano string out through her fingers. But the further they went, the more on edge Gryff became. He shied at shadows cast by the candles and backed up into Moll when the path forked. Something about the place unsettled him and the same uneasiness whispered inside Moll too. She turned to Aira and, just as she was about to suggest going back towards the cairns, something swung down from the tunnel roof in front of them.

Moll leapt backwards, crashing into Gryff. Hanging upside down from a loose root was the most extraordinary little man Moll had ever seen. For a start, he was green. A round, bald head set above an even rounder pot belly, despite his scrawny arms and legs, made him look like a series of cabbages placed one on top of the other. He wore a tattered waistcoat, undone to reveal his belly, and ripped trousers, but perhaps strangest of all were his ears which were four times the size of ordinary ears, and pointed. He blinked two black eyes at his visitors.

'Ladies,' he said, his voice high and reedy. 'Kittlerumpit, at your service. How kind of you to drop by.'

Aira drew breath to say something, but the goblin's words filled every space.

'Safe journey here? Didn't mind the front door too much?

126

Staying long?' He stretched out a thin green arm towards them. 'Allow Kittlerumpit to take your coats.'

Neither Moll nor Aira offered theirs up and Moll found herself gripping tighter on the piano string and feeling suddenly glad that she had trailed it in the shadows so that Kittlerumpit couldn't see it. Gryff bared his teeth as the goblin flipped his body upright and then dropped down into the tunnel.

'Come browse, come buy – the place is yours for the looking.' He strained a gleaming eyeball up against Moll and sniffed. 'Fresh from the moors, are you? Come for something in particular?'

Moll started to say something, but Aira cut across her. 'We'd like to browse for now. That's all.'

The goblin's gaze lingered on Moll for a moment longer than it needed to, then he clasped his hands in delight and skipped further down the tunnel.

'This way to Kittlerumpit's treasures,' he sang. 'Come along, come along.'

'Don't let on that we need the feather just yet,' Aira whispered. 'I don't trust him one bit.' She paused. 'And keep that piano string hidden.'

Moll tucked the reel into her pocket and kept just a single thread between her fingers, unravelling it into the shadows a little more with every step she took. On they went, following the goblin deeper into his lair, and as they rounded a corner into yet another passageway, Moll's eyes grew large.

Cut into the soiled walls were ledges and shelves, and

rammed into every space were dozens of rusted cages, each one holding something different: giant eggs, silver horns, rings carved from bone, golden furs, jewels as large as plates and cloaks made from butterfly wings. And there were wooden boxes hanging down from the roots in the roof laden with unusual treasures: a snowflake the size of Moll's hand, unmelted and perfectly formed; a slice of rainbow; clocks that read the time backwards and raindrops dancing inside a sealed jar.

Moll ducked beneath the boxes and squinted into the cages, but there was no sign of the burning wings. Aira drew out a purse of gold coins, but, as Kittlerumpit turned his head, he merely giggled.

'Put that away now,' he said, closing a cold, clammy hand over Aira's. 'Kittlerumpit does things differently down here.' He turned to Moll and then pointed to the cages and boxes around him. 'A dragon egg – it's yours in exchange for your dreams. A slice of rainbow – yours to keep at the cost of your sanity. A unicorn horn – a deal if you'll hand over your voice.'

Moll flinched at his words. They rolled off Kittlerumpit's tongue as if he was talking about the weather, but each deal the goblin sought to strike made Moll's spine tingle. Kittlerumpit stopped suddenly between two cages. In one lay a purse made from dark brown hair and in the other was a yellowy brown necklace.

He chuckled to himself. 'A wallet made from the nose hair of trolls and a necklace sculpted from imps' toenails – one day Kittlerumpit will find a bidder.' His eyes slid down to Gryff and his voice dropped lower. 'How much for your cat, little girl?'

Moll stood in front of Gryff. 'He's not for sale.'

The goblin stamped his foot, then he craned his head round Moll and steepled his fingers. 'Oh, but his fur . . . what a fine rug it would make for Kittlerumpit's poor, tired feet as he climbs out of bed each morning.'

Moll spat on the ground in anger and Aira stepped forward to prevent a fight. 'You heard the girl,' Aira said. 'The wildcat's not for sale.'

The goblin shrugged. 'Suit yourselves.' He opened the cage containing the necklace, slipped a hand inside, snapped off a nail and then raised it to his mouth. He chewed for a few seconds before swallowing. 'Naughty Kittlerumpit,' he giggled. 'But sometimes he just can't help himself.'

Moll tried not to think about how far inside the moors they'd walked with this detestable little goblin and drew herself up tall. Then she glanced at Aira who nodded.

'We're after a feather from burning wings,' Moll said.

Kittlerumpit blinked once, but his face betrayed no emotion. Then, after a pause, he chuckled. 'This way.'

They followed him down another passageway. There were fewer candles flickering on the walls here and long shadows covered many of the cages, but Moll could see something glowing at the end of the tunnel – not a candle this time, but something larger and brighter. She quickened her step, loosening more and more of the string as she hurried after

Kittlerumpit until they came to the cage she'd been searching for. It was bigger than the rest – it had to be – because inside it was an enormous pair of wings with feathers as gold as freshly minted coins.

Moll slotted the string into her pocket, pulled the catch back on the cage and reached inside. But as soon as her fingertips met with the feathers a sharp pain seared through her. She jumped backwards.

Kittlerumpit scowled and closed the cage. 'Touching a pair of burning wings before you've struck a deal with Kittlerumpit – tut-tut . . .'

Moll rubbed her hand and peered through the bars with Gryff and Aira while the goblin drummed his bony fingers against the cage.

'The feathers of the last phoenix to fly in our world.' The goblin's face crumpled into a smile. 'And one of these feathers will cost you . . .'

Moll leant forward. 'Yes? How much?'

The goblin closed his eyes for a moment and began counting on his fingers as if he was adding up a complicated sum. Then his eyes sprang open. 'A feather from the burning wings will cost you a page from your story.'

For a second, Moll thought she'd misheard him. 'A page from my story? I – I don't understand . . .'

Gryff sidled up to Moll, turning narrow eyes towards the goblin.

Kittlerumpit began to hop up and down, wringing his hands impatiently. 'What will it be, girl? A page from your story for the feather you crave? Or will you go home empty-handed?'

Aira shook her head. 'Be careful, Moll. We don't know what he means.'

Moll's mind spun. What Kittlerumpit was saying didn't make any sense. She didn't have any books with her. There was nothing to trade. But compared to the other deals she'd heard him muttering about this was nothing. And yet she knew the goblin couldn't be trusted, and something about his words made Moll's scalp crawl. She opened her mouth, ready to make her choice, then her eyes flitted to a smaller cage beside the one that held the golden wings. She blinked once, twice, then a third time just to be sure. Her legs wobbled beneath her and she bent down, her hands gripping tightly to the bars. Inside the smaller cage were things she recognised, things she'd been trying to hold dear though their memory was fading.

Here were Alfie's belongings: his jay feather earring, a lock of his cob's hair, an owl feather just like the ones that had fletched his arrows and a piece of parchment bearing some of the very last words he'd said to her: *'I'll always come after you, Moll.'*

'Go on,' the goblin said quietly, slipping a wrinkled hand down to open the cage door. 'You can touch this time.'

Moll picked up the earring and held it in her palm. She squeezed tighter and tighter as if by holding it she might somehow bring Alfie back, then she closed her eyes and tried to imagine that he was by her side. No image appeared in her mind though; it was as if his face was slipping from her grasp.

She turned to Kittlerumpit. 'Do you have him? Is Alfie here somewhere?'

Aira bent down next to Moll and whispered in her ear. 'Be careful. Trust your gut – not the illusions the goblin puts in front of you.'

Kittlerumpit glanced at the golden wings. 'It seems we have a choice.' He clapped his hands in delight. 'Kittlerumpit does so love choices. So, what will it be, girl? Your Alfie or your feather? And I'll keep it simple for you: whichever you choose, it'll cost you a page from your story.'

Moll shook her head. 'But ... Alfie. Is he *here*?'

The goblin scratched his head. 'So many cages, so many visitors.' He sniggered. 'Kittlerumpit forgets!'

Moll drew herself up. 'No,' she said firmly. 'You don't forget. You could never forget someone like Alfie. He's brave and good and – and – even though not everyone can see him you'd never forget him. Not ever.'

Kittlerumpit giggled. 'Alfie's belongings are here so maybe he is too. What will you choose: the feather or your friend?'

Gryff pressed up against Moll's legs and she wished she could find a way into his thoughts. Was Alfie here, somewhere, or was this all a trick? She looked at Aira.

'What do I do? Willow told me to find the feather, but ... if Alfie's here, then I have to go after him! I made a promise!'

'Go with your gut,' Aira said again. 'Even if it's not what's easiest.'

Moll looked at Gryff with desperate eyes. She hadn't asked to be part of the Bone Murmur, to be wrenched from the forest and tasked with beating the Shadowmasks. She thought of what lay ahead: finding the amulet, then destroying the last two witch doctors and the Veil to stop the eternal night. The quest was so *big* and, faced with the choice now, Moll wanted to give it all up and choose Alfie.

And yet ... she knew that the old magic was worth fighting for. Willow had told her to go after the feather and she had helped them in the forest when they were lost and in danger, and she had cured Oak's leg and helped their smuggler friend, Scrap. Moll couldn't just give up on the old magic, on something her own parents had dedicated their lives to.

'I – I can't choose,' Moll stammered.

Aira placed a hand on Moll's back. 'You have to, Moll. I'm here with you, but I can't tell you what's right.' She paused. 'If you think getting Alfie back will help us destroy the Shadowmasks, then choose him, but we don't know he's actually here.' She lowered her voice. 'And this goblin is bound up in the witch doctors' dark magic. Remember that.'

Kittlerumpit's eyes were black and shining. 'Oh, we're all having so much fun, aren't we?'

Moll looked at the earring in her palm, then at the horse hair and parchment in the cage. They sang of Alfie's story, but they were just objects, fragments from a time they'd had together, while in the other cage was the next step towards the amulet. Moll closed her eyes again.

This time though she saw Alfie.

He wasn't a blurred face or a half-remembered figure, as

he was in her dreams every night. This was different. She could see him clearly in her mind now and he was smiling, his fair hair flopped down over his eyes, his bow and arrow slung over his shoulder. Moll hardly dared move or breathe as she watched his mouth open a fraction and shape words she felt that she alone could hear. Then the image of Alfie faded and Moll's eyes sprang open – but his words were still ringing in her ears.

Find the amulet.

And somehow Moll knew in that moment that the feeling in her gut had been right. Alfie *was* alive and he had found a way to tell her so. She looked at Kittlerumpit and thought of how Alfie had sacrificed himself to destroy the Soul Splinter and she realised that she, too, would choose the old magic because, in finding the amulet, she *would* find Alfie again.

'The feather from burning wings,' Moll said at last. 'That's what I choose.'

'You're sure?' the goblin crooned.

Moll blinked, forcing down the tears that were prickling her throat at the thought of being wrong. 'The feather,' she said again, placing the earring back in Alfie's cage.

Kittlerumpit let the door of the larger cage creak open, then he gestured to Moll. 'Go on then. Take one.'

Hesitantly, Moll stretched out a hand. Her fingertips met with the soft gold feathers but unlike before they didn't scald her skin when she tugged at the largest one and lifted it out of the cage. It was the size of her arm and it glinted in the candlelight. Moll placed it in her quiver, next to her arrows, and tried not to look back at the rusted cage containing Alfie's things.

Kittlerumpit stooped towards a ledge and picked up a small yellowed animal skull. Moll noticed that it was filled with water.

'Now drink to seal our deal,' he said.

Moll took a step backwards, but Kittlerumpit clamped a bony hand round her wrist. 'Drink from the raven's skull or the feather stays here.'

Aira watched nervously as the goblin placed the skull into Moll's trembling palm, but, as she lowered her lips towards it, Gryff leapt up and tipped the skull towards him, draining the water in a single gulp. The wildcat hissed and then shook his head, but Kittlerumpit only raised one dark eyebrow.

'Interesting,' he muttered. 'Very interesting.'

The goblin picked up the raven's skull and set it back on a ledge and, as Moll watched, the despair she had felt that morning swelled up inside her again. What if the choice she'd made was wrong? What if they didn't really stand a chance of finding the last amulet and she'd missed her moment to get Alfie back? Had she let her friend down for a second time?

Aira placed a hand on Moll's shoulder. 'Let's go. We've got what we came for and we can talk up on the moors.'

'*If* you can find your way out,' Kittlerumpit chortled.

He was sitting on a cage he'd hauled out from a shelf and placed in the middle of the tunnel, blocking their way through. Moll dug a hand into her pocket for the piano string and felt it tingle inside her palm.

'Ooh, you don't realise how clever Kittlerumpit has been, do you?' the goblin smirked, swinging his legs back and forth.

And it was only when Moll looked down at his feet that she realised why he was grinning. On the ground, coiled up neatly in front of Kittlerumpit, lay the rest of the piano string glinting in the torchlight – the reel she'd so carefully unwound into the shadows so that they could find their way out.

Moll's heart skipped a beat. 'No,' she gasped. She hurried forward and snatched it up, then she glared at Kittlerumpit. 'You unpicked our way? But you haven't left our side. How did . . .?'

The goblin chuckled. 'Kittlerumpit's tunnels are full of magic. You didn't think he would let you go that easily, did you? Not when he has a bargain with the Shadowmasks to keep you here.'

His face darkened and, before Aira could slot a bolt to her crossbow, he melted into thin air. Gryff tore towards the cage he'd been sitting on, but Moll sprang forward and grabbed him back.

'No, Gryff! We need to escape,' she said, tucking the piano string back into her pocket. 'No fight. Not this time.'

Aira nodded, then she took a deep breath and they began walking down the tunnel together, past the cages stuffed with unusual objects and the boxes hanging above. They came to a fork in the passageway.

'Let's try right,' Moll said.

They turned down a wider corridor lined with yet more cages. From behind the bars, silver eyeballs followed their every move, a set of enormous black teeth gnashed and a snake made of diamonds hissed from the shadows. Moll shuddered and kept on walking, then the path split again.

'Left?' she ventured, trying to remember the way they'd come.

137

Aira nodded. 'Left.'

Moll could tell from her tone that she was far from sure. There were no cages in the passageway this time, just earth walls lined with candles. Gryff quickened his pace and Moll hurried on after him, then both of them slowed.

'Something's not right,' Moll whispered to Aira. And she stopped in her tracks. 'The walls! With every step we take, they're getting narrower!'

Gryff edged backwards because, sure enough, the walls were moving slowly, soundlessly in towards them.

'Run!' Aira yelled.

They hurtled back down the tunnel as the walls slid nearer still and Moll shrieked as she felt the soil brushing against her elbows. Gryff tore ahead and Moll and Aira pelted after him, then just as the passageway was about to close around them they burst out into a crossroads. The passageway sealed itself behind them and, to their relief, the tunnel they found themselves in next was still and spacious. But, from somewhere nearby, there came a high-pitched chuckle: the unmistakable sound of Kittlerumpit.

Moll threw her hands up in the air. 'He's bewitched it all! We're never going to find a way out before the Shadowmasks come for me and Gryff!'

Aira pointed to the passage on their left, her face shining with sweat. 'Come on. We can't give up.'

They hastened down another tunnel and this time the walls, the roof and the ground were completely covered in mirrors and in every direction Moll glanced she saw her panic-stricken face staring back at her. She tried to blank out her wild eyes, but wherever she looked they followed.

'Don't let that goblin's tricks scare you,' Aira muttered. 'Keep walking. And remember that if we can't see our faces right in front of us, that's good – it means there's a way through.'

Their boots clacked against the mirrored floor as the tunnel turned left and then right, then straight on through yet more mirrors. Moll scoured the glass, flinching as she caught sight of her face, while Gryff padded ahead, searching for a way out. But the further they went, the more disorientated Moll and Aira became, and they found themselves stumbling into walls, then staggering backwards. Moll looked around for Gryff, but all she saw staring back at her were two faces: one with a shock of short red hair and the other with a dark, tangled plait.

'Where's Gryff?' Moll gasped.

Aira whirled round, but it was just her and Moll in the tunnel now.

Moll blundered forward. 'Gryff!' she screamed. 'Where are you?'

But the wildcat didn't appear and the mirrors around them reflected faces full of terror. Moll and Aira rushed back the way they'd come, hands clawing at the mirrors to find their way through, then they burst out into an earth tunnel – but it wasn't the one they'd come from. This was the passageway where they'd found the golden feather. Moll tore beneath the hanging boxes right to the end of the tunnel. The small cage containing Alfie's belongings was now empty – but Moll didn't have time to think about that because the larger cage no longer held the wings of burning gold.

Moll stopped dead in front of it, rage flooding through her veins. Locked behind the bars, scrabbling at the lock with his paws, was Gryff.

'No,' Moll growled. 'Not this. *Not ever this.*'

When the wildcat saw Moll, he stopped struggling and his eyes grew large and afraid. Moll dropped to her knees and wrenched at the lock, but it held fast and she could only press trembling palms up to the bars.

Then the goblin appeared, walking slowly towards them from the way they'd just come. 'Kittlerumpit will let you both out if you leave the cat. And maybe the piano string too.'

Aira swung her crossbow down from her back, but Moll's temper was swifter and she darted forward. Eyes narrowed, she threw herself on top of the goblin, pummelling furious fists into his body and ripping at his clothes with her teeth. Cages and boxes clattered to the ground as the two wrestled back and forth across the tunnel.

'Get back, Moll!' Aira cried. 'I can't fire with you there!'

But Moll was deaf to Aira's words. All she could feel was her fury.

'No one locks Gryff up!' Moll panted, swinging a punch at Kittlerumpit's shoulder. 'He's wild. He belongs free!'

Kittlerumpit struggled backwards, his waistcoat torn and his nose bleeding. 'Don't forget, girl, Kittlerumpit is the only one who has a key to that cage. If you carry on like this, you'll never find it and your cat will be locked down here for ever ...'

Aira lowered her crossbow. 'What do we have to do to get the key?'

Before Kittlerumpit could reply, Moll was on her feet, her hair wild about her face. 'Listen, goblin,' she snarled. 'I'm through with your bargaining and your bullying and your horrid little tunnels.'

'Careful, Moll,' Aira whispered.

Moll blundered on, her anger hot and loaded. 'Gryff's not some *thing* to be locked up and traded! You'll free him or I'll tear you and this place to pieces.'

Kittlerumpit snorted. 'A little girl like you bringing down all these tunnels?' He rubbed his bruised elbow. 'Unlikely.'

Moll drew herself up over him. 'Everything you've got in here has been bargained for – traded – nothing's free. But Gryff came to me from the northern wilderness. He sought me out even though there was nothing in it for him. He gave his friendship *for free.*'

She took a few steps backwards and put a hand on the cage. Gryff nosed it through the bars and whimpered helplessly, then Moll got out her pa's knife from her belt and began sawing it back and forth against the metal bars. Behind her Kittlerumpit sneered.

'Is that the best you've got?' he scoffed.

Aira levelled her crossbow at the goblin. 'Leave her be.'

At first nothing happened and just the sound of scraping

141

metal echoed round the tunnel. Then, little by little, Moll's knife cut into the bars.

'It's working!' Aira gasped.

Kittlerumpit's face tightened. 'Impossible.' He wrung his tattered shirt like a spoilt child. 'That cage is enchanted. Its bars are made from iron forged in the depths of a volcano. Only *my* key can unlock it.'

Aira pulled back on her crossbow. 'Looks like we might not need you after all.'

Moll didn't look up. 'I don't care about your enchantments, goblin. That's my wildcat in there and I'm not leaving until he's free.'

One of the bars clanked to the ground and Gryff pressed closer to Moll.

'I'm up in the northern wilderness to find an amulet and to rescue my friends,' Moll muttered. 'I'm not here to play games. You've had your fun with the feather, Kittlerumpit. *Now let Gryff go.*'

Another bar snapped away and Kittlerumpit backed up against the tunnel wall, wringing his hands before Aira's crossbow. 'But how is she doing that? No one's ever broken into my cages.'

Aira took a step closer to the goblin. 'Well, you haven't met Moll, have you? This child's got more love and loyalty bound up inside her than you have in one of your crooked toenails!' she cried. 'And that counts for more than enchantments and sneaky deals.'

Moll sawed and sawed until her hand went numb and

every muscle in her arm ached, then another bar crashed down and Gryff burst from the cage, flinging himself against her. They crouched together, a tangle of paws and hair.

'We came down here for a feather,' Aira spat. 'And in a moment you're going to tell us how to leave.'

Kittlerumpit put his hands over his ears. 'Not listening! Not listening!'

Aira levelled her crossbow at him and the goblin's hands slid to his sides and he gulped.

'I want to know why you made Moll choose between Alfie and the feather,' Aira said. 'What were the Shadowmasks trying to do?'

Kittlerumpit chewed on his nails. 'Poor Kittlerumpit can't even disappear when he's as frightened as this.'

Aira took a step closer and jammed her crossbow beneath the goblin's chin. 'Tell me,' she growled. 'Or I'll make you disappear myself.'

Kittlerumpit blinked very quickly, as if struggling with an inner decision, but, when Aira placed a finger on her crossbow trigger, his words tumbled out.

'I never saw the boy she calls Alfie,' he spluttered. 'The Shadowmasks gave me his belongings because they hoped that the girl and her wildcat would come for the feather.'

'But why make her *choose*?' Aira growled.

'Because the Shadowmasks want her to give up on the boy. They said they needed to break her impossible dream to conjure their eternal night.' The goblin's bottom lip wobbled. 'Choosing Alfie over the old magic here would have proved that she had given up hope of finding him herself. That's all Kittlerumpit knows.'

Aira looked down at Moll who was still hugging Gryff, then she glowered at Kittlerumpit. 'We'd like to go now, goblin, and I don't care if the Shadowmasks told you to break Moll's hopes and hold her here. We're leaving and *you* are going to show us the way out.'

Kittlerumpit chewed his lip. For the first time, he'd been outwitted by one of his customers. 'The way home is always closer than you think,' he sniffed. 'Knock one and a half times on the slab in the roof and you'll be back on the moors in a second.' Aira frowned at the stone overhead. 'It's not the one you fell through earlier,' the goblin mumbled. 'Each slab in the cairns leads down to a different tunnel.'

Aira raised an eyebrow. 'How do we know you're telling the truth?'

The goblin looked down at his tattered clothes and at the cages strewn across the tunnel. 'Because Kittlerumpit doesn't want you or your friend or her wildcat in his tunnels any longer than he has to, whatever the Shadowmasks might have instructed him to do.'

Aira nodded at the slab. 'Open it. Now.'

Kittlerumpit scurried over to the wall, grabbed the ladder resting there and propped it up against the edge of the stone. He scampered up, knocked once, then as he was drawing his fist back to knock a second time, the slab wobbled and then crunched back, like a can lid opening, and the whiteness of the moors flooded in. A breeze rippled through the tunnel, shaking the stale world locked beneath the hills, and a handful of snowflakes drifted down.

Aira turned to face Kittlerumpit but, just as before, his small green body faded before their eyes and then vanished completely. Aira knelt by Moll and Gryff who were still huddled together on the ground.

'You did it, Moll!' she cried. 'You got Gryff out of the cage and we made Kittlerumpit show us the way home!'

But, as Aira tried to urge Moll up, she realised the girl wasn't smiling. Her eyes were red and swollen and large tears were rolling down her cheeks.

'When I closed my eyes before making my choice, I thought I saw Alfie telling me to choose the old magic,' Moll sobbed. 'But now everything feels confused again, as if maybe I didn't see him after all. What if he really is gone and I don't stand a chance of finding the last amulet?' She shook her head. Once again, it felt as if forces beyond her power were wrestling for control over her thoughts. She clutched Gryff to her chest. 'All that waits for me above these wretched tunnels is more dark magic.'

Aira didn't try to clasp Moll's hand – she remembered how the girl had withdrawn at Fillie Crankie – and, even though she knew they needed to leave the tunnels as quickly as possible, her words came softly. 'We can't know what's going to happen over the next few days or weeks or months,' she said. 'Most of the time when people hope, the odds are against them, but they keep on hoping anyway. However small and shaky you feel your hope is now, remember that it was enough to break through Kittlerumpit's cage. That fight inside you – that one

145

Kittlerumpit admitted the Shadowmasks are trying so hard to break – it's not dead yet, Moll.'

Moll let her chin rest on Gryff's back as the snow sprinkled down. 'But I might have lost my one chance of finding Alfie, for the sake of a magic that couldn't even make him real.' She tried to button her sadness in, but it spilled out, making her shoulders shake.

'Alfie was never down here, Moll. You heard the goblin. Even if you had chosen Alfie's belongings, it wouldn't have brought him back – it would have just hastened the Shadowmasks' eternal night instead. Only *believing* in your friend, holding fast to your impossible dream while keeping faith, can help you find Alfie.' She paused for a moment and then, very slowly, she lifted an arm to Moll's back. 'It's going to be OK.'

Moll didn't flinch this time and, as the tears flooded down, she leant into Aira's chest and let herself be held. She rocked back and forth in the darkness of the tunnels and cried for all the things she couldn't fix: for Siddy and Alfie and for her ma and pa who weren't there to comfort her now.

After a while, Moll looked up and wiped her eyes with her sleeve. 'I'm sorry for crying,' she sniffed. 'Usually I do it up a tree where no one can see me.'

Aira stroked Moll's hair. 'It's OK to cry.'

'No,' Moll said quietly. 'It's not. Because crying doesn't win wars and beat witch doctors. It gets you – *killed.*'

Aira smiled. 'Sometimes the bravest thing you can do is cry – because it's only afterwards, when your tears have dried, that you find you have the strength to fight on.'

Moll avoided Aira's eyes. 'Yes, well, if that's true, I'll be ready for lots more fighting now.'

Aira laughed, then she stood up and placed a boot on the first rung of the ladder. 'Come on. Let's get going. We don't want Kittlerumpit sending word to the Shadowmasks that we're still down in his tunnels.'

They clambered up the steps and emerged into a world washed white. The snow had almost stopped now and behind the clouds an orange dusk was pushing through. Moll stood amid the cairns and let the wind dry her tear-stained face. They'd been down in the tunnels almost all day and the dark, closed spaces had made her feel trapped. But out here, with the heather and the snow and the wind, Moll could breathe. She tickled Gryff's throat.

'No one will ever take you away from me,' she said softly. 'No one.'

Gryff blinked up at her, then the stone slab scraped back over the entrance to Whuppity Cairns, as if Kittlerumpit had never existed. Moll joined Aira, who had wandered over to the grazing ponies, but, as they shared out the sandwiches from their saddlebags, Moll heard a sound she wasn't expecting – one that made her head spin.

It was a voice, carried over the moors in a gust of wind, and it was calling *her name*. Moll knew this voice, almost as well as her own, and she scrambled to her feet.

'SIDDY!' she yelled. 'SIDDY!'

Chapter 18
Searching for Siddy

Moll surged forward, rushing over the heather on to the track and, with her boots skidding on stones, she hurtled down it, further across the moors towards Siddy's voice. Again and again he called out her name and with each cry Moll's smile grew wider.

'I'm coming, Sid!' she yelled as Gryff bounded level with her. 'Where are you?'

But only her name came back, carried on the evening wind. 'Moll! Moll!'

She could hear hooves now, but they were pounding on the track behind her and, as she twisted her neck round, she saw Aira riding Salt and gripping Pepper's reins.

Moll stopped, breathless, her hands on her knees. 'It's Siddy!' she panted. 'He's here, I know it, and—'

'Stop, Moll,' Aira said. 'Stop and listen to me.'

Moll scoured the moors, hardly able to focus on Aira as she drew the horses up in front of her.

'This isn't what it seems,' Aira said.

Moll strained her ears – past the meadow pipit's song and

the roars of rutting stags in the distance – and there was Siddy's voice calling out to her again.

'He's here, Aira. Listen.'

But, as they both did, Moll's face changed. Something about the voice sounded detached; it was more like an echo from many miles away than a voice right there on the hillside with them.

Aira looked down. 'Siddy's not here, Moll. That's an echo trapped in a knot of wind.'

Moll shook her head. '*His* echo. Siddy's. That means he must be close.'

But the voice didn't sound close. If anything, it sounded as if it was trailing away.

'You read Willow's letter,' Aira said. 'You saw what she said about the wind spirits carrying the parchment to you?'

Moll nodded.

'Well, sometimes the wind spirits also carry messages on the moors up here for those who know how to communicate with them.' She shook her head. 'And what you're following is not Siddy himself but his *voice*, trapped in a puff of wind.'

Moll closed her eyes and listened again. A gust of wind swirled around her, and with it came Siddy's voice calling out her name, then the wind drained away and was nothing more than a sigh. Moll's shoulders sank as the hopes she'd built were suddenly dashed.

Then the wind clamoured around them once more, scattering fragments of Siddy's words: *'Come to Greystone!'*

the voice inside the knot of wind cried. *'I know where the amulet is . . .'*

Moll blinked at the strangeness of it all. 'What does he mean? And how is Siddy doing this?'

The words echoed around them before crumbling into nothing as the wind withdrew.

Aira's eyes shone. 'I don't know how your friend has managed to communicate with the wind spirits,' she said quietly, 'but I know where Greystone is.'

Moll hands were fists inside her gloves. 'Where? Where is Siddy?'

'West of the moors lies the sea and a cluster of islands known as the Lost Isles.' Aira looked out over the hills. 'Greystone is the name of a castle on one of the Lost Isles, the one closest to the coast. I thought it was deserted, but it seems that's where your friend Siddy is – and somehow he's managed to get a message to you.'

'He's alive,' Moll breathed. 'And he knows where the last amulet is!' She frowned. 'Maybe Spud was wrong; maybe the Shadowmasks didn't take Sid from the moors after all. But his footprints . . . Spud said they stopped dead in the track and only magic could pluck him from the path like that.'

Aira was silent for a moment. 'The wind spirits are strong up here. They've been known to wrench people from the moors and cast them into ravines. But I've heard stories of them carrying people to safety too.' She paused. 'It's possible that the wind spirits rescued Siddy from a peatbogger and took him to the Lost Isles.'

Moll reached inside her coat pocket and drew out Willow's parchment: 'You'll find what you need one hundred years deep.' She looked at it for a moment. 'The ocean is deep . . . deeper than anything I know. You don't think,' her eyes grew large, 'that the amulet is at the bottom of the sea?'

'Wherever it is, Siddy knows.' Aira smiled. 'And we can't afford to spend a moment longer out here. Let's go and find your friend.'

Moll's face broke into a smile as she swung herself up on to Pepper, then they rode down the track, into the gathering dusk. The clouds pulled apart, letting the sunset slip through and bathing the snow in a deep orange glow. Burns and hills glimmered and Moll would have thought it beautiful had she not been thinking about the Shadowmasks, worrying that every time a covey of grouse or a herd of deer broke their silence it might be the witch doctors, spurred on after them at Kittlerumpit's word.

Eventually the path ended and just the moorland stretched out around them: heather, juniper bushes and gorse poking through the snow and a small loch reflecting the evening clouds.

'Proper wilderness now,' Aira said, nudging Salt on into the heather.

And yet Aira knew her way without the help of a map. The landscape was etched on her memory, each peat bog and gully locked inside her skull. Once or twice they slipped down from the ponies to fill their flasks from the burns, but the water was icy cold and Moll had to wriggle her fingers inside her gloves afterwards to fight the warmth back into them.

Soon darkness crept over the moors and Moll was relieved when Aira pointed to a bothy set before a copse of pine trees. It wasn't much, just a small hut made from timber to house any deer stalkers that passed this way, but it was a roof over their heads and, after they had fed and watered the ponies and tied them up, they traipsed inside.

Aira struck a match to the oil lamp on the table and it cast a hazy glow over two tattered armchairs set either side of a wood-burning stove and bunk beds piled up with blankets on the other side of the room.

'Bit cramped,' Aira said. 'But places like this are always unlocked and stocked with firewood. Up here on the moors we look out for one another.'

There was only one window, but on Aira's instructions Moll drew the curtains – they couldn't risk being found by the last two Shadowmasks – then she unpacked the supplies from their saddlebags while Gryff skirted the room for an unlucky mouse and Aira lit the kindling in the stove.

Before long, flames were flickering inside the wood-burner, heating the can of beans they had placed on top and the potatoes in foil slotted inside. Aira and Moll sank into the armchairs, letting the wall of heat seep right through them, and when the food was ready they ate silently.

There was plenty they could have said, but the events of the day and the journey across the moors had left them too tired for talk and, shortly after their meal, they flopped down into the bunk beds, heaping all of the blankets they could find on top of them. Moll placed the golden feather and the reel of piano string under her pillow in the bottom bunk, then she trailed a hand down to the ground. It was met, shortly after, by a paw.

Minutes later, Moll heard gentle snores coming from Aira's bunk, but Moll's mind wouldn't still and she lay staring at the flames behind the wood-burner door, watching them dance and listening to them crackle. She thought of Siddy's voice echoing on the moors and the possibility that tomorrow they might be together again – and for a moment her heart grew light. Then the darkness that had been lurking inside her since she'd come to the northern wilderness closed in and Moll's mind wandered to the sprawling moors outside – to the wilderness pressing in at her on all sides. She shuddered as she thought of how far she was from the safety of her wagon in Tanglefern Forest, then she blinked back her fear. Why was she scared? She was used to living wild; she'd grown up among the Sacred Oaks, but this felt different. Something about the enormity of the moors made her feel suddenly fearful.

Look the wild in the eye and face it: those were the words Oak had said to her every time she'd got scared as a child in the woods and Moll clung to them now as she wrapped her blanket around her and padded towards the window. Gryff followed and, as Moll pulled the curtain back a fraction, he snuggled against her legs.

The night was close against the window, a cold darkness pricked with stars. And above the copse of trees the moon was a slice of silver that, for a second, held the silhouette of barn owl out on its midnight hunt. Wind soughed through the pines and Moll clutched her talisman as she tried to look it all in the eye.

'It's just moorland,' she whispered into her blanket. 'There's no reason to be afeared.'

But these moors held cursed creatures and witch doctors vying for her life and, for the first time, Moll didn't feel a part of the landscape around her. She felt swallowed by it. She drew the curtain, closing off the night, and tiptoed towards the wood-burning stove. Then she sat down on the floor, huddled inside her blanket with her knees raised up to her chin. The wildcat nestled up to her side and purred.

'I don't feel like me any more, Gryff,' Moll whispered. 'Crying in the tunnel, feeling afraid of the wild . . . Ever since we came north, things have been collapsing.'

Gryff may not have had words to reply with, but he felt the loneliness inside Moll. He knew her as well as he knew himself and he understood that where grit and certainty had been there was something wavering, something desperately vulnerable, so he answered the only way he knew how: by placing two heavy paws on Moll's legs and nudging his head below her chin.

Moll felt the closeness of their bond. She might not have Alfie or Siddy or even Domino by her side, but she still had Gryff, and for now that was enough. She drew back the blanket, folded the wildcat inside with her, and for a while longer they just sat before the fire, watching the logs burn and wishing they were tucked up together in their wagon in Tanglefern forest.

Chapter 19
News on the Moors

Aira had been surprised to find Moll and Gryff curled up before the embers of the fire in the morning, but she hadn't probed and, after a quick bowl of porridge and a mug of heather tea, she and Moll mounted the highland ponies and urged them out on to the snow-scattered moors.

The sun rose behind them, bathing whole hillsides pink and glinting off the snow that flicked up from the ponies' hooves. Moll and Aira spurred Salt and Pepper over burns and through marshes and, after some time, they found a path that ran between a tumbled stone wall on one side and a bank of heather on the other. The ponies rushed up it, side by side, and, by the time they reached the summit, they were foaming at the bit. Moll and Aira reined them into a walk, but, as Moll looked up at the view in front of her, at what lay beyond the track that wound down off the moors, she gasped. It was the sea – and great mounds of land rose up from the water, dotted beyond the coastline like fragments of forgotten countries.

'The Lost Isles,' Aira said.

Moll's and Gryff's eyes travelled over them. Some of the islands were tiny and uninhabited – rocky outcrops with a few straggly trees – while others were larger and covered in frosted slopes where highland cows grazed and cottages lined wiggling tracks. And then there were the ones that burst out of the sea into jagged mountains tipped with snow. Moll marvelled at them all; it was like stumbling upon a secret kingdom.

Aira pointed to one of the closest islands – a small outcrop joined to the mainland by a humpback bridge. There was only one thing on the island, but it rose up in a jumble of stone turrets, gables and ramparts and Moll knew exactly what it was.

'That's Greystone, isn't it?'

Aira nodded. 'And Siddy's inside.'

Moll dug her heels into Pepper's flanks. 'Let's go before—'

Gryff turned suddenly and Moll's shoulders stiffened. 'What is it?'

The wildcat's ears were cocked towards the way they'd come and, as Moll wheeled Pepper round, her own ears snagged on what Gryff had heard: the pounding of a horse's hooves. Aira slid a hand to her crossbow and Moll reached for an arrow as a figure on horseback rode through the sunlight towards them.

Moll's heart thumped. What if this was the Night Spinner . . .?

Aira squinted. 'That's – that's Spud!'

Spud was galloping towards them, kilt flapping in the wind, ginger hair bouncing around his shoulders, and Aira threw up her hand and waved. But, as he drew closer, her expression changed.

Spud pulled up his horse in front of them, his face racked with worry. 'I came as soon as I could,' he panted. 'I followed your tracks in the snow.'

Aira leant forward. 'What's happened?'

'It's Angus – and Moll's friend, Domino.'

Moll flinched. How had Spud come across Domino?

'They're not in a good way.'

'What's happened?' Aira asked again.

'Apparently they'd been rebuilding the cottages in Glendrummie, helping those poisoned by the Veil and speaking to people about the old magic and its power over the Shadowmasks. Spirits had lifted a bit and those still fit and healthy had vowed to journey past the North Door with Angus and Domino to help Moll find the last amulet.' Spud shook his head. 'But the witch doctors must have sensed the threat ...'

Moll's stomach churned and Aira raised a hand to her mouth.

'The Shadowmasks sent a storm bigger than anything Glendrummie has ever seen,' Spud explained. 'The village was flattened by the winds, some of the people were killed and Angus and Domino ...'

Moll felt the landscape around her spin.

'They're alive,' Spud said, though from his face Moll could

tell there was more. 'When we saw the storm brewing, we rode out to the village and found the survivors fleeing south.' He paused. 'Morag recognised us and asked the Highland Watch to take her, Angus and the twins to the safety of Fillie Crankie. She vouched for Domino too, because he couldn't speak for himself, and—'

Moll leant forward. 'What's happened to him?'

Spud shifted in his saddle. 'The Night Spinner came in the midst of the storm – in daylight this time – and Morag said Angus and Domino tried to fight, but the Veil crept in and closed round them both.'

A chill rippled through Moll and Aira's eyes shone with tears.

'My brother,' Aira gasped, 'poisoned by the Veil . . .'

Spud hung his head. 'I'm so sorry, Aira.'

Moll swallowed as she thought of Domino, the boy she loved like an older brother, and Angus, with his steadfast faith in the old magic. How could both these men be trapped under the Night Spinner's curse?

'When we were riding to Fillie Crankie, we thought we could keep Domino and Angus going,' Spud said, 'just like they managed to do with the sick villagers. Both of them were crying out as if the forces of the old magic and the darkness were fighting inside them, but then their words – they – they stopped.'

Aira raised a hand to her mouth. '*Stopped?*'

Spud nodded. 'They haven't said a word since we arrived at Fillie Crankie last night. They won't eat or drink. It's

159

as if something inside them has given up. We don't know what to do, Aira. If we don't find a cure in the next few days, then ...'

Moll wanted to rush back with Spud and fling her arms round Domino, but she knew it wouldn't fix what the Shadowmasks had done. She gripped Pepper's reins to stop herself from shaking. 'I – I need to find the amulet,' she said. 'It's the *only* thing that can destroy the Night Spinner and his Veil and stop the eternal night.'

Aira glanced down at Greystone, then back to Spud until finally her eyes rested on Moll. She went to speak, but Moll knew what Aira would say, knew she'd go on with Moll if she asked. But one of them needed to find a cure – even if it was only temporary until Moll found the amulet – for Angus and Domino, and all those on the brink of death. So Moll spoke the words to stop Aira having to.

'Go back with Spud,' she said.

Aira shook her head. 'I can't leave you and Gryff alone out here.'

Moll nodded towards Greystone. 'We won't be alone soon. Sid's there. I know he is. Your brother and Domino need you more – you *have* to find a way to help them before it's too late and the darkness drowns them completely.' She bit her lip. 'And we both know where you'll find it.'

'Kittlerumpit,' Aira said. 'If there's anyone who has an antidote for dark curses, it will be him. And the Shadowmasks won't expect me to go back there.'

'Return with Spud and make that horrible goblin give you

a cure,' Moll said. 'And look after Domino for me. Tell him the stories of the old magic – make him believe again.'

Aira nudged her pony up to Pepper, then reached over and clutched Moll's hands. 'I've never met anyone like you, lass.' She smiled. 'I want you to remember what I told you: however small you feel, I know the toughness of your soul. I see your fight.' She lifted something over her head – a whistle carved from an antler on a length of string – and pressed it into Moll's gloves. 'This was handed down to my ancestors thousands of years ago from the giants up in the mountains – the folk who were there when the old magic first turned.'

She looked into Moll's eyes. 'See this whistle as a promise. If you need help from the old magic, blow it and it will come.' Then Aira picked up a ram's horn she'd tied to her pony's saddle, set her lips against it and blew. The sound blared, sharp and loud, and its echo drifted across the moors. 'And, when you hear that sound, you'll know that *I* have come for *you*.' Aira leant forward boldly this time and wrapped her arms round Moll.

Moll closed her eyes. 'Thank you for coming with me this far,' she said. 'And for believing in me.'

Aira squeezed tight. 'The Highland Watch never leave anyone behind.'

Moll turned Pepper away from the group, dug her heels in hard and, with Gryff by her side, she rode down the track towards the Lost Isles.

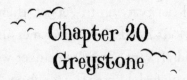

Chapter 20
Greystone

The sun was high in the sky now, winking off the icy bracken that poked through the heather either side of the track. Moll could tell Pepper was uneasy about breaking off from the others, but she urged the pony on, clicking her tongue and gripping his flanks with her legs. They followed the moors down to where the bracken petered out and a dirt road running parallel to the coastline began. It curved round a bend to her left, out of sight, but to her right it led straight on past a humpback bridge a mile or so further up the road and, although Pepper yanked his neck back round to the moors and whinnied, Moll edged him on to the track.

They hadn't taken more than a few strides before a cart rumbled round the bend and Pepper reared up, sending Moll crashing down into the bracken. She grappled for the reins, but Pepper shied, then bolted back towards the moors and Moll cursed as she remembered Aira's words about the highland ponies: *The only time you've got to watch them is if they leave the moors because they get spooked by carts and cottages.* She watched as Pepper galloped further and further up the path, but she didn't have time to go after him because the cart was drawing near. Gryff sank his teeth into Moll's coat, tugging her down into the bracken with him, and then they waited, Moll's heart throbbing as she peered through the ferns.

The cart was filled with crates of vegetables, sacks of potatoes and a large bundle of firewood and, to Moll's surprise, a boy a few years younger than her sat up front behind the horse, his legs tucked beneath a blanket. Moll crouched lower in the bracken as he pulled the cart to a stop beside them. The boy was bundled up in an overcoat and a scarf, but beneath his woollen hat she could make out two dark eyes and a shock of white-blond hair. Moll considered him. He looked perfectly harmless, but Kittlerumpit the goblin hadn't looked much either, so Moll didn't want to take any chances.

The boy narrowed his eyes in Moll's direction. 'I see you can,' he said, then he shook his head as if he'd realised there was something not quite right about his words. He tried again. 'I can see you.'

Moll said nothing and kept absolutely still beside Gryff. The boy said nothing also and, just as Moll was contemplating flinging herself out into the road with her catapult in one hand and her bow in the other, the boy spoke again.

'Are you who?'

Moll could feel the beads of sweat inching down her back. She was unsure of the boy – she knew that strangers were often not to be trusted – and she couldn't work out why he was speaking in such a jumbled way.

The boy smacked his head. 'I mean, **WHO ARE YOU?**'

Moll stood up slowly, her bow raised. Beside her, Gryff bared his teeth.

'The question,' she growled, setting an arrow to her string, 'is who are *you*?'

The boy backed up in his seat. 'A-a-am I Bruce?' he stammered.

Moll's squinted, but she kept her bow raised to her chin. 'I don't know. You tell me. Are you Bruce?'

The boy nodded hastily. 'Yes, yes. **I AM BRUCE**. I'm not much good with words. Better with food. I'm the book – the **COOK** – up at Greystone.' He reddened. 'Sorry – it's worse when I meet new people.'

'Greystone,' Moll muttered. 'Is that where you're going now?'

'No. I mean, **YES**.' Bruce threw his hands up. 'Can you put your bow and arrow down, please? It's putting me off!'

Gryff snarled beside Moll. He didn't seem to trust the boy, but Moll could see Greystone now. She was so close to Siddy.

She lowered her bow. 'I'm meeting someone at Greystone,' she said evenly.

Bruce's eyes lit up. 'Siddy? You're meeting Siddy, aren't you?'

Moll's heart skipped a beat.

Bruce smiled. 'Mrs Grey ate him for breakfast.'

'WHAT?' Moll spat.

'Oh, no! I mean, he's **HAVING BREAKFAST WITH MRS GREY**. That's what I mean.'

Moll breathed a sigh of relief. 'Who's Mrs Grey?'

Bruce was silent for a moment, as if planning his words very carefully. 'She inherited the castle years ago. Keeps herself to herself, but she's got a good heart and she believes in the old magic. She's spent the last month trying to come up with ways to destroy the quail – I mean, **VEIL** – and she knows the wind spirits in the north better than anyone. When they whispered of a boy lost on the moors, she commanded them to bring him here.'

Bruce beamed, clearly pleased with his string of successful sentences. 'You're Moll, aren't you? Siddy speaks about you a lot.'

Moll nodded.

Bruce leant forward. 'I would like to lift you.'

Moll raised an eyebrow. 'That would be awful.'

Bruce shook his head and looked rather glum. 'I meant to ask if you'd **LIKE A LIFT**?'

Moll glanced at Gryff who eyed Bruce up and down, then reluctantly slunk round the back of the cart and leapt up between the crates. Moll clambered in after him and Bruce spurred his horse on.

'Come far?' the boy asked, craning his neck round.

Moll thought about it. She'd ridden north as a stowaway on a train, braved a gorge full of witches, survived moors full of peatboggers and escaped a goblin's lair.

'Quite far,' she mumbled.

165

Bruce shrugged. 'I'm local. Born on the Lost Isles.'

He turned back to his horse and started whistling and, after a while, the cart veered left on to the humpback bridge. Moll's gaze fell upon the castle looming in front: a square fortress with ramparts skirting the highest level and four turrets rising from each corner. The cart crept closer still and Moll took in the tall windows lining the façade and the large wooden door, criss-crossed with iron bands. And then she heard a sound that set her heart reeling.

'Moll! Moll!'

It was Siddy. Not an echo of his voice trapped in a knot of wind. This was *him*, right here on the Lost Isles, and, as he cried out again, Moll's face broke into a grin.

'Sid!' she yelled. 'I'm here!'

She scrambled down from the cart with Gryff before Bruce had even pulled it to a stop, then she darted towards the door and rapped the brass knocker. She waited, hopping from foot to foot at the thought of seeing Siddy, but no one came. She knocked again. Still no answer. Then she turned round to find that Bruce and his cart were nowhere to be seen.

Gryff's hackles rose. Something didn't feel right. They'd heard Siddy cry out just a moment ago and yet no one had come to the door. Moll followed Gryff's gaze, back towards the shore, and gasped.

'How on earth . . .?'

The humpback bridge had completely disappeared and Moll gulped as the realisation crept in: they were cut off from the mainland now. She turned back to the door and, just as she was about to knock a third time, somebody screamed. Moll's head jerked up towards the window where the sound had come from and there was Siddy, at last, but his face was white with terror. And through the glass Moll heard his muffled voice.

'It's a trick, Moll!' he shouted. 'Get away from here! Run!'

The window was darkened suddenly by a whirl of grey cloak and then Siddy was gone. Moll reached behind her for an arrow and it was only then that she discovered it wasn't just Bruce and the bridge that had vanished.

The golden feather was gone too.

Chapter 21
The Lost Isles

Panic tore through Moll. Had the feather fallen out on the moors? Or had Bruce stolen it when her back was turned in the cart? Moll thought of her quest in Kittlerumpit's lair, now all for nothing, then she pinched her leg to stop her thoughts spiralling. She needed a plan. She had to work out how to hold everything together – to free Siddy and find the feather – because she wouldn't leave her friend again, no matter what he said.

'What do we do now, Gryff?' she asked.

Without a moment's hesitation, the wildcat prowled towards the door and, quite of its own accord, it groaned on its hinges, then creaked open before him. No one appeared from behind it, as if the castle itself was inviting them in. And, with an arrow set to her bow, Moll breathed in a lungful of courage and stepped over the threshold with Gryff.

They glanced around the stone hallway. It was empty and unlit, but a sliver of sunlight spilled through the door, glinting off the crossed swords fixed to the walls and casting a path towards an opening ahead. But the passageway beyond wasn't marked by a door, as Moll had expected. Stretching the height of the hallway was a huge face carved into the stone. The eyes were filled with jet-black jewels and as Moll edged closer she could have sworn she saw them swivelling in their sockets, following her every move. What frightened Moll most, though, was the enormous mouth hanging open in a silent scream. The only way on into the castle was through the middle of that gaping mouth . . .

Moll reached for Gryff and thought of Siddy and the golden feather and all that needed to happen to beat the Shadowmasks once and for all. Then together they stepped through the mouth. In front of them was a staircase which spiralled upwards into the gloom and they began to climb it, glancing every now and again through the latticed windows at the grey sea beyond. Moll placed a hand on the wall and grimaced. The stones were coated in cobwebs, soft and sticky, and they draped across the walls like the skin of a ghost. Tucking her elbows in and raising her bow still higher, Moll carried on climbing.

Then the shouting began.

'No! Get away from me!'

It was Siddy. Moll and Gryff raced up the staircase towards the sound, winding round and round, before charging off the final step and bursting into a large room. Hundreds of shelves lined the walls from the floor right up to the ceiling and each one was cluttered with different-sized glass bottles. Some were small and curved with long necks while others were rectangular with cork stoppers – and every bottle was filled with liquid: ivy greens, candlewax reds, sapphire blues, burning yellows. A long, wooden table stretched the length of the room and on it were candelabra sagging with cobwebs. Above them, hanging from the roof, was an enormous chandelier made entirely of antlers, and inside that, bound in a giant cobweb, was Siddy.

Moll rushed towards him. 'Sid!' she yelled. 'Oh, Sid!'

He wriggled his body round inside the antlers, only his head free from the shroud of cobwebs.

'Moll,' he said quietly. 'I told you to run away.'

'I couldn't leave you, Sid. No matter what you said.'

Siddy smiled and Moll noticed a tear trickle off his chin.

'Well, well, well,' said a voice from the far end of the room.

Moll turned round and readied her bow, but what she saw was not a terror of leathery wings or a mask with a forked tongue, as she'd encountered a few weeks ago down by the sea. On a balcony was a throne coated in spiderwebs and on it sat a very old woman. She was hunched over as if time had bent her closer to the grave, and her grey robes were covered in dust. Instead of skin on her face, cobwebs stretched over her cheekbones, sucked into empty pockets where eyes and a mouth should have been. Immediately, Moll knew this was a Shadowmask, not the kindly Mrs Grey that Bruce had invented.

The witch doctor tilted her head towards Moll and the bones in her neck cricked. 'And so you have come at last, Molly Pecksniff.' Her voice was a rasp, as if there were only a few words left inside her.

Moll noticed Bruce kneeling by her side, his head bowed low and the golden feather at his feet.

'You lied to me,' she snarled.

Gryff pounded his paws against the flagstones and hissed, but, when Bruce lifted his head, his eyes were dark and afraid.

'Orbrot, she – she made me,' he stammered.

The Shadowmask stood up. 'Skull, Hemlock, Ashtongue, Darkebite and now me, Orbrot . . .'

Moll's insides clenched as she thought of the sinister pattern the first letter of each of the witch doctors' names spelt: **SHADO**. The word was almost complete.

Orbrot went on. 'I am the fifth Shadowmask. I—'

But Moll didn't wait for any more. She thought of the fight inside her and willed on her impossible dream, then she drew her bow back and fired. The arrow sailed through the hall, but Orbrot leapt aside just in time and the arrow struck the far wall and clanged to the ground.

Orbrot reached down and snapped the arrow in half. 'That's not a very polite way to begin now, is it?'

'Don't listen to her, Moll!' Siddy cried. 'She'll try to make you feel weak and useless, but you're not. I know you're not!'

Moll watched in horror as the cobwebs tightened round her friend, fixing him still.

'Free Siddy and hand over the golden feather,' Moll said, 'or I'll fire again and this time I won't miss.'

Orbrot let the broken arrow clatter to the stone floor, then she shrugged and walked very slowly down a flight of steps.

Her cloak rustled like old felt as she crossed the flagstones and paused at the other end of the long, wooden table.

'Arrows, words, catapults, fists.' She laughed but the sound was hollow, like a dead man's call. 'None of those are going to help you now.'

Moll raised her bow again, but her insides quaked with dread. How many times were her arrows going to fall short? Where was the fight inside her that Aira had been so sure of? The strength that Siddy thought she had? Even Gryff was edging to hide behind her now. It was as if the fifth Shadowmask had some unseen power that drained them both of courage.

Orbrot wrapped her wrinkled fingers round the back of a chair. 'You see these bottles all around us, Molly?'

Moll scanned the cluttered shelves.

'Ignore her, Moll!' Siddy gasped, trying to break free from the webs that held him. 'Block your ears—'

The cobwebs crept over Siddy's mouth and gagged the rest of his words. Moll tightened the grip on her bow and raised it to her eye to focus on Orbrot, but with every word the Shadowmask muttered she felt her courage wane.

'These bottles are filled with *your* hopes and dreams, Molly.'

Gryff whimpered and then cowered beneath the table as Orbrot continued.

'Your connection with the Bone Murmur has meant that I have been able to steal them without you noticing.' She paused. 'I couldn't tap into your wildcat, though – a predator like him is too hard to penetrate from afar – but, now that I have him here in Greystone, I see my words are having quite the desired effect.'

Moll's thoughts crashed down as realisation dawned. It had been little seeds of doubt at first – worrying that the quest was too big for her in the Clattering Gorge, feeling her search for Sid was hopeless while saddling Pepper outside Fillie Crankie, being unable to let Aira's words of comfort in as they rode to Whuppity Cairns and watching her arrows fall short against the peatbogger. Then the worries had grown: the overwhelming guilt at losing Alfie *and* Sid, her despair in Kittlerumpit's tunnels and her fear of the wilderness around her in the bothy the night before. There had been a reason why Moll hadn't felt like herself in the north. Orbrot had been stealing her hopes and dreams; she had been slowly draining Moll's fight.

The Shadowmask walked over to the shelf nearest Moll and, as her hands crawled out of her cloak, Moll noticed her nails. She shivered. They were long and brown, curling under each fingertip like sharp, rusted hooks, and Orbrot let them clink against the bottles as she walked past.

'Each bottle contains a thought you've had, Molly – a pointless little thought for your friends or for your quest to save the old magic.'

The witch doctor stopped for a moment beside a square bottle with a glass stopper that held a dark purple liquid, 'What have we here? A token thought for Domino – a little wish that he'll be on the mend soon?' Orbrot moved on to the next bottle. 'A spot of homesickness in this one, I think.' Her cobwebbed mask tilted towards Moll. 'Aw, missing Oak and Mooshie, were we?'

Moll edged back towards the spiral staircase, her bow now limp by her side, and beneath the table Gryff began to shake.

Orbrot stalked on to the next bottle. 'A plea for your precious Gryff trapped inside Kittlerumpit's cage,' she sneered. 'How sweet. Oh, and a prayer for Siddy whom you abandoned on the moors, whom you scorned for being useless and whom you laughed at on top of a train with Domino. Not much of a friend, are you?'

Moll shook her head at the chandelier that held Siddy. 'It wasn't like that, Sid. You know that, don't you?'

But the cobwebs had bound Siddy tight and he could only blink frightened eyes at her.

'You may have relied on bows and arrows and catapults before,' Orbrot muttered, 'but they count for nothing in the face of a Mind Warper.' She crossed the room towards Moll. 'I can break into your thoughts, Molly. I can lift every hope you have right out of your body.'

Moll inched behind the table, but still Orbrot followed, her robes shuffling over the flagstones after her.

'Every hope you've had since coming to the northern wilderness I've taken.'

Gryff cowered by Moll's legs, making soft moaning sounds, and, as Moll looked up at Orbrot's cobwebbed mask gliding towards her, she felt the hopes she'd had outside Greystone – of

174

being reunited with Siddy and finding the last amulet – drain from her chest. She stood, trembling, at the end of the table.

Orbrot stopped suddenly. 'There was *one* hope I didn't manage to steal.' Her voice had a bite to it now and the cobwebs pulled taut across her face, sinking about the eyes and darkening into the holes. 'Somehow you managed to cling on to this sorry little thought.'

Moll's mind raced. What hope of hers had been strong enough to withstand the Mind Warper's curses?

'Just like Kittlerumpit, I'll offer you a trade,' Orbrot sneered. 'I'll free Siddy, and give you back your golden feather, if you'll hand me the dream I crave.'

Then Moll remembered the goblin's words to Aira in Whuppity Cairns: *the Shadowmasks . . . said they needed to break her impossible dream to conjure their eternal night.*

Orbrot's mask tilted to one side and Moll could almost see her anger pulsing behind the cobwebs. 'All of this can be over if you hand me *your impossible dream.*' She steepled her fingers in front of her robes, her nails bent round like a vulture's talons. 'You admitted your other fears, Moll. You said them out loud. Now it's time to admit this one. Give up your hope of finding Alfie again, of making him real. Just say the words – *I give you Alfie* – and I'll free Siddy from my web and hand over the feather.'

Moll felt the words Orbrot wanted hovering on her tongue. It would be so easy. Just four words and she would have Sid back and the feather they needed to find the last amulet. And yet something inside her quavered at the thought of giving up her impossible dream, the one she whispered before bed every night, the one she clung to when almost everything else was falling apart. And she couldn't help but wonder what it was about Alfie – or her memory of him – that Orbrot needed. Alfie had been tied up in Shadowmasks' magic from the start – they'd used him to create their Soul Splinter – so what if they needed to use him again in their plans for an everlasting darkness?

The Shadowmask stepped close to Moll and she could see each cobwebbed filament coiled round the woman's neck and smell the stale tang that seeped from her mouth. A spider crept between the folds of her robes and Moll shrank back with Gryff.

'You clung on stubbornly in Kittlerumpit's tunnels,' Orbrot said. 'You chose the old magic over Alfie because you believed – because you *hoped* – that it would help you find him again. But your impossible dream has always been too far out of reach. Alfie's in the Underworld now – in a place you cannot follow him to. He's gone, Molly. You let him die when you forced him to destroy the Soul Splinter.'

Moll let the poison of the Shadowmask's words drip inside her. No one had admitted that Alfie might be gone for ever, that maybe it *was* all her fault. Her nightmares had been full of this awful possibility, but none of her friends had voiced the darkest whispers of her dreams. And yet, if Alfie was dead, why had she felt so sure that she had seen him in her mind in Kittlerumpit's tunnels . . .?

'Let him go, Molly,' Orbrot muttered. 'You killed him

because of your obsession with the old magic, a magic that is all but lost now. Alfie might still be alive had it not been for your selfishness, your quest for glory, but now he is locked forever in the darkness of the Underworld – and you cannot help a boy who is already dead.'

Moll could hear Siddy struggling inside the chandelier, groaning beneath the spiderweb gag, but her eyes were glued to the shelves, to all her hopes and dreams trapped in Orbrot's bottles. And, as she looked at them, she felt an emptiness swell inside her, a hole opening somewhere close to her heart where she stored her impossible dream.

Her bow dropped to the ground and she fell to her knees and clung to Gryff. Then she closed her eyes and thought of Alfie and their last few days together: of how he had rescued her from Ashtongue's trap and followed her out over the sea to destroy Darkebite and the Soul Splinter – *of his own accord*. Moll shook her head. Orbrot hadn't been there on the eagle's back with Alfie. She hadn't heard Moll's promise to him: that she'd follow her friend wherever he went and whatever the Shadowmasks had in store for them. And she hadn't seen Moll weep as Alfie disappeared. She didn't know the real story . . .

And, once again, as Moll thought of her friend with her eyes clamped shut, an image of Alfie hardened inside her mind into something so real she felt that if she rushed forward and reached out her arms he would be there inside them. Moll kept absolutely still and, in the emptiness of her closed eyes, she watched Alfie walk towards her through a swirl of shadows. And then he stopped, his scruffy blonde hair and bright blue eyes so close that Moll could almost feel his breath on her cheeks. The shadows rose up suddenly and, as Alfie raised his arms towards Moll, she felt her own arms stretching out – two souls searching for each other in the dark – then the pitchblack thickened, drowning Alfie out, and though Moll's heart beat with panic as she watched her friend disappear, she knew without a trace of doubt that Alfie was still in her world and she would *never* give up her impossible dream.

Moll didn't dare open her eyes to look at Orbrot – all that waited for her there were fear and loathing. Instead, she crouched close to the surest thing she knew, to Gryff, whose love and loyalty had roots deeper than the hatred that throbbed around them. She listened to the wildcat's heartbeats clamouring against her own, drowning the sound of the Shadowmask calling her name, and, slowly and cautiously, Moll dared to hope again as Alfie had in the face of the Soul Splinter. She felt Gryff's strength build up inside her, stronger than Orbrot's words, stronger even than the Night Spinner and his Veil, and with it came an idea. It was a small idea, and full of risk, but the hope inside it flickered like fire. Moll opened her eyes and stood up.

'You're going to give Alfie up in exchange for the golden feather, aren't you?' Orbrot said.

Moll nodded and the Shadowmask clasped her crooked hands in delight.

'A wise choice, Molly. No point in chasing dying dreams.'

She looked at Gryff who was sitting beside Moll, his green eyes sparkling. 'It seems even your cat agrees.'

Moll took a step towards Orbrot, then, to the witch doctor's surprise, Moll began to walk in a circle around her.

'You stole my parents from me,' Moll said quietly as she circled the Shadowmask again. There was a tremor to her voice, but she pushed it down.

Orbrot nodded. 'Many will die as the dark magic is forged.'

Moll carried on walking, around and around. 'Your curses wounded Oak and they blinded Gryff.'

Orbrot nodded. 'A small price to pay for our powers to rise.' Her cloak twitched. 'Are you ready to surrender your impossible dream now?'

Moll didn't answer. She kept circling Orbrot and, though the Shadowmask couldn't see it because the room was so gloomy, Moll made sure that with each step she took she unravelled a little more of the near-invisible piano string from her pocket. It wound loosely round Orbrot's cloak and every time it did so Moll felt the hope inside her grow.

From the balcony, a side door opened and Bruce slipped from the room, but Moll was bent on her plan now and she saw nothing of his sly disappearance.

'The Night Spinner and his Veil poisoned my friends, Domino and Angus,' Moll said.

She was walking faster now, her voice strong like steel and her eyes fierce, and from the far end of the room a bottle on one of Orbrot's shelves cracked and the blue liquid inside it vanished. Orbrot was so intent on Moll giving up her

179

impossible dream that she didn't notice, but Moll heard the sound and with it her courage grew.

'Your dark magic conjured creatures that attacked me: peatboggers and witches in the north, owls and kelpies down by the sea.'

Another bottle on the shelves tipped over and broke, a spool of red liquid disappearing as Moll's voice rose into a shout and her steps quickened.

'You burned our camp to the ground in Tanglefern Forest and sent storms to flatten the homes of the people in the north! But I won't give in!' she cried. 'I won't sit back and let you rip this world apart,' Gryff leapt up on to the table and hissed, 'and all those who fight on the side of the old magic with me won't either! Because they've been with me the whole way, making sure you won't win! Mellantha helped me unravel the first bone reading though it cost her her life. Cinderella Bull called upon the sea spirits to protect us in Little Hollows. Oak guided me from the beginning and nearly died from a dark magic curse! Mooshie kept us all safe in the forest and in the cove! Scrap led the Tribe to the second amulet despite the smugglers out to kill her! Puddle hid us from the Shadowmasks in his lighthouse!'

More and more bottles toppled from the shelves and clattered to the floor, their colourful liquid melting into the air. But Moll wasn't finished yet.

'Domino led us north!' she roared. 'Angus took us in while the storm raged in Glendrummie! Aira helped me in

180

Kittlerumpit's tunnels! Siddy and Gryff have been there with me every step of the way! And Alfie, *my* Alfie, who you want me to give up on, destroyed the Soul Splinter even though it meant he might die! Me, Sid, Gryff and Alfie – we've fought past tree ghouls and wolves! We've sent arrows into cursed eels and we've brought down four Shadowmasks already!'

Orbrot drew breath to speak, but Moll was practically running around her now, loosening a little more of the piano string with every stride, her voice growing in strength and volume as she ran.

'We beat vapours and Alterskins! We outwitted mer ghosts and marsh spirits! And the only reason we did any of that was because we didn't give up! We kept on hoping!'

A whole row of bottles on a shelf to Moll's right shattered into tiny pieces and the liquid inside them fizzled away. Orbrot shifted her weight and the cobwebs around her face stiffened. Then Moll stopped in front of her, face flushed and breath ragged.

The Shadowmask folded her arms. 'Quite finished?'

Moll spat. 'I'm not even getting started.'

She yanked hard and the piano string she'd wound round Orbrot tightened suddenly, snatching in her robes and sending the witch doctor crashing to the ground.

'That's for Alfie,' she hissed, 'because you're wrong about him and, no matter what you say, I'm going to find my friend and make him real.'

Hundreds of bottles burst apart on the shelves and the room sang with the sound of smashing glass. Moll tossed the string she was holding to Gryff who caught it in his mouth, then pounced on Orbrot and held her still.

'Those are *my* hopes and dreams you've stolen! *Mine!*' Moll yelled, seizing her bow from the ground. 'And I'm going to take them back.'

More and more bottles toppled to the floor, but Moll wasn't just going to wait for them to break apart. She pulled back on her arrow until the string was taut, then she thought of her impossible dream, took aim at the shelves on the right-hand side of the room and fired. The arrow careered into the bottles, and the Oracle Spirit ballooned out the whole length of the room, sending fragments of glass sprawling across the flagstones. Moll fired another arrow into the shelves on her left and it ripped through them – and as the liquid inside disappeared Moll felt something familiar burn in her soul. It was the fight that Aira had seen, the unconquerable toughness that Moll knew after seeing Alfie just a moment ago could never be beaten. She whirled round to face Orbrot.

'Get your cat off me!' the witch doctor howled.

Moll dipped her head at Gryff who leapt off the Shadowmask's chest and padded over to Moll's side, the piano string still gripped between his teeth. Moll slotted another arrow to her bow, glanced briefly down to Gryff, then she pointed her weapon straight at the Shadowmask.

'Gryff's not a cat,' she muttered. 'He's a *wild*cat.'

The arrow shot out and the Oracle Spirit billowed round the witch doctor. But, as Orbrot's body crumpled into a heap of matted cobwebs and dead spiders, her voice threaded through the room: 'You think you've defeated me, but my castle is filled with enchantments that will trap you here until the Night Spinner comes.' Her words were thin and hoarse, growing weaker and weaker with every word. 'And when the last Shadowmask arrives he will bring such deadly curses that you will abandon your impossible dream once and for all before the Veil swallows you in its darkness.'

With the last of Orbrot's words, the room fell silent, a tomb of broken glass and cobwebs. Moll looked towards the balcony and noticed for the first time that Bruce had vanished, but she and Gryff had other things on their minds. The wildcat dropped the piano string at Moll's feet and, while Moll wound it up and pocketed it, Gryff jumped up on to the table. He bounded down it before soaring up into the chandelier and ripping at the cobwebs with his teeth and claws as he tried to free Siddy.

Moll hoisted herself up on to the table and ran towards the chandelier as Siddy squeezed his body between the antlers of the cage. And then they were all there together: a wildcat pressed between two hugging friends who had tears coursing down their cheeks.

Chapter 22
A New Friend

Moll, Siddy and Gryff sat on the table beneath the chandelier and for a moment they were just glad to be together.

'I didn't mean to leave you on the moors, Sid,' Moll said. 'I rushed on because I wanted to find Angus' sister and the amulet, but I should've waited. I never should have left you.'

Siddy dusted the cobwebs off his flat cap. 'My fault for trying to make friends with a highland cow; I was talking to one, then I turned round and you were gone.'

Moll smiled. 'And you know I didn't mean what I said back in the Clattering Gorge, don't you?'

Siddy nodded. 'A few cross words don't mean a friendship's over.'

Moll glanced at Gryff, then back to Siddy. 'Our friendship – the three of us – it's stronger than iron, Sid. If we tried to smash it with a hammer, it wouldn't break. It wouldn't crumble. It's *that* strong.'

Siddy nodded again. 'You're right.' He paused. 'But being stranded on the moors, swept away by wind spirits cursed to do a Shadowmask's commands, then locked in a dungeon before being bound up in cobwebs and shoved inside a chandelier – that's an experience I'd rather not repeat if we can help it . . .'

Moll laughed, then her words rushed out as she told Siddy about everything that had happened since they'd parted and of her visions of Alfie and her firm belief that he was still alive.

'I let you out of my sight and you're off making deals with goblins?' Siddy cried.

Moll squared her shoulders. 'I gave him a nosebleed right afterwards.'

Siddy rolled his eyes. 'Where's the golden feather now? Because we'll need all the help we can get to make it past Orbrot's enchantments and escape before the Night Spinner comes.'

Moll picked at her coat. 'Orbrot's wretched servant, Bruce, stole it.'

Siddy's face darkened. 'He was the one who brought me meals when I was locked in the dungeon. Whenever Orbrot was around, Bruce was horrid to me: kicking over my food, pinching me when I was fast asleep – he even cut up my bow and arrows and burned them!'

Moll felt a rush of anger towards Bruce at the way he had treated her friend.

'But one night I heard him crying outside my cell door and cursing Orbrot's name,' Siddy continued. 'I don't think he wants to be here either, but somehow he's under the dark magic's power. Bruce is just a rotten coward really. We'll get the feather back from him before the Night Spinner comes—'

'—and the eternal night rises,' Moll finished. 'What do you think it is about Alfie or my hope in him that the Shadowmasks need so much?'

Siddy shrugged. 'I don't know, but staying in this castle a moment more than we need to isn't going to help us solve that puzzle.'

Moll looked over her shoulder towards the staircase she'd come up earlier, but to her surprise it was no longer there. Just a wall of stone looked blankly back at her.

'The staircase has vanished!' she spluttered.

'This castle's got a mind of its own,' Siddy replied, sliding off the table. 'Orbrot treated it like a living thing – always stroking the walls and whispering into corners.' He shuddered and pointed to the door up on the balcony. 'Bruce must have left that way. Come on, let's go after him.'

They walked towards the staircase leading up to the balcony, but Moll stopped Siddy just before it, her eyes narrow. 'Your ears are wiggling,' she said. 'You're keeping a secret from me, aren't you?'

Siddy reddened, then he glanced down at his coat pocket and Moll noticed that there was something moving inside it.

'I – I was going to tell you after we'd escaped . . . because he can be a bit overwhelming when you first meet him.'

'Who can?' Moll said slowly.

A burst of dark brown fur shot out of Siddy's pocket and

an animal with a long, thin body and a twitching pink nose began leaping up and down the stairs in a series of strange hops and sideways jumps.

'A *ferret*?' Moll cried. 'What on earth are you doing with a ferret, Sid?'

Gryff licked his lips and stalked towards the stairs and Siddy hastily positioned himself between the wildcat and his new pet.

'I found him skulking around the dungeons; I think he must have crept in, looking for food.'

The ferret careered into the back of a step, then let out a soft clucking noise before repeating his hops and jumps.

Moll raised her eyebrows. 'What *is* he doing?'

'For some reason, Frank dances when he's feeling enthusiastic,' Siddy replied, looking a bit sheepish.

Moll watched the ferret's little legs scampering back and forth. His black eyes gleamed in delight at the attention and Moll threw her hands up. 'At least Porridge the Second and Hermit were quiet and didn't make a fuss when they tagged along. But *this*—'

Frank shot out a leg, then shimmied to the right.

'—this is going to be exhausting!'

Siddy watched his ferret dance. 'No more exhausting than spending time with you.'

Moll scowled.

'Cheer up,' Siddy added. 'I could've ended up with a highland cow.' He stooped to pick up Frank who snuggled against his cheek before diving back into Siddy's pocket until just his tail flopped out, wagging back and forth like an excited dog's.

'Fine,' Moll said, following them up the stairs. 'But, just so you know, Frank's a girl.'

Siddy dug his hand into his pocket, lifted the ferret upside down and gasped. 'You're a *girl*, Frank!'

Frank curled herself into a ball and licked Siddy's hand.

He smiled. 'Isn't it great how well Frank takes to change? You could learn a lot from him, Moll.' He paused. 'Her.'

Done with chatting about ferrets, Moll pushed past Siddy on to the balcony. She opened the door that led off left and then staggered backwards, clutching at the walls.

'Sid,' she whispered. 'Look . . .'

Ahead of them were thirteen stone steps, each one half a metre long and wide, floating in the air. They spread out towards a huge wall opposite and then they stopped at a stone platform before a door framed by two large torches. Moll peered down and felt suddenly sick. Far below them, maybe thirty metres beneath, was a pit scattered with bones, only just visible through the layers of cobwebs that laced the space between the two walls.

Siddy gulped. 'This is the only way on, isn't it?'

Moll scrunched her hands into fists. 'I think so. And we've got to move fast with the Night Spinner on our trail.'

Chapter 23
The Floating Steps

Frank stuck her head out of Siddy's pocket and gave an excited squeak at the challenge that lay before them. Moll shot the ferret a withering look, but then her attention shifted to Gryff. He had lifted a tentative paw towards the first stone.

'Be careful,' Moll whispered.

The wildcat laid his foot on the step, but the moment he did so the stone wobbled beneath him. Gryff snatched his weight back and watched as the step dropped silently from the air and then landed with a smash, seconds later, on the floor below.

Moll slid a look at Siddy. 'There must be a way across. It's the only direction Bruce could've gone!'

Siddy pointed. 'Look, Moll. There are letters on the slabs.'

Moll squinted into the gloom and saw that each of the twelve remaining steps bore a letter.

She said them aloud in a half-whisper: 'O. K. R. S. B. P. R. F. O. C. D. T. That's not even a word!'

Siddy's eyes darted back and forth between the letters, then Frank wriggled from his pocket and leapt out past the gap where the first stone had been before landing on the slab marked 'O'.

'No!' Siddy cried, palms raised to his mouth.

But the stone held Frank's weight. The ferret tapped her claws on the slab before wiggling her tail and jumping on to the next step. This time she wasn't so lucky though, and, as the stone wobbled beneath her then fell away, Siddy and Moll shrieked. In the nick of time, Frank hopped to the next stone, and again it held her weight.

'Every second stone,' Moll said slowly, trying to find the pattern. 'Perhaps you can only step on those ones if you want to make your way across.'

'But why do the slabs have different letters on them?' Siddy asked.

Moll shook her head. 'We haven't got time to think on it, Sid; we need to keep moving.'

She blew out through narrowed lips and tried to keep her eyes on the stones, instead of the terrifying drop beneath, then she followed Frank's path, leaping on to the step marked 'O'. It held her weight and Moll focused on her balance, her palms tickling with nerves, before jumping on to the third step. She scooped up Frank, then glanced down and felt her stomach swing. The floor far below seemed to rise up beneath her and the walls felt as if they were swaying. Swallowing back her fear and clutching Frank tightly, Moll braced herself to follow the pattern, jumping to the fifth step, then the seventh and ninth – each holding her and Frank's weight.

'Every second stone – it *is* the pattern!' Moll called back to Gryff and Siddy. 'Come on!'

Tentatively, Gryff jumped across the stones in Moll's path and Siddy followed a few steps behind.

Moll turned to the stones ahead of her and, as she landed on the eleventh step, the slab began to wobble and her blood ran cold.

'No!' she screamed.

But the step tumbled away beneath her.

~ Chapter 24 ~
Orbrot's Enchantment

Frank shot out of Moll's hands and soared over the last stone on to the platform, but Moll was already falling.

In desperation, she flung out her hands to grab hold of the twelfth step and, with her heart thudding in her throat, she clung to the stone with white fingertips.

'Hold on!' Siddy cried.

Moll's body rocked in the air as she wrestled for a stronger hold. 'Quick, Sid! Help me!'

But it was Gryff who came to the rescue first, landing just beyond her fingers on the stone she held on to. He placed his paws on Moll's hands and she bit her lip as she felt his claws digging into her skin. The wildcat winced at the pain he saw he was causing; if he held on much longer, he'd draw blood from Moll's hands.

'I'm coming!' Siddy shouted from behind her. 'But there's not enough space for me *and* Gryff on the stone! He'll have to jump back on to the platform before the door so that I can jump on to your stone and pull you up!'

Moll blinked at Gryff and her words came in a rasp. 'Go back,' she said.

The wildcat whimpered for a moment, unwilling to leave Moll hanging so precariously. But then he glanced at the platform behind him, where Frank was, and sprang on to it, leaving Moll dangling from the slab. Moll gripped tighter, her arms burning under the strain, then Siddy landed on the stone she clung to and hauled at Moll's shoulders until she could drag her own body on to the step. Siddy jumped back to the platform to join Frank and Gryff while Moll, heart thundering, clambered on to the slab.

Then she leapt on to the platform with the others and watched in horror as the second, fourth, sixth, eighth and tenth steps fell away and the torches shone upon the remaining letters inscribed into the stones: **O. R. B. R. O. T.**

'It's obvious when you see the letters without the other slabs,' Moll panted. 'The only stones we could stand on were the ones that spelt out Orbrot's name – every second one, to start with, and then a change at the end—'

'—to keep us on our toes,' Siddy finished, holding his cap with shaking hands. 'I thought you were a goner, Moll. I never thought that stone would hold us both.'

Moll ran a bruised hand over Gryff's ears. 'When we get back to Tanglefern Forest, I'm going to make you and Gryff a Tribe medal for that rescue.'

Frank sniffed the large wooden door behind them, then squeaked.

Siddy picked himself up and, tucking the ferret back

into his coat pocket, he took a deep breath. 'I wonder what Orbrot's got in store for us next . . .'

Moll turned the handle, expecting the door to be firmly locked, but it opened.

'Good start,' Siddy said, rubbing his hands.

But Moll's eyes were wary. 'I prefer doors you have to smash down. Ones that open for you always lead to badness.'

They all edged inside and found themselves in a small, office-like room. A threadbare rug lined the floor and against the far wall there was a mahogany desk. On it was a lamp, still lit, and an empty bottle, like the ones that had lined the shelves in the room before. Cobwebs clung to everything. They draped over the desk, twisted round the chair and hung like a veil over the glass cabinets behind.

'Looks like Orbrot's study,' Moll said.

Siddy nodded. 'And I reckon she was planning to lock your impossible dream inside that bottle.'

Moll frowned. 'I don't understand. There's only one door – the one we just stepped through. If we go back out, we'll just be trapped in the room we came from! Bruce can't have escaped this way . . .'

'There must be another door,' Siddy replied. 'We just have to find it.'

There was something about the room that made Moll want to tiptoe and whisper and, as she made her way towards the cabinets, her shoulders rose. Behind the glass were dozens of wooden cases and each one was filled with the same thing: dead moths. Their delicate brown wings had been splayed and fixed with pins and beneath them wiry legs poked out.

Siddy recoiled. 'Those white circles ringed with black on the wings – they look just like eyes . . .'

Moll nodded. She couldn't help feeling that, although they were alone in the study, someone or some*thing* was watching them. She looked around at the walls and frowned. 'The wallpaper,' she said slowly, 'it's a giant map.'

Sure enough, the whole room was pasted with sepia rivers, forests, seas and moors. Moll walked over to the wall and ran a hand across a large patch of what looked like woodland. 'It's – it's Tanglefern Forest!' she cried, and a longing to be tucked inside her wagon in the clearing swept through her.

Siddy stood next to her and peered closer. 'There are rips in the map . . . Look here – in the forest – great slashes across the parchment where our camp should be.'

'And here,' Moll said. 'Out on the heath above the sea – it's the same thing, as if the map has been hacked at with a knife.' A coldness settled at the back of Moll's neck as an image slipped into her mind. 'Orbrot's nails,' she said slowly. 'Maybe she ripped the map apart.'

Gryff's ears flattened to his head and Frank sank lower inside Siddy's pocket.

Moll followed the map around the room, back towards the door, with Siddy close behind her. There was no sign of another door, but on the wallpaper map there were rips right through Little Hollows, the cave they'd hidden in down by the sea, and great chunks had been shredded by Inchgrundle, the seaside village where they'd gone to look for the second amulet.

'The map's only torn in the places the Shadowmasks and their dark magic attacked us,' Moll said.

Siddy clutched Moll's arm. 'The thresholds! They sound like paper tearing when they open! Maybe Orbrot has been controlling the thresholds from *here*. Ripping the map with her nails, in the exact places she wanted her darkness to pour in from the Underworld.'

Moll stopped short in front of the door they had come through because hanging from the back of it was a portrait of a girl with black hair and bright green eyes.

'It's me,' she whispered and her insides churned as she took in the slashes that marred the face of the portrait. The eyes had been scratched out, the hair was ripped to shreds and deep marks punctured the neck. Gryff rubbed his body against Moll's knees.

'I think we know how Orbrot got inside your mind, Moll,' Siddy said. 'Like the maps, she only needed to scratch this painting for her dark magic to slip in.'

They continued to follow the map round the other side of the room as it moved on to show the Clattering Gorge and the North Door. A slit ran right through the middle of the trees just beyond the North Door, marking the spot where the witches had attacked them. And then Moll and Siddy stopped where the moorland met the coast and a scattering of islands jutted out into the sea.

'The Lost Isles,' Moll whispered. 'That's where we are now . . .'

The silence swelled around the room and Moll's heart quickened. There was a slash right through a small island joined to the mainland by a humpback bridge. Gryff's tail sank low to the ground, a growl grew in his throat, and then the map burst open at the tear and dozens of thin, wiry legs clawed their way into the study.

Chapter 25
Gifts From the Underworld

Gryff leapt in front of Moll as dozens of creatures hurtled out of the map, a frenzy of flapping wings and furred bodies. The wildcat thrashed with his paws and, as Moll and Siddy struggled backwards, they realised what the animals were.

'Moths!' Siddy cried. 'Gigantic moths!'

The creatures were the size of eagles and, though their wings beat against Moll and Siddy with a restless whirring, they were not lined with blades, as the owls' wings had been up on the cliffs, and the moths had no razored teeth or claws. Moll flung her arms up and forced them back, then she reached for her bow and tossed Siddy her catapult.

A moth dropped down on to the floor in front of him, its feathery antennae quivering. It flexed its wings and lowered them slowly, almost like an invitation, and Siddy's gaze fastened on to the white circles ringed with black. The pattern glared up at him – a cold, slate eye – and, as Siddy looked upon it, he screamed.

Moll spun round and her face drained of colour. Siddy's

whole body had stiffened mid-stride, as if someone had frozen him to the spot.

'Don't look at the wings!' he yelled.

There was a crunching sound and Moll watched in horror as Siddy's feet turned grey, followed by his legs, the little ferret in his pocket, his torso—

'No!' Moll shouted, rushing towards him.

—*and his face.* Moll's palms met with Siddy's hands only they were no longer warm and soft and beating with life. They were cold, and hard like marble. She stumbled backwards and clutched at her mouth.

Siddy had been *turned to stone.*

She knelt by Gryff, her eyes clamped shut, as more and more moths spilled through the map. 'Don't look at the eyes on the wings, they'll—'

A moth shunted into her side and knocked her over. Moll kept her eyes squeezed shut, but Gryff's instinct to fight and protect outweighed all else and he leapt towards the creature. The moth flicked a wing down over Gryff's head and instantly Moll's eyes sprang open – she could sense that something was wrong. And, as the moth fluttered upwards, Moll felt as if someone had punched her in the stomach. Before her was another statue: of a wildcat frozen mid-pounce.

The blood roared in Moll's ears, but she struggled to her feet and raised her bow. This was a fight worth having and she was going to give it to them. Forcing her eyes away from the creatures' wings, Moll released arrow after arrow into the throng. The Oracle Spirits rushed out – her aim was keen and strong once again – dragging the moths down into heaps of broken wings. But, for every moth she killed, another appeared through the threshold.

Eyes fixed to the ground, Moll rushed towards the wall and raised her hands to the rip. But palms weren't enough to hold the dark magic back and the furious wings beat on through. The din throbbed and Moll raised an arm over her eyes to shield them from the insects, then an idea came to her. What if she destroyed the map itself? Maybe that would not only stop the moths but also put an end to *all* the dark creatures pouring in from the Underworld. And what better way to destroy paper than fire ...

Eyes closed and arms lashing, she felt her way back towards the door, yanked a torch free from its bracket, then staggered back into the study. The heat from the torch beat at her skin, but she surged on, forcing a way through the moths and feeling for the walls.

Gasping for breath, she set her flame against the part of the map where the moths were scrabbling in. A second later, there was a great *WHOOSH* as the fire ripped up through the threshold, crisping it to shreds, but Moll didn't stand and watch. Prising her eyes open, she raised her bow to bring down the moths that had already clawed their way through. Again and again Moll pulled back on the string and, though the moths were fewer, the fire was rippling around the walls now, enclosing her and the stone statues in a den of raging flames.

Moll placed a hand on Siddy's shoulder. 'Come back!' she pleaded. 'Please come back to me, Sid!'

She turned away and fired her bow into another moth and then another until there was just one insect left. The moth circled the room and glided low, presenting its cursed wings before Moll. She felt her eyes drawn to the patterns, then she blinked hard, raised her arrow and fired. The final moth crumpled to the ground and Moll rushed over to Gryff.

'Come on!' she cried. 'Come back to me!'

As the flames leapt around the room, racing up the curtains and hauling them down, cracks appeared in the stone statue, spreading outwards like veins.

'Yes,' Moll breathed. 'Yes.'

Had killing the last moth put an end to Orbrot's curse? The stone began to break apart and great chunks crumbled from the wildcat's body. First his head shook free, then his front limbs wrenched out of the casing and the rest of the stone crunched to the floor. Moll whipped round to see a network of cracks splitting down the stone around Siddy and then his head and arms burst out as the statue shattered. But there was no time for an embrace. The fire was tearing through the room and Moll was looking beyond Siddy now, to the glass cabinets behind Orbrot's desk. She squinted into the flames, then she grabbed Siddy by the arm and urged Gryff on.

'This way! I think there's a door – between the cabinets – it must have been blocked by a layer of cobwebs before, but the smoke and the flames have stripped that away!'

They sprinted towards the cabinets and, sure enough, tendrils of cobwebs hung down either side of an old wooden door. They yanked it open, then ran up a spiral staircase which led them out to the castle ramparts. The night sky folded around them, cool and crisp and full of stars. But the fire Moll had started was already spreading, shaking great shadows out across the gravel.

'We need to find a way down!' Moll cried, following the ramparts round.

Siddy shook his head. 'But I don't understand – how did you stop the moths and free us from being statues?'

Moll's eyes were bright against the night. 'I set fire to the castle.'

The ramparts bent left along the wall that faced the mainland and they hurried down it.

'The fire was *you*?' Siddy cried and from his hand Frank rolled two little eyes. 'Not another enchantment?'

Moll shook her head. 'No. That was all me.' Her eyes skittered around the ramparts. 'It was the best plan I had . . .'

Siddy groaned. 'Why—'

His words were cut short as he stumbled into Moll and Gryff who had stopped suddenly where the ramparts turned left again, back towards the sea.

There, huddled in the corner, was Bruce. And he was holding their golden feather.

Chapter 26
Bruce's Plan

'You!' Moll snarled. 'We ought to kill you.'

She raised her bow and Siddy pushed Frank down into his pocket as he drew out Moll's catapult, but Gryff slunk past them both and stood before the shaking boy – and something about the wildcat's look made Moll regret her words. Since seeing her hopes and dreams locked away by Orbrot, a new fight had stirred inside her – one that made her even hungrier to avenge her parents and her friends and set all this right – but Moll could read Gryff well and she knew the message in his eyes.

Forgive, he was saying. *Forgive.*

'I didn't clean or feel your heather,' Bruce said. He winced at his words, then punched a fist into the wall beside him.

Moll glanced at Siddy. 'I think he's allergic to words.'

Siddy nodded. 'I figured as much when I heard him crying in the dungeons.'

'I was trying to say that I didn't **MEAN** to **STEAL** your **FEATHER**,' Bruce mumbled. 'It was Orbrot. She made me.'

Moll drew herself up tall. 'We've set fire to the castle and you've got a matter of minutes before the whole place goes up in flames. So, tell us why I shouldn't stick an arrow in your miserable body right now.'

Moll wasn't sure whether that was the level of compassion Gryff had been hoping for, but she was still cross that Bruce had tricked her so it would have to do for now.

At the sound of the roaring flames below, Bruce's words tumbled out. 'Orbrot stole something from me and she told me the only way I could get it back was if I brought you into the castle and stole your golden feather.' He glanced at Siddy. 'The only reason I was cruel to you was because I was trying to groove myself – **PROVE MYSELF** – to Orbrot.'

The fire raged on inside the castle and a chunk of stonework where they'd climbed up on to the ramparts fell away with a deafening crash.

'Speak faster, Bruce,' Moll spat. 'We need you to get us out of here before we're burned to a crisp, but we have to know whether we can trust you first.'

Bruce wailed. 'I'm not a boy at all!'

Moll nodded. 'No, you're not. You're a pathetic little coward.'

Bruce shook his head. 'You don't understand. I'm not a *boy*. I'm a selkie.'

Siddy frowned and Frank's whiskers twitched.

Bruce turned his woollen hat over in his hands. 'I'm a selkie trapped in human form by Orbrot! Oh, the hopelessness of things . . .' He stumbled to his feet and sniffed, then took a deep breath and Moll realised that he was thinking through his words as best he could. 'Selkies are seals who can shed their skin on land to become human for a few hours,' he said slowly.

Moll's gaze travelled over Bruce's large black eyes and his near-white hair. If you squinted hard enough, she realised, and tried not to think about the overcoat and the scarf, Bruce *did* look a little like a seal pup.

'One full moon last year I shed my sealskin to see what it would feel like to be a toy – a **BOY**, I mean,' Bruce said. 'But Orbrot stole it. And without my sealskin I can't change back. I can't hunt for fish or dive into the neeps – **DEEPS** – to find my family. I'm trapped as a boy with words I can't even use right and forced to obey the person who stole my skin.' He held up the golden feather and handed it to Moll. 'I thought if I rolled in the heather,' he shook his head, '**STOLE THE FEATHER** for Orbrot then she might give me back my sealskin.'

Moll tucked the feather into her quiver. She knew what it felt like to be dragged into dark magic when you wanted nothing to do with it. 'Shadowmasks don't do deals, Bruce. They just take. Orbrot wanted a slave to do her dirty work for her – to trick and steal and lie.' She glanced nervously over the ramparts, then at Siddy. 'We need to get out of here, and we need to use this feather to find an amulet one hundred years deep. That's the only way to stop this dark magic.'

Bruce's eyes lit up. 'I have been one hundred years asleep – **DEEP**! Us selkies know every bit of the Lost Isles.' He paused. 'We'll need a boat and—'

Siddy leant forward eagerly. 'You know where we can find the amulet?'

Bruce jumped as a window below them exploded and great billows of smoke belched upwards, blotting out the stars. 'I think so, but Orbrot said the Shadowmasks' purse – I mean, **CURSE** – would kill me if I told my secrets to the child and the beast from the Bone Murmur.'

Moll's face fell. 'So you can't tell us where to look?'

'Not yet, but the witch doctor's power over me will fade if I take my true form. Help me find my sealskin and I can take you one hundred years deep.'

Siddy turned to Moll. 'How do we know for sure that we can trust him? So far, he's helped keep me prisoner and tricked you into battling with a witch doctor.'

Moll nodded. 'I don't know, Sid. But we've not got much of a choice . . . he's our only way of escaping from this castle and of finding the amulet.'

Siddy wrung his hands. 'What's our other option?'

Moll shrugged. 'Get burnt.'

'What's your plan, Bruce?' Siddy asked. 'How do we get out of here?'

Bruce pointed right and beckoned them to follow. The group hurried down the ramparts, their faces glowing from the fire coursing through the castle, until they came to a large wooden contraption. It had a triangular frame and pivoting on top of it was a long, wooden beam. On one end a weight had been attached and on the other there was a sling.

'*That's* how we escape,' Bruce said.

Siddy cleared his throat. 'I think you've got your words muddled again.'

Bruce shook his head. 'It's a trebuchet – like a giant catapult. Normally it fires flaming cannonballs, but,' Bruce glanced from Siddy to Moll to Gryff, 'tonight it's going to fire a bus, I mean, **US.**'

Moll shuddered as Bruce jumped up, grabbed the sling and brought it down level with the group. 'Who's going first?'

Frank shot out of Siddy's pocket and began dancing inside the sling.

Moll raised an eyebrow. 'At least this pet is braver than Hermit . . .'

Chapter 27
The Selkie

Smoke bulged from the sides of the castle, pouring out where windows had once been and painting the night sky grey. Siddy crouched in the sling of the trebuchet, one hand gripping Moll's catapult, the other wrapped round Frank.

'See that tiny island? About fifty metres out and left from Greystone?' Bruce said.

'To the *right* of Greystone?' Siddy asked. 'The rocky outcrop?'

Bruce smacked his head with his hand. 'Yes, to the right. It's called the Rock of Solitude. Swim for that.'

Siddy glanced at Moll. 'This is *even* worse than the train jump.'

But, before Moll could reply, Bruce leapt up on to the weight attached to the other side of the wooden beam. It sank with him and the sling containing Siddy and Frank rose a few metres, then the beam see-sawed for a moment and Moll cottoned on. She jumped on to the weighted side with Bruce and it crashed down on to the ramparts while the other end shot up, flinging Siddy and Frank into the air. Moll watched, aghast, as Siddy soared off the castle ramparts, arms flailing, legs scrabbling, before plunging into the sea some way short of the Rock of Solitude.

He surfaced, clutching Frank and the catapult. 'I'm alive!' he cried. 'I'm alive!'

But Siddy's voice was almost completely drowned by the sound of crumbling stone. The ramparts to the side of them juddered and a large block fell away from the corner, crashing down into the water.

'Go now!' Siddy roared. 'Before it's too late!'

Bruce scrambled into the sling with Moll who reached out to grab Gryff. But the wildcat shied away and Moll glanced back at Bruce.

'How do we fire it?' she asked. 'There'll be no one left to push down on the weight.'

Bruce's face turned pale. 'I hadn't thought of that.'

A huge flame licked up over the ramparts, a pulsing wall of heat against Moll's skin, and she stretched out her arms again for Gryff. But the wildcat had other plans and Moll's eyes widened as she realised what they were.

'No!' she shouted, throwing one leg over the side of the sling.

Bruce held her firm. 'We have to go now!'

Gryff leapt up on to the weight on the other side of the beam just as a piece of stonework crumbled inwards, landing beside him and forcing the wildcat and the weight to the ground with a thud. Moll and Bruce screamed, then the sling lurched up, propelling them both out into the sky.

Moll didn't even flinch as the icy water closed round her and as soon as she surfaced she shouted out for Gryff. The wildcat was just a silhouette against the burning sky, right on the edge of the ramparts, and Moll's throat choked. She'd seen Gryff jump, seen him leap from the tallest trees in Tanglefern Forest and land unscathed, but an enormous drop from a castle? He'd have to clear metres of jutting turrets, not to mention the rocks that lined the shore.

'Gryff!' Moll cried again, clinging to the golden feather in her quiver, and battling against the waves that pulled her back and forth.

The wildcat watched for a moment from the ramparts and then turned slowly away before padding out of sight.

'He's – he's *gone*,' Moll gasped.

Siddy swam close, his teeth chattering. 'Maybe Gryff knows another way down … maybe …'

His words trailed off and Moll knew what he was thinking. There was no other way down. Moll felt the tears build up behind her eyes and then – through the flames and smoke – came a silhouette, a furious pounding of limbs on stone.

'He's going to jump!' Moll cried.

Bruce shook his head. 'He won't make it. You have to make him turn back!'

But Moll's belief in the wildcat was unshakable, like the roots of the very oldest oak tree back in Tanglefern Forest, and she willed him on with all the strength in her soul. 'You can do it, Gryff!' she yelled. 'I know you can!'

The wildcat surged forward and then leapt from the

ramparts and for a second it seemed to the three children in the sea that he was hanging amid the fire, forelimbs stretched out, nose inching towards the water. Moll watched without breathing and then Gryff was tumbling through the air and smashing down into the sea. He ploughed through the waves towards the others, his eyes fixed on Moll.

'He's something, that wildcat of yours,' Bruce murmured.

Moll splashed towards Gryff and with her free arm she held him close for a second. 'He's everything,' she said quietly. '*Everything.*'

Chapter 28
The Rock of Solitude

The swim to the Rock of Solitude was slow, and the cold Moll hadn't felt before now numbed her through. But Bruce had kept his word; they were free of Greystone and its enchantments, and eventually Moll felt stones beneath her boots. She hauled herself and her soaking clothes out on to them. The rocks were crusted with barnacles and limpets and strewn with driftwood, but beyond them, lit up by the blazing fire that was Greystone, was a much larger rock that arched up over the whole island. And it was completely hollow inside.

'Into the cave,' Bruce said. 'We'll be safe in there for a while and we need to rest and make a plan.'

Shaking with cold, the group traipsed inside. The roar of flames from the burning castle in the distance was hushed, but from the shadows cast by the fire Moll could make out chalked dashes on the walls by the entrance to the cave.

Bruce followed her gaze. 'I come here to be a bone – **ALONE**.' He sat down on a ledge of rock and sighed. 'Every mark is a day I've spent as a boy – a useless boy who gets his words all tangled.'

Siddy sat down next to him. 'You're not actually that useless, Bruce. You just helped us escape from a burning castle and you seem to know where we need to go next. You're—' he thought about it for a moment and Moll realised that both she and Sid were beginning to trust the selkie now, '—like a guide! And that's not something useless at all.'

Moll watched as Gryff melted into the shadows of the cave, then she turned to Bruce. 'You've helped us, Bruce, and now we're going to help you find your sealskin.'

She shivered inside her drenched clothes and, noticing her chill, Bruce scampered outside, returning moments later with an armful of driftwood. He rubbed the driest sticks together and, before long, a spark appeared. The group huddled close as the warmth of the flames spread out and Moll and Siddy gasped as Bruce's secret hideout came into view.

On every ledge surrounding the cave there were small wooden carvings. Some were no bigger than Moll's thumb while others were taller with little sticks slotted into holes to act as whiskers. Moll squinted into the half-light and she saw that each carving was a seal.

Bruce gazed at the wooden figures. 'My family and friends,' he said sadly. 'I shaped them out of driftwood.'

Moll's eyes widened as she took in an enormous wardrobe fashioned and carved from driftwood and tucked into the far end of the cave. It was slightly lopsided and the wood was chipped and weathered, but there was something beautiful about the waves carved into the two closed doors and the shells fixed to the handles.

'You carved a wardrobe too?' Moll exclaimed.

Bruce stood up and walked towards it, then he opened the doors and smiled. 'It's a bed.'

Moll and Siddy gathered round him to see an enormous bed of feathers – white and brown flecked – and a mound of blankets bunched up in the corner.

'Eider duck feathers,' Bruce said. 'I've been collecting them since Orbrot stole my sealskin.'

Moll smiled. The more Bruce spoke to them, the safer he seemed to feel and the easier he appeared to find it to hit on the right words.

'Why did you build a bed behind doors?' Siddy asked.

Bruce looked down. 'So that no one would see me crying at night.'

He closed the door and wandered back to the fire and, after the flames had warmed them through and dried their clothes, the three children stole outside, their palms clasped round stones to bash as many limpets as they could from the rocks. They crept back into the cave a while later, dropping armfuls of limpets into the bucket of seawater Bruce had collected. Gryff came to join them and Moll drew out the flask of water Aira had tucked inside her quiver and they ate and drank, safe for a little while inside the Rock of Solitude.

When the wildcat had eaten his share, he stalked off towards a scoop in the rock and curled up inside it, but Moll stayed by the fire, watching the sea lurk beyond the cave. She tightened her scarf around her neck as she thought about the last Shadowmask hastening after them and the full moon just one night away. Then she looked at the others – at Siddy trying to get Frank to eat a limpet and at Bruce carving a seal into the handle of her catapult – and smiled. She might be hundreds of miles from home, but she was with friends and the comfort of that warmed her in a place even the heat from the fire could not reach.

'Your sealskin,' Moll said to Bruce. 'Have you any idea where Orbrot could have hidden it?'

Bruce blinked. 'I know where it is. A selkie always feels drawn towards his shin – I mean, **SKIN**. It's reaching it that's the problem.' He pointed upwards and Moll noticed a very small hole in the cave wall, right near the roof. 'In there,' he said. 'Orbrot kept it there because she knew it would draw me back here every night and keep me out of her way so that she could work on her enchantments. But the space is too small for me to fit my hand inside, though every night I try.'

Moll was silent for a moment, then her eyes flicked to Siddy.

'Don't some people use ferrets for hunting?'

Siddy nodded. 'They send them down burrows to flush out rabbits ...' He trailed off as he realised what Moll meant and he drew Frank out of his pocket, propping her on his knee. 'Frank, we have a job for you.' Frank wagged her tail and wiggled her ears and Siddy looked from Moll to Bruce. 'I think she's on a natural high after the trebuchet ride.' Scooping her up in one hand, Siddy used the other to balance his weight from rock to rock until he reached the hole in the wall. He plopped the ferret down on a ledge in front of it. 'In there, Frank. Bring out anything you find.'

The ferret wriggled inside the hole, then, seconds later, she appeared again with a tiny pebble in her paw. She offered it up to Siddy who shoved it in his pocket. 'Again, Frank,' he whispered. 'Try again.'

Frank disappeared and down below Bruce paced about the cave. 'She won't manage it. I'm doomed to stay a boy for ever.'

Frank's bottom poked out of the hole suddenly and began bouncing up and down.

Moll rolled her eyes. 'Dancing. There's no time for that now, Sid. We need to find Bruce's skin and move on ...'

But Siddy could see more than Moll. 'Keep going, Frank!' he urged. 'Keep pulling!'

Little by little, Frank shuffled backwards out of the hole, and Bruce gasped as he glimpsed the silver-white fur the ferret was tugging with her teeth. She hauled it free and Siddy scooped it up. It was soft and shining and, at the sight of it, Bruce's eyes welled with tears.

'My sealskin!'

The ferret was panting, clearly exhausted, but she had just enough energy for a celebratory cartwheel before slinking into Siddy's pocket and falling fast asleep.

Siddy scrambled down the rocks and handed the sealskin to Bruce, who fell to his knees.

'Thank you, thank you!'

He hugged the skin to his chest, then he left the cave

and walked down to the water's edge before holding it round his shoulders like a cape. Then he slid into the sea and disappeared beneath the surface.

Moll looked on from the entrance of the cave. 'You don't think Bruce has left us, do you, Sid? Now that he's got what he wants?'

They watched the sea, a dark stillness cast orange in parts by the dwindling fire at Greystone, then a small silver-white head popped up, scattering ripples, and a seal pup blinked large black eyes at them.

Siddy's face broke into a smile. 'Look! He's a selkie again!'

For a moment, Moll wondered at the strangeness of things – how she'd set out to destroy the last of the Shadowmasks and had somehow stumbled upon a boy just trying to find his way home. She thought of her own home, her wagon deep inside Tanglefern Forest, and how she, too, wanted more than anything to be back with her friends under the cover of ancient trees.

The seal pup dipped beneath the water, then resurfaced closer to the shore. Its whiskers twitched and, as Moll, Siddy and Gryff looked upon their new friend, they knew he would keep his promise: he'd take them to wherever it was that lay one hundred years deep.

Siddy smiled. 'Go find your family now, Bruce. Moll, Gryff and I will need to make a boat if we're going to be able to follow you to the amulet. Come back at first light.'

The selkie slipped down into his underwater world and the others turned back into the cave. Moll looked around doubtfully, then her eyes caught on the pile of logs tucked into the far corner. 'The driftwood. We could make a raft out of it.'

Siddy shook his head. 'We don't have any rope to tie the logs together.'

Moll raised her eyebrows. 'But we've got string.' She dug out the last note of the witches' song from her pocket. 'It's as strong as metal, Sid. No matter how hard I pull, it never breaks.'

Siddy thought about it for a moment, then he stood up. 'We need to make this raft fast so we're ready for when Bruce comes back; we can only afford a few hours' sleep . . .'

They built a base from the three largest planks of wood they could find, then they strapped a dozen logs across it before using their penknives to chisel two smaller pieces of driftwood into oars. It was gone midnight by the time they had finished and their eyes were heavy with sleep, but they had a vessel, a raft large enough to hold Moll, Siddy, Gryff and Frank, and Siddy had gathered enough sharp stones for the catapult he'd borrowed from Moll.

Moll stoked the fire, then they all climbed into the box bed, spread the blankets over Bruce's feathers and shut the wooden doors. Moll listened, half hoping, for the sound of Aira's horn – a sound that might mean she'd cured Domino and Angus and had come back to help them – but only the waves answered, lapping against the stones. Moll whispered her promise to Alfie, then she pulled a blanket over her before closing her eyes and drifting off to sleep.

*

A little further up the coast, the final Shadowmask was awake. He had sensed the Veil weaken for a moment and he knew immediately what that meant: somehow the child and the beast had killed Orbrot and the witch doctor's soul was no longer bound up in the quilt of darkness. And so, after locking the monastery very carefully, Wormhook had left the Rookery with the Veil.

He rode the quilt towards the sea and he smiled. The thresholds might have closed, but Orbrot had been slipping creatures from the Underworld into the Lost Isles since she'd settled at Greystone. Wherever Molly Pecksniff and her wildcat were hiding, they wouldn't stand a chance against what waited for them in the depths of the northern sea.

The Veil sailed over the snow-capped mountains and Wormhook clasped his hands in delight as he thought of what he would find down by the shore. He glided on into the night, his cloak trailing out behind him, until finally the mountains receded and he touched down on a shingle beach. He dismounted the Veil, stroked it fondly, and then he advanced towards the sea, his boots grinding against the stones.

He stopped and looked out over the water – dark and shining like oil – then he stooped and brushed a sack hand through the shallows. A few minutes later, two bulging eyes surfaced: black orbs the size of plates set below hoods of green skin. A body followed behind, large and rounded, all covered in slime, then a huge tentacle burst from the sea, suckers shaking, before thrashing down against the waves. Wormhook didn't flinch. Instead, he let his mask fall level with the giant squid's head, a stone's throw away from the enormous tentacles that writhed beneath the surface, so that he could finish what Orbrot had started.

'Swim fast, kraken. Search every corner of the sea from here to the Lost Isles. I want the girl and the beast brought to this very spot so that I can squeeze that impossible dream from Molly Pecksniff's heart.' He glanced behind him and beckoned the Veil over with one finger. 'Then, when her hope is finally drowned, we will finish what we started.'

The kraken's eyes swelled and then it sank beneath the surface and only a circle of foam rocked where its monstrous head had been.

Chapter 29
Braving the Lost Isles

The first thing Moll and Siddy saw when they opened the doors around their box bed at the crack of dawn were the mackerel: six of them by the entrance to the cave, their rainbow scales glittering in the sunlight. Gryff was already standing over them, whiskers quivering.

'Did Bruce leave these for us?' Moll asked quietly.

Then she followed Siddy's gaze to a rock outside the cave on which a seal pup with silver-white fur lay. It shuffled closer on its belly and croaked.

Moll walked towards it, glancing left and then right as she peered out of the cave. Greystone was now a smoking heap of rubble – it wouldn't be long before any locals still left on the coast came to investigate what had happened at the castle – but neither the Veil nor the Night Spinner seemed to have arrived. Just the sea stretched out around them, a never-ending sheet of steel blue.

Moll knelt before the seal pup. 'You brought us the fish, didn't you, Bruce?' The selkie's grey nose twitched and Moll smiled. 'Thank you!'

Gathering up the mackerel, she, Siddy and Gryff rushed back into the cave and, after eating quickly, they heaved their raft into the icy sea.

Moll stood on the rocks, gripping the reel of string still left in her hand, while Bruce watched from the water as the rest of the group manoeuvred themselves on to the raft. Then Moll jumped aboard, tossing the string to Gryff who caught it in his teeth and prowled to the far end of the raft to keep watch. Frank positioned herself at the opposite end of the vessel and Moll adjusted the quiver on her back. She was low on arrows after the moths – there hadn't been time to snatch them from the fire – but the golden feather was still there, and slotted inside Siddy's coat pocket was her catapult, its handle now inscribed with a seal pup, courtesy of Bruce's handiwork.

Moll glanced at the Lost Isles to the north of them. They were larger than the Rock of Solitude, taller and wilder, jutting out of the sea in jagged peaks, while on the mainland, where the moors ended, mountains cloaked in snow began. Moll turned towards Bruce's sleek head bobbing before the raft and watched as it sank beneath the water, spilling ripples, and then appeared, a minute later, slightly further up the coast between the islands and the mainland.

Moll took a deep breath. 'Into the heart of the Lost Isles.'

Siddy reached out and stroked Frank's head and nodded. 'Towards the last Amulet of Truth.'

They paddled on after Bruce, inching up the ragged coastline, and, though they passed caves cut into islands and mountain peaks lost amid frayed clouds, Moll kept her eyes trained on the seal. The crags either side of them grew taller still, until they blocked out the sun and cloaked the raft in shadows, and it was then that Siddy lifted his paddle out of the water and glanced at Moll.

'What – what are they?' he stammered, pointing into the sea ahead of them.

Grey fins sliced through the water towards the raft and Moll snatched her oar in and huddled closer to Siddy. But she saw that Bruce wasn't in the least bit frightened. Instead, he rolled his body playfully into the fins and then several long, blunt noses poked up. Moll breathed out.

'Dolphins,' she said. 'Like the ones we used to see back in Little Hollows.'

The pod swam alongside the raft for some time and Moll was almost glad of their company in among the stillness of the Lost Isles, but after a while the animals spiralled into deeper waters and once again the group was alone. Siddy and Moll pulled their oars on through the water, past cliffs full of puffins and guillemots and slabs of rock where seals basked, while Gryff and Frank kept watch either end of the raft.

Occasionally, they glimpsed a cottage at the foot of an island, but mostly the coast felt wild, home to the calls of the birds and seals that hung in the wintry breeze. Moll felt the air bite through her gloves and nip at her ears and she gripped her oar tighter and tried her best not to think about the Night Spinner and his Veil. But, when Bruce stopped swimming and turned questioning eyes back at the raft, Moll knew something wasn't right.

She glanced at Siddy. 'It's gone quiet. Listen ...'

They strained their ears for the groans of the puffins or the yapping kittiwakes, but the birds were still and silent on the crags and only the waves sounded, thumping against the cliffs. Bruce slid closer to the raft until his furred chin was touching the planks of timber. And suddenly Moll realised why. Where Bruce had been the waves no longer rolled. Instead, they swirled in a circle, a spin of water that was gathering pace to form a hollow drop in the middle.

'Whirlpool!' Siddy screamed.

They dug their oars into the water and back-paddled, but the whirlpool only grew in size. The birds tore from the cliffs, shaking the silence with terrified cries, and Moll's insides squirmed.

Because there, in the middle of the churning water, was a head – a pulsing mass of slithery skin with two rolling eyes. Moll knew instantly that this was a kraken, the beast from the depths of the sea that Aira had spoken of, but it was fused with all the horror and curses Orbrot had mustered from the Underworld.

Bruce shot beneath the surface and Frank dived into Siddy's pocket. But Gryff, the piano string still gripped between his teeth, growled from the end of the raft and as he did so a giant green tentacle reared out of the sea, its suckers glistening in the sunlight. Moll felt her limbs go weak and Siddy moaned, but when Gryff stamped his forelimbs on to the raft, his eyes blazing and his muscles rippling, they knew it was a call to fight.

'Weapons!' Moll shouted, hurling down her oar and snatching an arrow from her quiver.

Siddy grabbed Moll's catapult and, as Moll yelled 'Fire!', his stone and Moll's arrow shot out at the same time. The kraken drew up more tentacles from the depths, great suckered limbs that curled into the air like chains, and just before Moll and Siddy's missiles hit its squid-like body a tentacle whipped round and thrashed the weapons away. The kraken's eyes narrowed and it twisted its tentacles together creating a terrible squelching sound. Sensing what was coming next, Moll and Siddy back-paddled desperately, but the kraken smashed a tentacle towards the raft. It missed them by millimetres, but the movement jolted the vessel, sending Moll, Siddy, Frank and Gryff sliding to the very end as the whole thing tilted downwards. Then it bounced back up, spraying water over them, and the group scampered into the middle.

'Reload!' Moll cried. 'We have to try!'

Once again, Moll nocked an arrow to her bow and Siddy loaded his catapult with a stone and they fired, but the kraken hurled the weapons out of its path and sank beneath the surface. Just the whirlpool remained, edging closer and closer to the raft ... and then it exploded.

Water burst from the sea, spattering on to the planks of wood, before the kraken rose up again, great ropes of drool hanging from its suckers. Moll and Siddy quaked in fear as they stared up at the creature. Then it slammed a tentacle down on the vessel, hurling Gryff into the sea.

'No!' Moll cried, rushing to the edge of the raft.

The end of the piano string was floating on the surface and Moll yanked it up, but there was no sign of the wildcat. Her eyes scudded across the waves, then Siddy wrenched her backwards.

'Watch out!' he yelled.

The kraken lunged forward, ripping several arrows from Moll's quiver and flinging them into the sea. Siddy hauled Moll further back and she clutched her quiver tight, desperate to keep the golden feather safe. The kraken withdrew for a moment to gather its full strength.

'Gryff!' Moll panted. 'Where is he?'

She whirled round, searching for the wildcat, then saw Bruce nosing him through the water towards the raft. Quickly, she bent over the edge and lifted Gryff up, then Bruce tried to clamber aboard too – he wasn't giving up on them yet and he was ready to help with the fight. Moll heaved the seal pup on to the raft as Siddy fired stone after stone.

But the monster loomed before them still, tentacles quivering, and Moll realised they couldn't fight what was coming. With a single stroke, the kraken would drown them all . . .

And then Moll remembered something Willow had told them about their bows, something she'd completely forgotten about until now. There was another way their arrows could be used – to fire a protection charm instead of a weapon if they thought hard enough about the Otherworld – but they only had *one chance* at this in their lifetime. She'd had hers when they were searching for the second amulet, but Siddy still had his – and she still had one arrow left . . .

'Use my bow and think of the Otherworld!' Moll yelled. 'Will it on and the arrow will fire a cocoon to protect us!' The kraken lumbered forward and Siddy whimpered.

'You can do it, Sid!' Moll cried. 'I know you can!'

Fingers trembling, Siddy raised Moll's bow and, as the kraken's tentacles lunged towards them, he fired. The Oracle Spirit burst out, but, instead of careering towards the beast, a shell of hard white light enclosed the raft and everyone on board. Tentacles slammed against the cocoon and suckers squelched against the sides, but the Oracle Spirit was strong – stronger than the Shadowmasks' magic – and, like a shield of glass, it withstood the kraken's blows. Not even the waves that pounded against its sides could topple the little raft now that it was encased and it stood firm, a glowing light amid the shadowed cliffs, blocking out all noise and danger.

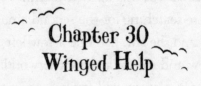

Heart clamouring, Moll turned to Siddy. 'Well done, Sid! You did it!'

Siddy set his bow down and watched, wide-eyed, as the kraken wrestled its suckered tentacles over the cocoon. 'It worked,' he panted as Frank emerged from his pocket and licked his chin. 'It actually worked.'

Moll nuzzled into Gryff's fur, then reached out a hand to touch the cocoon. It was cool and hard and, though the kraken wasn't giving up, Moll knew that the beast didn't really stand a chance against the old magic now. She smiled at Bruce.

'Thank you for rescuing Gryff. You're fast becoming the most impressive selkie I've ever met.'

Bruce clapped his flippers together in delight, but then the kraken slid a large, throbbing eye right up to the cocoon, and the seal pup flattened himself to the raft, his fur bristling.

'We can't stay like this forever,' Moll said. 'We only have one more night until the full moon rises ... What do we do?'

The sun was sinking now and, although they couldn't see it through the maze of islands, its light spilled through the gaps, scattering orange on the sea.

'It'll be night soon,' Siddy said quietly. 'What if the Night Spinner creeps up on us . . .?'

Frank scurried over the raft towards the cocoon, bashed it with her paw and then let out a little growl at the kraken. But, when the beast barged its slimy body against the shell of light, the ferret shot backwards before clattering into Moll, getting her legs and claws tangled up in Moll's hair.

'Urgh, Sid, control your ferret! You don't see Gryff prancing around all over people's faces.'

Siddy went to grab Frank. 'She's got her paws stuck in something . . . What's that hanging around your neck?'

Moll glanced at her chest as Siddy yanked the ferret free. Hanging from a piece of string was the whistle carved from antler that Aira had given her. Moll ran her thumb up and down it. 'Sid,' she said slowly, 'I may have an idea how to get us out of this.'

He nodded. 'So long as it doesn't involve being catapulted off another burning building, I'm in.'

Moll held out the whistle. 'Aira gave this to me – she said the giants up in the mountains, the ones who were *actually there* when the old magic first turned, gave it to her ancestors. She said if I was in need I should blow it and the old magic would come to help.'

Siddy threw his hands in the air. 'And you didn't think to give it a quick *toot* when I was turned to stone or when

229

the castle was burning down or – or when the kraken nearly ATE US?'

Moll's cheeks reddened. 'I forgot. There's a lot to remember with golden feathers and piano strings.'

The kraken slid its face down the cocoon and Siddy edged closer to Moll. 'Blow the whistle. Now.'

Moll raised it to her lips and blew but the sound that came out was reedy and thin and she felt a stab of doubt that something so small could help them now.

Siddy shook his head. 'Blow the whistle like you mean it, Moll. Like you believe it'll help – just as I believed when I made the cocoon.'

Moll blew again, mustering up all the belief that she could, and the sound blared within the cocoon, high and shrill and full of hope. And, even after Moll had lowered the whistle from her lips, the sound rang through the Lost Isles.

'There's magic coming,' she whispered. 'I can feel it.'

Siddy nodded and then Gryff slipped from Moll's side to the front of the raft. He looked out towards the passage of sea cutting through the islands, as if he could sense something beyond their vision. A cluster of dark shapes appeared in the sky: a dozen large birds swooping low through the islands towards them, their wings a flash of brown and white against the fading sun.

'Ospreys,' Moll murmured, then she looked at Aira's whistle. 'Do you think we – we *called* them?'

'Even if we did,' Siddy said glumly, 'birds won't be much use against a kraken.'

Moll watched as the ospreys soared towards them before circling above the sea monster. She craned her neck to get a better view. 'What are they doing?'

And then her stomach plunged. The ospreys were diving – bolts of talons, claws and orange eyes plummeting straight towards the cocoon.

'No,' Siddy breathed. 'The Shadowmasks must have called the birds! Not us!'

The kraken drew back, its tentacles raised in glee as the birds descended, but instead of hammering their talons against the cocoon the birds stretched out their wings at the very last moment, suddenly breaking their dives. Moll held in a scream as the raft wobbled and the endless battering of waves stopped.

'What's happening?' Siddy wailed.

Moll glanced up to see the ospreys clutching the cocoon, which was now soft like cloth and gathered inside their talons like scrunched-up silk.

She raised a hand to her mouth. 'I think we're . . . *flying!*'

The two children rushed to the edge of the raft and when they looked out they saw the kraken far below them, thrashing at the sea with its tentacles. They climbed higher and higher into the twilight, up above the jagged peaks and into a sky strewn with amber clouds. The raft rocked back and forth to the beat of ospreys' wings and, safe inside the silver-white tent, Moll picked up the whistle and smiled.

'The old magic came to help us,' she said.

The birds carried them silently through the clouds, past

waterfalls crashing off jutting crags, on up the coast above a copper sea, until eventually the Lost Isles shrank to a few scattered mounds, dark shapes against the dying light. Moll glanced at Bruce who was watching through the cocoon, unblinking, but he made no signal to imply they were going the wrong way. It seemed he wasn't the only one who knew where the place Willow had called *one hundred years deep* lay.

There was nothing to be done now but to trust that the birds knew where they were going. So Siddy and Molly sat together, talking long into the night – of what might be waiting for them ahead and of what the last amulet might be – but also of their tree fort and their wagons deep in Tanglefern Forest and of everything they planned to do together once all this was over. And as the ospreys flew on into the night, below a large pale moon, they spoke of Alfie and hoped that wherever he was, he was safe.

Chapter 31
One Hundred Years Deep

Gryff tugged at Moll's coat sleeve and she opened one eye.

'Brrrooooooo.'

She let the wildcat's greeting call rumble in her ears, then she sat up and yawned. Siddy was lying beside her, snoring, with Frank curled up on his chest and, at the far end of the raft, Bruce was peering out through the cocoon. Moll followed his upward gaze. Brown-flecked feathers rippled in the wind and far below the ospreys the sea sprawled out towards an unknown horizon. Sunlight bobbed on the waves and it was so warm and snug inside the cocoon that it might have been a summer's day had the coastline to their right not told another story. White mountains rose up from the sea, their bases ringed with ice, and wisps of snow unfurled from the peaks.

Frank stirred from Siddy's chest and, on seeing Moll and Gryff awake, nibbled on Siddy's ear.

'The mountains,' Siddy murmured, rubbing his eyes as he looked out of the cocoon. 'They go on forever.'

Moll nodded. For as far as they could see, peaks and ridges jutted across the land. They were colossal, like the bone structure of a mighty dragon, and they reached such dizzying heights it looked as if they were propping up the sky itself. Moll swallowed. Somehow they had to find the last amulet among them *tonight* . . .

There was a sharp cry from above and suddenly the ospreys tucked in their wings, the raft swung to one side and the birds bulleted towards the sea.

'Hold on!' Moll yelled, clutching Gryff with one hand and digging her nails into the raft with the other.

Her stomach swung to her throat and her eyes streamed as the birds plunged down, down, down – then the raft hit the water with a jolt, the silk around them hardened into a glass-like cocoon again, and once more they felt the familiar push and pull of the tide around them. Using their beaks, the ospreys nudged the raft up to the base of the nearest mountain before launching into the sky and gliding away over the mountains. But, where the ospreys had been on the ledges of rock, there was now a person: a woman whose face told of magic and undiscovered worlds.

'Is – is that . . .?' Moll's voice trailed off in disbelief.

The messenger from the Otherworld was exactly as Moll remembered her: blue swishes of colour looped from her cheekbones up over her brow, pale green dots curved beneath her eyes and a long silver plait hung down over her dress. The only change was the fur cape she wore which curled round her body like folds of fresh snow.

Siddy pressed his palms up against the cocoon. 'Willow!'

The woman dipped her head towards them and something in the gesture reminded Moll of how Gryff greeted her after time apart. Willow took a deep breath and as she exhaled, the cocoon around them faded and then vanished. Moll shivered at the sudden chill of air.

'I do not have long,' Willow said. Her voice was quieter than it had been in the forest when they'd first met. It was almost a whisper, like a trail of words carried loosely on the wind, and now that Moll looked more closely Willow's body looked different too – faded at the edges as if the Oracle Spirit was only just in Moll's world. 'The dark magic is trying to hold me back even now,' Willow continued. 'But, when you destroyed Orbrot, the Shadowmasks' power weakened for a moment and I was able to find a way through to you.' The markings around her eyes tightened. 'Keep hold of your bow, Moll.'

Moll frowned. 'But I lost the last of my arrows and—'

Willow cut through her words. 'Keep the bow and follow the selkie.'

She leapt from the rock out on to the raft and Moll and Siddy held their breath at the sight of magic so close and so full of urgency. Willow leant forward and touched the whistle hanging around Moll's neck and Moll gasped as she watched the Oracle Spirit's touch transform it into a small key carved from bone. Engravings ran down each side.

'Oracle Bone script,' Moll murmured, turning it over in her palm.

Willow nodded. 'Magic does not fix as one thing for very long. You only need to blink or turn away and it disappears, but it is never gone for good. Look after that key, Moll. You will know when to use it.' She drew herself up, her body fading in the sunlight before them. 'I must leave you now – the Night Spinner's dark magic isn't far behind – but we will meet again. That much I know. When you have found what lies one hundred years deep, head north on foot. Over the Barbed Peaks.' She paused. 'And know, as ever, that the old magic is willing you on every step of the way.'

She twisted her hands above her head, as if running them over invisible objects, and then, from Willow's fingertips, silver shapes swirled into the air, like wisps of smoke, and as they drifted slowly down to the raft they hardened into objects the group couldn't have been happier to see: goblets full of steaming hot chocolate, bowls of warm milk for Gryff and Frank, fresh fish for Bruce and trays laden with porridge, fresh fruit and buttered toast. But where Willow had been there was nothing – just the feel of magic glimpsed and then lost.

Siddy glanced around. 'Do you think we have time to eat it? The Night Spinner could be here any moment.'

Moll considered. 'I think it's important to eat breakfast before tackling dark magic; Willow wouldn't have conjured it all up otherwise.'

Siddy picked up a goblet. 'I agree.'

They ate hungrily, scraping at the bowls of porridge and draining the hot chocolate in glugs, and, when they had finished, the mysterious feast vanished, just as Willow had done.

Moll watched the sea for a moment, ruffled by the morning breeze, then, as Bruce slipped back into the water, she and Siddy dug their oars into the waves and followed the selkie as he swam further up the coast. Hours drifted by with Gryff and Frank keeping watch at both ends of the raft again and, though Moll's hands were blistered inside her gloves, she kept on paddling – always north – with the cries of the kittiwakes in her ears.

Eventually Bruce slowed. They had approached a gap between the cliffs and, as the raft edged closer to it, Moll and Siddy realised it was in fact a fjord cutting inland to form a giant loch. Bruce stopped and as Moll looked at the slice of water within the mountains she saw that it was frighteningly still, like glass, washed white by the reflection of snow from the cliffs either side. The selkie's nose twitched, but he did not go any further. Instead, he hovered before the loch as if it was something important but also something to fear.

'Bruce has come to the end of his journey,' Moll said, slowly understanding.

Siddy nodded. 'And I have a feeling ours is only just beginning.' His eyes travelled the length of the loch. 'One hundred years deep. Why do I have a feeling that whatever we want is down at the bottom?'

Bruce swam up to the raft and placed a flipper on the wood and Siddy and Moll crouched before him.

'You were very clever back at Greystone,' Moll said.

Siddy nodded. 'And very brave with the kraken.'

Bruce croaked and then to Moll's surprise Gryff prowled close, dipping his head before the seal pup. Feeling left out, Frank joined the group and did a little leg kick before the selkie, and Moll smiled. Her and Siddy's journey had been fraught with peril, but it had also been full of unexpected friends, of people they'd grown to love and trust and without whom they would never have made it this far.

'We won't forget you, Bruce,' Moll said quietly.

Siddy nodded. 'Back in our camp we tell stories around the fire and, when all this is over, when me and Moll are back with our family and friends, we're going to tell *your* story.'

Moll stroked the seal pup's head. 'And it'll be the finest story anyone has ever told.'

Bruce placed his flipper over both Moll and Siddy's hands and then he croaked again before sinking beneath the water to make his long journey home.

Moll and Siddy squinted into the mid-morning sun as they looked out across the loch.

'Don't even ask if I have a plan for how we get the amulet,' Moll said, 'because I don't.' She shuffled closer to Gryff as she thought of an endless deep falling away beneath their raft, then she glanced at the two dark-haired shapes bobbing up by a rock further out in the ocean.

'Sea otters,' Siddy said, following her gaze. 'Back in Little Hollows, Oak told me that they hold hands when they sleep so that they don't float away from each other.'

Moll looked at the great white stillness in front of them,

then she reached out and squeezed Siddy's hand. He squeezed back, and then together they picked up their oars and steered the raft into the cliffs.

Moll took in the mountains either side of them, great shields of snow that climbed vertically upwards into dizzying heights, boxing them in on all sides and blocking out the morning sun. There were no gulls bobbing on the water, no fish nosing the surface. This was a place of stillness and silence.

They paddled on, Gryff pressed close to Moll's side and Frank perched on Siddy's knee, until Moll pointed to a wooden jetty leading out from the base of the cliff at the far end of the loch. There was a small shingle beach there and what looked like an old fishing hut.

'Let's make for that,' Moll said. 'I think we should get off the water.'

Finally, they came to the jetty and, using the piano string to tie the raft to a mooring ring there, they hoisted themselves up and sat on the dock, legs tucked up under their chins and heads down to fight the cold.

'We're at a dead end, aren't we?' Siddy mumbled. 'How can we get down to the bottom of this loch without freezing – or without breathing – before the Night Spinner finds us?'

Moll watched as Frank hurried up and down the piano string that moored the raft, then she turned to Siddy. 'Willow's letter said: *steal the last note of the witches' song then take a feather from burning wings and you'll find what you need one hundred years deep.* Maybe we need to *use* the things we've found to get the amulet,' Moll said. 'The piano string is endless and even though it's almost invisible there's a weight to it, so we could use it like a fishing line to reach the bottom.' She paused. 'We know the string's magical so maybe it'll have the power to tie itself round the amulet and haul it up for us.'

Siddy nodded, then he looked out across the water. 'This loch is huge and we don't even know what we're looking for. It could be anywhere . . .'

But Gryff and Frank were already down on the raft again, clawing the string away from the driftwood.

'They're unpicking it,' Siddy said slowly.

Moll nodded. 'They're right. We don't need the raft any more – Willow told us to go on by foot.' She glanced at Gryff who had managed to loosen the first log. 'Come on, let's help them – we need to move fast.'

When there were just a few planks left, they jumped back up on to the jetty and Moll wound in the last of the string. She clutched the reel in her gloves and then little by little she let it out again, dropping it slowly through the water. It lengthened before their eyes, a silvery thread glistening in the splice of sunlight that edged over the cliffs, before sinking into the milky water. Down and down it went as Moll unravelled it through her fingers, but, after ten minutes, she slid a nervous glance to Siddy.

'What if we never reach the bottom?'

'Keep going,' Siddy said firmly. 'It's our only hope.'

Moll loosed more and more of the piano string and then,

across the great silence of the loch, music started. It wasn't like the haunting melody in the Clattering Gorge. This was different: a single, low note that thrummed between the cliffs as if it might be summoning someone or something from very far away. Moll gripped the piano string tightly so that it couldn't unravel any more and instantly the music stopped.

Siddy's shoulders hunched and Frank tiptoed back inside his coat pocket. 'You may not have hit the bottom, but you've disturbed something . . .'

Moll's eyes glazed with dread. 'Not witches again?'

Siddy shook his head. 'I don't think so. This feels different somehow.'

Moll nodded, then Gryff nudged her arm and, with shaking hands, she released more of the string into the loch. Again the note sounded, rich and low and filled with foreboding. Moll jumped.

'What is it?' Siddy cried.

'There's something on the end of the string.' Moll peered over the edge of the jetty. 'I can *feel* it – a weight tugging hard.'

'Do you think it's the amulet?' Siddy asked hopefully.

Moll kept pulling and then ripples started spilling out around the string and Siddy huddled close. The ripples quickened, the piano note swelled and then it cut to silence as a webbed hand burst out of the water.

'It's a monster!' Siddy screamed. 'And we've gone and woken it up!'

Chapter 32
Waking Murk

'Yank the string!' Siddy yelled. 'It might go away!'

But as Moll jiggled it about it was clear the monster was here to stay. Clumps of seaweed rose out of the water and Moll's muscles seized with fright as she realised what the tendrils of algae actually were. *Hair.* And, beneath them, the face of a very old woman: crinkled grey skin that hung in sagging folds and gills that marked either side of her neck. Gryff growled, but still the webbed hands clung to the piano string and all Moll could do was cling back. Because this strange creature – whatever it was – was their only link to the amulet.

'Why have you disturbed my sleep?' the old woman wheezed.

Siddy swallowed. 'We want to—'

Moll's hands tightened round the piano string. '—drag you up here and pin you down until you hand over the last Amulet of Truth.'

'What – what my friend means,' Siddy stammered, 'is we'd like to talk to you because we're looking for something very important.' His voice was trembling, but he forced his words out. 'We don't have much time and we wondered if you could help us.'

The old woman blinked two pale eyes. 'Well, you'd better pull me up then, hadn't you?'

For a moment, Moll did nothing. She didn't trust the woman, with her webbed hands and gills, but they needed to find the last amulet and so, warily, Moll nodded to Siddy and together they heaved on the string. Little by little, the old woman emerged from the loch: she was small, like a child, with a pointed chin sprouting grey hairs, dripping rags made from cockles and clams, and two thin, webbed feet.

Moll blinked as the woman clambered up on to the end of the jetty, raised herself upright and glared at them. The skin around her mouth was puckered, forcing her lips to droop, and the bags beneath her eyes sloped on to leathery cheeks.

Moll tucked the piano string into her pocket and, just as she was thinking that this creature was the most miserable-looking thing she had ever laid eyes on, the old woman shot out a webbed hand and grabbed Moll's arm.

'You want me to help you?' she sneered. 'Silly children, what on earth would make you think I'd want to do that?'

Her dry lips curled back to reveal a row of jagged teeth, then Gryff barged into her side and she staggered backwards.

Moll twisted free and surged forward. 'Run!' she cried. 'Run!'

They tore down the jetty towards the fishing hut and

behind them the slop of webbed feet traipsed closer. Siddy flung open the door and Moll, Gryff and Frank piled in before slamming the door shut behind them and pressing their backs against it.

'Now what?' Moll panted.

Siddy glanced around at the broken chairs and the battered table, then at the broom propped up against the wall. Moll followed his gaze.

'You think we can fight that creature with a *broom*?'

Siddy lurched towards his weapon. 'You got any better ideas?'

Moll grabbed her catapult from Siddy's pocket and stooped to collect a few splinters of wood as ammunition, then she crept up to the window. But, when she looked out through the glass, she screamed. The old woman's face was right there, her cold eyes blinking back at Moll. Moll scampered away, Siddy raised his broom and from behind the glass the creature from the loch hissed.

Gryff's whiskers flared and the old woman slid back from the window, but, when Moll heard the cockles and clams clinking together, she knew that the creature was skirting the hut towards the door. There was a scratching at the entrance and Moll, Siddy, Gryff and Frank listened, wide-eyed, to the rasping breaths of the woman outside.

Then the door scraped open and she stood before them, hunched and scowling. But she didn't launch herself at the group, as Moll had expected. She was still and quiet as the water dripped from her rags down on to the floor.

'So, you grotesque little humans,' she muttered, 'are you going to give me a reason why I should help you or are you just going to turn tail and run?' She coughed and a glob of water, grit and seaweed spattered on to the floorboards. Moll recoiled in disgust and gripped her catapult tighter. 'Well?' the woman asked.

'Because a dark magic is spreading across our land,' Siddy gulped, 'and we think you might have something that can help us fight it.'

The old woman's eyes lit up for a moment at the mention of fighting the dark magic, then she shook her head and drummed her fingers against the door frame. 'No one visits me for hundreds of years, then I'm called up from the depths twice in one winter.' Her words dissolved into more coughing, great barks that racked her body and bent her double. 'The first visitor who summoned me last month wasn't very nice to kind old Murk and now you come along and I'm expected to *help*?'

She stumbled forward suddenly, but, instead of making to grab them, she grappled for the back of a chair, missed it and crashed to the floor. She curled up in a ball and moaned and Moll was suddenly struck by how small and frail the old woman looked.

'Sid,' Moll whispered, watching a tear roll down the loch monster's cheek. 'Murk's not angry . . . She's upset.'

Moll bent down, trying not to breathe through her nose as the watery stench of fish and seaweed hit her. But, when she reached out a hand to help Murk up, the old woman batted it away and kicked out with her feet. She coiled up again into a shaking lump and this time Siddy stretched out a hand and placed it on her back while Frank nuzzled against her thigh.

'We want to help you,' he said. 'We want to put an end to the dark magic that is spreading across this land.'

Murk looked up through bloodshot eyes. 'So you've said – but earlier you were running away from me . . .'

She shuffled backwards and as she did so Moll noticed something in the old woman's rags that she hadn't seen earlier. Hanging down against the cockles and mussels, but wedged deep into Murk's side, was something long and thin and silver.

Moll slid a glance to Siddy. 'That's an arrow,' she said. 'Only we can't see the tip because it's buried in Murk's side. She's *in pain*.'

Murk sniffed. 'A masked man came with the arrow; he said it was made of indestructible metal and, because he couldn't destroy it, he wanted to bury it one hundred years deep so that *no one* would find it.' The old woman shifted her weight and grimaced. 'No one finds me, not usually, but he had dark magic on his side.'

Moll flinched. 'The Night Spinner.'

Siddy's eyes grew large as he turned to Moll. 'Do you think this arrow is the last amulet?'

The thought niggled inside Moll. When they had found the other two amulets, she had *felt* their magic, but she didn't sense anything now. 'I don't know,' she said quietly.

Murk hung her head. 'The masked man laid a curse on me. He said that if I ever tried to draw the arrow out I would die.'

Moll was silent for a moment, then she pulled the golden feather from her quiver. 'A phoenix has life-giving properties,' she said slowly. 'When one dies, another is born from its ashes.'

Murk shrugged. 'And? What use is a phoenix feather to me?'

'Maybe it can counter the curse,' Moll said. 'Maybe it can bring you life instead of death when the arrow is removed.' She glanced at Siddy. 'It would be like the string; we'd be using an object we found on our journey.'

Murk shuffled backwards. 'What if you're wrong?'

Moll didn't blink. 'What if I'm right? You could walk free from this curse and Siddy and I could be in with a chance of claiming the last amulet and forcing the dark magic back once and for all?'

Murk chewed on a strand of seaweed. 'How will you remove the arrow?'

Moll took a deep breath. 'Siddy's going to yank it out and—'

Siddy frowned. 'I am?'

'Yes, you are,' Moll replied. 'Please keep up. And I'm going to lay this feather over the wound straight after.' Murk's wrinkles slid closer together. 'This might be your only chance to break free from the curse. And time is running out – there's an eternal night waiting to happen if we don't act now.'

The old woman took a deep breath, then she sat up, looked at Siddy and nodded. Siddy leant forward, biting down on his lip as he placed a hand on the arrow, then pulled hard.

Siddy's hand shot back and he shook his head. 'I can't do it. It's hurting her too much.'

But it was Murk who answered through clenched teeth. 'Go on, boy.'

Siddy heaved again and Murk's whole body tensed, then she threw back her head and howled as Siddy wrenched the arrow free. Moll slid the golden feather over the gaping hole and for a few seconds nothing happened and Moll winced as the old woman sobbed and blood seeped through the wound. But then the feather began to glow, as bright as a burning star, and Murk stopped crying. She looked down at her waist, then at the feather which was no longer covered in blood, and her face broke into a smile.

'I'm not in pain any more!' she gasped.

Moll lifted the feather away and, where the wound had been inside the rags, there was now unbroken grey skin. Murk staggered to her feet and chuckled and Moll wondered how she had ever thought this strange little creature ugly.

'Thank you,' Murk said. 'You're not such grotesque little humans after all.'

Moll smiled as she slotted the golden feather back inside her quiver and Siddy laid the arrow on the table.

'The last amulet, the one that contains an unknown soul that we have to free.' Siddy paused. 'It doesn't feel right. It's not like the other times when we *knew* that we'd found the amulets.'

Moll glanced at Murk. 'Do you know where this arrow came from?'

The old woman shook her head. 'The man just arrived with it one night.'

Moll narrowed her eyes. 'Willow said I'd need to use my bow again. Perhaps this arrow is what I need to kill the Night Spinner and stop his Veil.' She paused. 'I think the amulet's still out there waiting for us, Sid.'

Moll picked the arrow up and placed it in her quiver beside the golden feather, then she glanced through the window towards the mountains barring their way north, a blur of white as fresh snow fell, drowning out the midday sun.

'*Head north – over the Barbed Peaks*, that's what Willow said.'

Siddy bit his lip. 'It's time for us to find the last Shadowmask now, isn't it?'

Moll nodded. They had spent so much time running away from the witch doctors, desperate to stay out of sight. But now, as the end of things drew close and the eternal night loomed near, they had to seek the darkness out. They had to run helplessly into its arms.

Murk shuddered. 'You'll need to leave as soon as you can if you're going to attempt to climb the Stone Necklace in daylight.'

'The stone *what*?' Siddy asked.

'Necklace,' Murk replied. 'It's the name given to the peaks

that line the north side of this loch because they curve right round from the coast inland.' She sighed. 'But even if you do manage to climb the Stone Necklace, which you won't, I doubt very much you'll make the crossing over the ridges beyond it. They're called the Barbed Peaks for a reason.'

Moll's face fell.

'I'm sorry,' Murk said. 'It's just – you're so small and,' she glanced at the cliff face outside, 'and that great wall of rock – I've never heard of anyone scaling it . . .'

Siddy scooped Frank up and the ferret licked his cheek. 'Why does everything have to be so difficult?'

Gryff prowled beneath the window, then he looked up at the Stone Necklace and Moll sensed his determination, his refusal to give in, even though the challenge ahead hung large and almost impossible. She clenched her teeth.

'The old magic may not be the easiest way, but it's almost always the *best* way,' Moll said. 'And, even if it leads me up dangerous cliffs and into the hands of the Shadowmask, I'll keep on following it. Step by step.'

Siddy tucked his scarf into his duffle coat. 'We're with you, Moll. Let's get going.'

Gryff dipped his head and Frank raised a paw which might, or might not, have been a salute.

But, not so far away, spurred on by the thought of an eternal darkness, the Veil continued to scatter its curse, a poison seeping into the heart of the land.

Chapter 33
Scaling the Stone Necklace

They emerged from the fishing hut into a world dusted white. The jetty was a plank of snow and Moll and Siddy tensed as they glimpsed the loch, now covered in great sheets of ice that creaked and groaned into the silent fjord.

'This is no ordinary weather,' Murk muttered as still more snow fell.

Moll nodded. 'This is the Night Spinner's doing. My friend Aira from the Highland Watch told me the dark magic has conjured the worst mists and snows the north has ever seen.'

They walked across the pebbled shore until they were standing at the foot of the Stone Necklace.

'See?' Murk said glumly. 'It's too big. Far too big.'

Moll let her eyes travel from its base right up to the jagged ridge. It was a giant wall of rock, covered in snow and polished, in parts, with ice. She blinked as the snowflakes sprinkled down, peeling from the peaks in shifting ribbons.

'Enormous. Colossal. Gargantuan,' Murk mumbled. 'Never seen anything the size of the Stone Necklace.'

Moll turned to the old woman. 'I thought once the arrow was out you'd cheer up.'

Murk shook her head. 'It's in a loch monster's nature to be gloomy. And what I see in front of me is the gloomiest of things yet.'

Siddy rolled his eyes and from his pocket Frank stuck out a little pink tongue at the loch monster.

Moll tugged her cap down over her ears. 'Right,' she muttered. 'Let's get climbing.'

Murk nodded. 'Terrible idea but yes, off you go. And good luck! Though it probably won't help.'

'Goodbye, Murk,' Siddy said. 'I hope you enjoy the depths of the loch now.'

Murk nodded. 'It'll be splendid. Unless the selkies crowd in and bother me. Or the ice covers my surfacing spots. Or everyone forgets I exist and no one comes to visit me for another one hundred years. Goodbye!'

The old woman waved from the shore, a resigned grimace plastered on her face, as Moll, Siddy, Gryff and Frank walked to the base of the Stone Necklace. Gryff set off first, his claws gripping fast on the rocks beneath the snow, but, when Moll and Siddy tried to follow, their boots slid on the icy crags, their gloves scrabbled for holds and they tumbled back to the shore.

Murk called after them. 'See what I mean? Completely hopeless, as I said. Might as well just sit and wait for the Shadowmask to have his wicked way . . .'

Moll watched the wildcat springing between ledges of

snow, up to places where she couldn't follow, then she threw herself at the cliff face again. But, when she landed, with a thump, at Siddy's feet, he shook his head.

'It's not going to work. We need something to hold on to as we climb.' Siddy glanced at Moll's pocket. 'I think I've got an idea.'

A short while later, Moll was pulling back on her bow, the silver arrow taut against it, and a knot of piano string wound round its tip that then trailed into Siddy's hands.

'Aim for the highest point you can, Moll,' Siddy said. 'And fire hard so that it sticks into a crag.'

From behind them, Murk let out a strangled wail, then covered her eyes with her webbed hands. 'Oh, I can't watch. It's too awful.'

But Moll wasn't listening any more because poised some way up the cliff was Gryff, and he was waiting for them to follow. She watched him for a moment and then her gaze flicked upwards, to the highest point of the cliff, and closing one eye, she drew the arrow back against her chin, and fired hard.

The arrow shot upwards, the string in Siddy's hands materialising out of thin air and unravelling as it went. A glint of silver racing through the snow, the arrow soared up and up and up the Stone Necklace until it struck the cliff top and dug hard into a crag.

Siddy grinned and Murk peeped out between her fingers and raised her eyebrows in surprise. 'Well done! But you'll probably break your legs on the next bit.'

Moll grabbed hold of the piano string, visible only because of the flakes of snow which landed on it. She tugged hard and knew that it would take her, Siddy and Frank's weight – because the old magic was something they could rely on, even in the face of a towering mountain.

She set her boots against the cliff, looked up at the peaks, almost lost in the swirl of snow, and began to climb after Gryff, her gloves wrapped tightly round the piano string. And, though her toes and fingers were numb and snowflakes smudged on to her eyelashes, she kept on climbing – over ledges and overhangs, across chasms and crevasses – feeling Siddy and Frank behind her in the way the piano string moved. Once or twice, her boots skidded on the ice and she stumbled several metres down, but every time the string held fast and Moll carried on going.

The summit came almost as a surprise. The sky was white and full of snow and, set against the Stone Necklace, the two things were hard to tell apart. But Gryff was there, nuzzling against Moll's side as she threw her body on to the top. The wind was wilder here and as Moll took in the view ahead she gulped. The mighty ridge that was the Stone Necklace curved round from the sea far inland, but spread out in front of her, for as far as her eyes could reach through the falling snow, were mountains – vast peaks with plunging sides and crests that scored the horizon. Frozen waterfalls had been sculpted over some crags while others were a haunting maze of snow and rock and ice.

Moll shivered. 'Somewhere out there is the last Shadowmask.'

Siddy clambered up on to the ridge beside her, his cheeks red from the cold and the climb. He collapsed in the snow. 'We did it!'

Frank leapt excitedly from Siddy's coat, but promptly sank into the snow and had to be picked back up and pocketed. Then Moll, Siddy and Gryff peered back over the cliff edge. They could just make out a dark dot on the shoreline.

'What do you think Murk would say if she was up here with us now?' Siddy asked.

'That if we don't break our necks in the Barbed Peaks the last Shadowmask will come and break them for us.'

Siddy nodded. 'Probably.'

They watched as the dot shuffled out across the ice and then sank through a hole and disappeared into the loch. Then they turned back to the Barbed Peaks and, through the screen of snow, they watched a covey of ptarmigan pour over a ridge and then drop down into a hollow. Moll yanked the arrow from the crag and tucked the string into her pocket, then she took a deep breath.

'We stay together out here in the mountains – all of us. You, me *and* Gryff.'

'And Frank,' Siddy added as the ferret raised a defiant chin towards Moll.

Gryff led the way on to a ridge that wound out from the Stone Necklace. The snow gusted around them and lay thick about their boots, but they plodded north, as Willow had told them, following the highest points of the mountains to avoid the snowdrifts gathering in the folds. Some of the ridges were so narrow they had to go single file, edging round crags and leaping over drops, but they trudged on and little by little they made their way through the Barbed Peaks.

Somewhere behind the papery skies was the fading sun, but, even if it had been able to push through the clouds, they didn't have long before darkness fell. The sky was turning – a backlit blue spliced with orange – and soon the moon would be riding high and the last Shadowmask would be just hours away from casting his eternal night. Moll shuddered inside her coat. They didn't even know where they were heading and yet *they* were the ones tasked with halting this everlasting darkness.

Moll blinked as a hare skimmed the ridge, its amber eyes glinting against the sifting snow, then Gryff stopped on a rocky crag. His ears swivelled, his whiskers twitched and then he grunted and kept on walking. Moll chewed her lip as she tried to work out some sort of plan, but, moments later, Gryff stopped again, pausing mid-stride before scrambling backwards into Moll's legs. Moll felt the wildcat's heartbeat clamour against her legs. Something wasn't right.

'What is it?' Moll whispered, crouching beside Gryff.

The wildcat's ears were flattened to his head, then he growled and began to run back the way they'd come.

Siddy strained his eyes towards the next peak and Frank's head darted this way and that from his pocket. 'But – there's nothing there!'

Moll grabbed his arm and yanked him back. 'I don't care! Gryff's never wrong!'

They hurtled back up the pass, their boots skidding

through the snow and scree, but, before they reached the peak, the whole mountain beneath them began to shake. Gently at first, like a tremor from a distant earthquake, and then stronger so that the force was enough to knock Moll and Siddy to their knees. They clung on to the crags with Gryff and Frank and the snow whirled around them.

'An earthquake?' Moll shouted.

But, as the entire mountain shook itself free from the ground and reared up into the air, Moll realised that this wasn't an earthquake and they weren't clinging to an ordinary crag. They were hanging from a leg and that leg belonged to an enormous man built from the rock itself.

The blood pounded in Moll's temples as she remembered Aira's words.

In among the Barbed Peaks, there were *giants*.

Chapter 34
The Ancient Ones

Moll, Gryff, Siddy and Frank clung on in terror as the giant's voice boomed out.

'Who disturbs the Ancient Ones?'

The voice was so low and loud that its vibrations sent whole chunks of snow sliding off the peaks around them. The giant took a huge stride forward and Moll felt her body slam against his rocky thigh. She gripped tighter, hardly daring to breathe, and glanced up. The giant's torso loomed above her, a tower of mighty rocks, but it was the face that scared Moll most: great caverns for eyes, a jagged ridge for the mouth and shards of ice for hair.

She could feel Siddy shaking beside her. 'What do we do?'

But the answer didn't come from Moll. Again the giant bellowed and the sound echoed across the mountains, filling the sky and the sea and every living thing around them.

'Arise, Ancient Ones!' it cried. 'There are imposters in our midst and they have broken our slumber.'

All around them the mountains juddered, shaking off clumps of snow before rising up into stone pillars. Ten giants lumbered forward, stepping over ridges as if they were pebbles, and the words ran dry in Moll's throat. The giants were so enormous they could have perched on the Stone Necklace and paddled their bouldered feet down in the loch below.

Moll pressed herself into the giant's leg, her eyes closed. 'Don't move,' she whispered to Siddy. 'Whatever you do, don't move. They might not have seen us yet.'

The giant turned his body this way and that as he searched for the intruders and, with each swing, Moll, Gryff, Siddy and Frank swayed back and forth, fingertips and claws clutched tight. He stooped down and peered beneath a boulder before flinging it aside and, with her heart thundering, Moll opened one eye. Her muscles tensed. Frank was climbing out of Siddy's pocket and to Moll's horror she saw the ferret had interpreted the advancing giants as an invitation to play. Frank dropped down to a narrow ledge – the giant's knee perhaps – and began to dance.

'There!' a giant roared.

The voice was female, but it was loud and fierce and Moll's insides churned as she realised who it had come from: a giant to the right of them with long, daggered icicles hanging down either side of her face and knuckles the size of bricks that dragged across the ground. Her mouth opened, wide and black like the entrance to a cave.

'On your leg, Wallop!' she screamed. 'They're on your leg!'

The giant they were clasping on to, Wallop, glanced down and Frank scampered back up to Siddy, Moll and Gryff who then shrank as far as they could into a crevice. But there was no escaping now.

'Two smidglings, a wildcat and a ferret?'

Moll felt the rush of Wallop's breath on her cheeks, as cold as the bitter north wind, then the giant swung a hand towards the group, swiping them clean off his leg and into his rocky palm. He unfolded his fingers and drew his prisoners up to his face, squinting into the fading light. Moll clung to Gryff. Wallop's mouth was a den of darkness and, as he raised the group up to his nose and sniffed them, Moll's whole body slid towards it, sucked in by his heaving breath. Then Wallop's face scrunched, his eyes narrowed and he roared, sending Moll, Gryff, Siddy and Frank tumbling back over themselves against his fingers.

'They have the Oracle Arrow!' he hollered.

There was a rumbling and a grunting among the other giants, then one raised its fist. 'Then they must be the ones who stole the Ancient Book from our cave too! Thieves! Thieves!'

Moll staggered to her feet. 'We haven't stolen your book!' she shouted. 'And we only have the arrow because—'

The female giant strode forward and the icicles around her face jangled. 'Eat them, Wallop,' she said.

Another giant nodded. 'Munch their bones!'

The giants' rage grew.

'Chomp their stupid brains!' cried yet another.

'Chew their pointless toes!' It was the female giant again, bent on absolute brutality.

Wallop raised a hand and the chanting faded. 'We are

the Keepers of the Ancient Book, the manuscript that holds the full story of the old magic,' he said. 'We are not barbarians.' He glanced at the female giant who looked rather disappointed. 'Please remember that, Petal. These smidglings deserve a fair trial.'

Siddy rose to his feet beside Moll. 'Thank you – thank you!'

The giants sat down on the mountaintops in a circle around Wallop, who held his prisoners up in his hand.

'Smidglings, you are charged with stealing the Ancient Book and the Oracle Arrow. How do you plead?'

Moll looked at Siddy and together they said, 'Not guilty.'

Siddy took a step forward. 'We're trying to protect the old magic – just like you. We found the arrow stuck inside Murk, the creature in the loch, and we haven't even heard of your book before. You need to believe us so that we can stop the last Shadowmask from conjuring the eternal night!'

There was a momentary silence and all Moll could hear was the shuffle of falling snow. And then the giants began to laugh.

'Murk lives one hundred years deep!' Wallop guffawed. 'A couple of smidglings like you couldn't have summoned her from all the way down there. So, it seems you are liars as well as thieves ...'

'Gobble their bottoms!' Petal roared. 'Snaffle their earlobes!'

Moll tried to keep calm. 'But we *did* summon Murk!' she cried. 'The old magic sent us clues to follow and, even though

261

the last Shadowmask buried that arrow one hundred years deep, we found it!' The two rocky ledges above Wallop's eyes lifted and Moll spun round to Siddy. 'They don't believe us, Sid! After everything we've gone through, they think *we're making this up!*'

Siddy could feel Moll's temper rising. 'Don't do anything rash, Moll,' he begged. 'We'll make them understand.'

But Moll was way past *rash*. Out came the catapult, in went the stone and, with fiery eyes, she raised her weapon towards Wallop's forehead. 'Listen here, Wallop!' she snarled. 'You better put me and my pals down or—'

The giants were on their feet again, punching their fists in the air.

'Eat the angry smidgling first!' Petal roared. 'Swallow her whole!'

'But – the – the trial!' Siddy stammered. 'You promised us a fair trial!'

Wallop grunted. 'That was before missy here got out her catapult.'

Siddy yanked Moll's weapon down. 'Apologise!' he cried. 'They're *giants*, Moll!'

Moll wrenched her arm free and drew back on her catapult pouch. 'He called us liars – after all we've done to protect the old magic!'

Siddy flung himself against Moll. 'Don't do this!'

But she wrestled her arm free, pulled back on her catapult – and fired. The stone clipped Wallop's forehead, then clattered off his body before dropping to the ground.

Siddy bit his lip. 'Oh, Moll, why do you never learn . . .'

The giants stamped their feet then threw back their heads and bellowed.

'Squash them!'

'Trample them!'

'Flatten them!'

Petal clapped her hands. 'Mince them in the snow! Gobble their guts!' She was in her element now.

Wallop drew his hand up to his face and then opened his mouth. Siddy hugged Frank, Gryff began to hiss and then Moll grabbed Siddy's arm.

'Listen!' she cried.

Above the hollering giants was the unmistakable sound of a horn. It blared out across the mountains and Wallop's hand stopped in mid-air. Next came a thundering of hooves. And then voices shouting. Moll's heart leapt. Could it be? The other half of a promise made on the moors before the Lost Isles?

And then, tearing over a ridge to the east of them, only just visible in the dusk, came a woman with ginger hair and a crossbow slung over a tartan cape, and a young man, dark-haired, full of fight, clasping a pistol.

'Aira!' Moll screamed. 'Domino! Help us!'

Chapter 35
Kittlerumpit's Cure

The relief at seeing Aira and Domino made Moll stagger backwards in Wallop's palm and, as her friends rode closer still, right up to the peak of the mountain behind the giants, Moll saw that Domino looked just as he had when they'd said goodbye to him at the North Door; he was no longer a slave to the Shadowmasks' darkness! Instead, he held himself tall and Moll's chest swelled with pride. *This* was the Domino she remembered. This was the man she'd come to regard as an older brother. Moll readied herself for the fight, but then a strange thing happened.

Aira slid from her horse and threw Wallop a large smile. 'How are you, pal?'

Wallop shrugged, 'Nae bad, Aira. About to eat some lying smidglings, that's all.'

Aira led her horse closer to the giant. 'See, I wouldn't eat those smidglings if I were you.'

'Why not?' Petal grumbled. 'They look delicious.'

Wallop nodded. 'And they stole the Oracle Arrow from

our cave which we were meant to protect until the child from the Bone Murmur came for it.'

Aira smiled. 'Well, for a start the girl's far too spicy to sit comfortably with your digestion – I know what you're like, Petal – but also because that girl *is* the child from the Bone Murmur. And the wildcat there is the beast.'

The giants glanced at one another and then Petal groaned. 'Can we eat the boy and his stupid ferret instead then?'

Siddy promptly fainted, but Domino only smiled. 'Siddy here has helped Moll and Gryff on their journey to save the old magic. These are the children you've been waiting for. *They* are the ones who will force the Night Spinner and his Veil back.'

At the sound of Domino's voice, Moll wanted to leap down from Wallop's hand and throw herself into his arms – if only to block the mocking laughs she knew would come from the giants at the idea that *she* was the child from the prophecy – but the Ancient Ones didn't laugh. Instead, they crunched down on to one knee while Wallop settled Moll, Siddy, Gryff and Frank on the peak beside Aira. Then Wallop, too, knelt in front of the group, his head bowed. And Moll stood, baffled, on the snow-strewn mountaintop, because surrounding her in a circle of mighty stone was a ring of giants swearing an oath to help her.

'Keepers of the Ancient Book before you kneel,
We pledge to you an oath which our words do seal.
The arrow that you carry must slay the Spinner's Veil
And we will fight beside you, as goes the old sung tale.'

The giants rose to their feet and Moll would have remained where she was, blinking in disbelief at talk of ancient books and old sung tales, had Domino not rushed towards her and swallowed her up in his arms. Moll leant into his thick coat and breathed in the familiar smell of campfires and trees.

'You're OK,' she whispered.

Domino squeezed her tighter, then he bent down and tucked Moll's hair back from her face. 'The dark magic couldn't crush my soul, Moll. It couldn't crush Angus' either, not when we both knew you and Sid and Gryff were out there.'

Moll shook her head. 'But *how*? Did Aira and Spud find a cure?'

Domino nodded. 'They took me down into Kittlerumpit's tunnels with them – that mangy goblin said he wouldn't hand over the cure without seeing the patient first.' He paused. 'Unicorn tears. Turns out only a creature that pure can lift the darkness of a Shadowmask's curse.'

Moll shifted. 'What was the price? I can't see Kittlerumpit giving that out for free.'

Domino brushed the snow from Moll's coat, then he smiled. 'It's not important. Not now.' He tightened his spotted neckerchief. 'A few of the Highland Watch are travelling south and along the way they're giving the cure to all those poisoned by the Veil, but Aira heard your call so we knew you needed our help.'

They turned to see Aira helping a dazed Siddy to his feet

and Frank hopping excitedly between Gryff's legs. Domino hugged Siddy tight and Aira put an arm round Moll.

'I see you've been keeping up the fight,' Aira said.

Moll smiled as Gryff slunk to her side and rested his head beneath her hand. 'Trashed a castle, killed a Shadowmask, escaped from a kraken, found the Oracle Arrow ...' She looked at Siddy who had recovered enough to give a shaky smile. 'We're not doing too badly.'

Wallop lowered his head so that it was level with the mountaintop. 'I'm sorry for almost eating you all – and for Petal's attitude. She's usually a vegetarian, but this has been a long, cold winter with very little food.' He looked north suddenly, into the encroaching darkness, then turned back to the others. 'If the Night Spinner stole the arrow, he must have taken the Ancient Book too.'

Siddy frowned at Moll 'Why steal the book?' He scooped up Frank who had done so many cartwheels in the snow she was now hyperventilating. 'What use is an ancient story to the last Shadowmask?'

Moll shrugged. 'I don't know. But it's night already and, if we don't destroy the Night Spinner and his Veil before the full moon drops, the sun won't rise tomorrow and everything we've done will have been for nothing.'

Wallop placed a hand down on to the mountaintop, spraying an avalanche of snow over the group.

'You need to keep heading north,' he said. 'That's where the dark magic is coming from.'

Moll knelt down beside Gryff and held him close and,

although she knew that somewhere within the Barbed Peaks the last Shadowmask was waiting for her, she wasn't afraid. They had the Oracle Arrow, Domino was OK and the giants had sworn to help them. They were closer than ever to finishing all of this – and to getting Alfie back.

Chapter 36
Wallop's Oath

Aira gathered up the reins of the horses, but as she did so, Moll and Gryff's gaze slid to the giants. Every single one of them was standing absolutely still, facing the darkness of the north, as if their enormous eyes were picking up sights far beyond even Gryff's vision.

Moll screwed up her eyes into the snow. 'What is it?'

There were mumblings among the giants and one or two picked up large boulders from the foot of the mountains.

'Something's coming from the north,' growled Wallop.

The giants fell silent and through the quiet Moll heard a rattling, scuttling sound. She reached into her quiver for the Oracle Arrow and slotted it to her bow. But it wasn't the Night Spinner and his Veil that crested the mountain; it was a herd of stampeding stags. They bore no resemblance to the magnificent beasts Moll had seen on the moors with Aira – these were the skeletons of deer whose bones clattered and knocked and whose antlers shook from side to side like clawed branches.

The giants lumbered towards the beasts, hurling their

rocks into the herd. Aira raised her crossbow and Domino seized his pistol, but, when Moll went to fire her arrow, Siddy clamped a hand on her arm.

'Save it,' he said. 'Remember, you'll need it to destroy the Veil and the last Shadowmask.'

Moll backed towards Gryff as more and more stags spilled over the peaks and ridges in a wave of dark magic. Aira sent a bolt careering towards them and Domino fired his pistol, then Moll threw up her hands.

'We can't just stand here and watch!'

The stags streamed closer, white against the night and flooding beneath the giants' legs. Domino fired into the throng and a stag rushing up the mountain buckled, then collapsed into a rubble of bones. But more kept coming and Moll scrambled backwards into the snow as a stag surged forward and scooped her up with its antlers. Gryff leapt at the beast, lashing out with his claws until he'd wrestled Moll to the ground, and then Aira shot a bolt into the stag and it lay still in the snow. Moll lifted herself up and Siddy slotted a stone into Moll's catapult, but, when it was raised to his chin, he and Moll froze.

There, hanging above a distant peak and only just visible against the snow and the night, was something dark and glittering – and mounted on it was the unmistakable silhouette of a cloaked figure.

'The Veil!' Moll shouted. 'And the Night Spinner! They've come for us!'

Domino ushered everyone behind the line of giants, who

were now blocking the stags from climbing the mountains, and through their rocky legs they peered out.

'The Veil isn't moving towards us,' Domino said slowly. 'It's going away . . .'

'But why?' Siddy asked. 'The Night Spinner will have seen this fight. He must know Moll and Gryff are *here*.'

Wallop bent down to the group; his huge ears hadn't missed a word. 'The Night Spinner will know that we giants pledged an oath to help you. He will have sent the stags to detain the Ancient Ones with the hope that Moll and the wildcat will follow without us.' He thrashed his arm against several stags that crept close, then he turned to Moll. 'He wants you to journey over the Barbed Peaks alone so that you arrive weak and exhausted, but I swore an oath to you and I'm not going to let you down now. My giants can hold the stags from pouring south for a while, but we need to move fast.'

Moll looked up. The snow was easing and in its place was a mountain range washed blue beneath a bright, swollen moon. They had only a few hours to force the dark magic back.

'Now quickly, climb into my hands,' Wallop said. 'One stride of mine is an hour's walk for you.'

Aira glanced at the highland ponies. 'And my horses?'

'Petal will look after them. She's kinder to animals than she is to smidglings.'

Amid the din of broken rocks, roaring giants and clattering bones, the group hoisted themselves into Wallop's fists: Aira and Domino in one, Moll, Siddy, Gryff and Frank in the

271

other. Then Wallop raised himself to full height, crushing a stag as it charged between his legs.

'Hold on tight,' he muttered, closing his palms around those he'd pledged to help. 'This is going to be a bumpy ride.'

Moll pressed herself into the crevice of Wallop's thumb, then she felt the world slide as the giant set off, bounding over mountains and ridges, ever north with each lurching stride. On and on Wallop ran, leaping over peaks and racing along ridges until Moll lost all sense of time. She only knew that, when the giant opened his palm, she'd have to face the last of the Shadowmasks and his deadly Veil.

'Are you scared?' Moll found herself whispering to Siddy.

He clutched her hand in his. 'Yes.'

Moll pressed his palm. 'I am too, Sid.'

'You've never really admitted that to me before.'

Moll gathered Gryff close to her until she could feel his heartbeat chiming with hers. 'I always thought you'd think less of me if I told you.'

They careered right as Wallop headed further inland.

'I'd never think less of you, Moll. You catapulted a giant in the face and even then I knew I'd never leave you.'

'But being brave is my *thing*,' Moll said. 'I don't have much else.'

'Don't have much else?' Siddy scoffed. 'Being brave is only a little part of you. You're loyal and funny and kind – at least you are when you're not cross.' He huddled up next to her. 'People have more than just one *thing*. This Bone Murmur and everything that's happened since we took up our fight against the dark magic, that's only a small part of you. Once all this is over, there'll be tree forts and wagons in the woods and you and me and Alfie all back together again.'

'Do you really think we can do it?' Moll asked. 'You reckon the Tribe and that arrow in my quiver are enough to force the last Shadowmask magic back for good?'

Siddy fell quiet, but when he did speak Moll wanted to hold his words close and store them in her pocket for ever. 'We're more than enough, Moll. Together, we can do *anything.*'

And, as they crouched inside the giant's palm, Moll saw Siddy's courage clearly: up against the giants he had fainted and on the train north he'd nearly buckled, but at the end of all things – in the face of the crushing of their hopes and dreams and a sun that might never rise – Siddy was brave. There was a sureness to his words, a grit, and it counted for more than any weapon ever could.

'If something happens,' Moll said after a while, 'anything at all, you should know what a brilliant friend you are, Sid. I might have lost my temper and said things I didn't mean, but I wouldn't have wanted anyone else with me and Gryff.' She paused. 'There aren't many who can say they've done what we've done and seen the things we've seen.'

Siddy laughed as Frank cuddled up in his arms. 'Tree ghouls, kelpies, smugglers, krakens. What a journey this has been.'

Moll smiled into the darkness, then she thought of Alfie,

of how he'd been with them every step of the way until they'd set off for the northern wilderness, and an ache spread out inside her. She leant her head against Gryff's fur and, as his purr rumbled deep inside her body, Moll wondered whether it was possible for anyone to love their friends as much as she loved Gryff, Siddy and Alfie.

Hours passed and, when the giant did eventually stop and open his palm, the night was thick around them. A single cloud shifted across the moon, coating the mountains in darkness, but when it slid back Moll gasped. Wallop was standing on the top of a snow-covered ridge and climbing the height of the mountain in front of them was a staircase carved into the rock. It wound higher and higher up the cliff face, the snow puckered by footprints, until it reached a monastery perched on the very top of the mountain. Its icy walls and spiral turrets shone silver in the moonlight.

'The Rookery,' Wallop panted. 'We thought this monastery was abandoned, but I followed the Veil straight to the staircase before the Night Spinner stepped off and crept up.' He paused. 'This is where I leave you. I need to get back and help the Ancient Ones against the stags because, if those beasts spill over the Stone Necklace, the Highland Watch will be unable to contain them and the people of the north won't stand a chance.'

Wallop set the group down in the snow and Moll swayed at the sudden stillness of the mountain.

'Thank you, Wallop,' Aira said. 'From all of us.'

Wallop nodded, then he bent down opposite Moll. 'Keep an eye open for the Ancient Book. You may not understand why, but you'll play a part in restoring it to us.'

Moll glanced over her shoulder at the Oracle Arrow. 'I'll do my best not to let you down.'

The giant smiled, the cracks in his face wrinkling about his eyes. 'You're a rare sort of girl, Moll. There's a determination buried inside you that the bravest of my giants would crave.' He rose up to his full height and his icicled hair sparkled in the moonlight. 'Travel well, my friends, travel well.'

He bounded back across the mountains, striding over peaks as if they were molehills, and, when the dark finally swallowed him up, Moll turned to face the Rookery. She took a deep breath, felt for Gryff and then together they walked down the ridge towards the stone staircase.

Chapter 37
Beyond the Staircase

G ryff went first, pausing every now and again on
the steps, ears cocked. Moll followed close behind,
trying to ignore the sheer drop to her right as they
made their way up. The moon was blocked by a layer of cloud,
but every time it broke apart light shone down, picking out
the footprints on the steps that the Night Spinner must have
made. Moll was surprised to see how small they were – only
a bit bigger than her own – perhaps the last Shadowmask
was old and shrivelled, like Orbrot had been.

Eventually they came to the top of the staircase and
Gryff paused before an archway. A rook croaked from the
stonework above them, making Moll jump, then it took off
and once more silence fell. Moll craned her neck as far as
she dared.

'Looks like a courtyard,' she whispered. 'With open arches
for windows and a door on the far right wall leading into the
monastery itself.'

Moll held her breath as Gryff slipped through the archway
and hid in the shadows against the wall, then the rest of the

group followed. The courtyard was large and lit by flaming torches and Domino had to put a hand over Moll's mouth to stop her from gasping as she took in the creatures that held these lights: stone gargoyles that leant out from the walls, with hooded eyes, snouts and claws framed by jagged wings – and inside their gaping mouths flames flickered. There was a fountain in the middle of the courtyard, the tinkle of water the only sound to scrape the quiet night, and sitting on the stone lip, raising a cup to his mouth, was a figure draped in black robes. By his side hung the Veil, a quivering blanket of death.

Siddy flicked the catch back on the pistol Domino had given him, then he turned to Moll and in a whisper so quiet it was almost just a breath, he said, 'Go for the Night Spinner first. We can finish off the Veil afterwards.'

Silently, Moll lifted the Oracle Arrow from her quiver. It felt heavy in her hands and her heart was thundering so fast she felt sure that she would drop it. But, when Domino placed a hand on her back, urging her on, she gripped it hard before slotting it against her bow. The flames danced all around them, the fountain trickled on and Moll knew in that moment that she would never get a more perfect shot than this. The Shadowmask's back was turned – she had the advantage of surprise – and in a single shot she could avenge her parents' death and put an end to the witch doctor's magic.

Siddy was there beside her and Gryff's body was pressed against her legs. *Now.* This was her chance. Moll pulled back on the bow until the string was taut, then she closed one eye, took aim at the figure's back, where its rotten heart would be – and released the Oracle Arrow.

The silver bolt thrummed from her bow, sailing through the air before digging deep into the Night Spinner's back. The Shadowmask slumped to the ground, the arrow too quick for one final cry, but any joy Moll felt was short-lived because what she saw next made her blood run cold.

A figure emerged from the doorway leading into the monastery: dark, robed and with a mask of stitched-up sack. The mask tilted, then a laugh slithered out as the Veil glided towards him and the shock brought Moll to her feet.

'No!' she cried.

Aira turned panicked eyes to Domino. 'You said there were only six witch doctors! So who is . . .?'

The laugh grew, drowning out Aira's words until it filled the courtyard and the flames inside the gargoyles' mouths shivered with pleasure. Then it dropped to a snarl. 'I am Wormhook, the last of the Shadowmasks.'

Moll glanced at the figure by the fountain; something about it was strangely familiar . . . She thought of the footprints in the snow on the staircase that had only been a bit bigger than her own. Could they have belonged to a child? A child bound up in the Shadowmasks' curses?

'No!' Moll cried again, her stomach churning as the horrifying possibility leaked open before her.

Wormhook tutted as he raised a finger towards the slumped figure. 'And I think Molly knows all too well who *that* was.'

Moll's throat tightened as she raced forward. *No, no, no,*

beat her heart. She fell to her knees and turned the body over. A black hood covered the face, but when she tore it away she threw back her head and wailed. Here was the face that had stolen into her dreams every night since she'd last seen it down by the sea: a scruff of fair hair above two shining blue eyes.

Tears rolled helplessly down Moll's cheeks as she flung her arms round the body. 'Oh, Alfie, Alfie! What have I done?'

The others rushed close and Gryff bent low, nuzzling Alfie's cheek.

'Alfie's connection to the Soul Splinter meant that when it was destroyed he also disappeared,' Wormhook crooned from the door of the monastery, 'down to the depths of the Underworld. But I plucked him from the shadows before they claimed him for good. I made him real, just as you wished for, Molly Pecksniff.'

He paused, as if relishing the irony, and Moll sobbed into Alfie's lifeless body.

'I made him my *Night Rider*,' Wormhook muttered, 'a cursed soul without any memories of his past, to carry the Veil through your land while Orbrot sent witches, peatboggers and goblins to find you and I conjured storms. The Veil's victims awoke jabbering about the Night Spinner, about *my* power to come, but no one ever suspected *your* little friend might be behind the poisonings. To think that you thought *I* was riding the Veil all that time when I only ever rode it once, to pay a visit to a kraken on the coast . . .'

Wormhook ran a cloth hand over the Veil and sniggered.

'Alfie's soul was cursed from the moment we stole his tears to make the Soul Splinter, Molly, but your ridiculous hope in him – your *impossible dream* – meant that a little part of him belonged to you. Your belief in your friend stopped me from claiming him completely, but, now that you've killed him, you have no impossible dream to believe in any more! Alfie's body will fade, but his shadow, his damned soul, will remain and that will *belong to me completely* – and a soul that has been corrupted from innocence to darkness is more powerful than any other kind.'

Wormhook's straw hair glinted in the torchlight.

'I will have Alfie's shadow join with the Veil to form a cloak of darkness so terrifying that it will drown out the sun and the stars and the moon. Then, under an eternal night, the Veil will call up the creatures of the Underworld so that I can begin my rule of terror.'

Siddy clenched his jaw. 'Alfie's soul was good and strong and *your* curses made him into a monster! He would never have done anything like this!'

But Moll was beyond the rights and wrongs of what the Night Rider had done under Wormhook's command. This was her friend, the boy who had stormed into her life in Tanglefern Forest and helped to open up her closed heart. She buried her head in Alfie's chest.

'Come back,' she sobbed. 'Please! I kept my promise. I crossed moors and mountains to find you. I've come to make you real!'

Domino lifted Moll away and slipped a hand beneath

Alfie's back. He drew out the arrow, placed it in Moll's quiver, then he felt for Alfie's wound. His hand stilled and he glanced up at the others.

'There's no blood,' he said quietly. 'I can't even feel where the wound should be.' He stood up and glared at Wormhook. 'You didn't make Alfie properly real . . . You cursed whatever was left of him when he destroyed your Soul Splinter, then you used him as a puppet to poison people's spirits – and, when neither Orbrot nor your hideous beasts could hold Moll back, you had Alfie lure her here.' Domino spat on the ground in disgust. 'You're pathetic. Moll never gave up on Alfie – she never surrendered her impossible dream – because I know that girl and nothing, not even death, could make her give up on her friends!'

And, as Domino said those words, Moll realised they were true. Even though Alfie lay motionless before her, she still hadn't given up her hope in him. Moll ran a hand over his hair, then she gasped as she realised Alfie's robes were fading. But he didn't shrivel to a shadow, as Wormhook had implied. His body lay there still, but his robes vanished and Moll could see that he was now clothed just as he had been the last time she had seen him: in a duffle coat over ripped shorts and old tattered boots. *This* was her Alfie, not the slave to dark magic Wormhook had made him. But he didn't move, didn't breathe. What life he'd had left was now gone.

'Time to admit that you've given up on him once and for all,' Wormhook goaded.

Moll shook her head and rose to her feet. 'You let him die

when he never did you any wrong!' The pain beat inside her as she said the words aloud, but, despite what they meant, she still clung to her impossible dream, her belief that somehow this might not be the end for Alfie. 'It's *me* you want. Not Alfie. And I came for you. I was ready for the fight . . .' Moll's voice began to crack and Siddy touched her arm.

'Moll,' he cut in.

Moll twisted free as the tears coursed down her face. 'You're a monster!' she screamed, setting the Oracle Arrow to her bow again. 'How could you make me kill my best friend?'

'Moll,' Siddy said, louder this time, firmer. '*Alfie's still alive.*'

Moll's bow dropped limp by her side and she looked down. Her heart quickened. Alfie's body had faded around the edges now, but it hadn't disappeared like his robes had. He was paler somehow, almost transparent, and to Moll it felt like looking at the ghost of a boy or an old photograph of someone from the past – but none of that mattered because Alfie's chest was rising and falling. She had kept her belief in her impossible dream and *somehow* that had kept Alfie alive.

Aira raised her crossbow at Wormhook. The leader of the Highland Watch knew that it had to be Moll who destroyed the last Shadowmask, but Aira's guard was up because Moll's heart and mind were far from the witch doctor now and they couldn't let him escape.

'Alfie,' Moll whispered, shaking him by the arms. 'Alfie.'

His eyes met hers, but they were dull and glazed.

'It's me . . . Moll.'

Alfie blinked once and then his eyes travelled over Moll

282

and Gryff and finally Siddy. But no flicker of recognition stirred; it was as Wormhook had said: all memories of his past were gone. Moll went to shake him again, but her hands fell right through him and she stumbled forward. Alfie was there still – *just* – but his body was nothing more than a wisp.

Siddy turned to face Wormhook and Frank bared her teeth from his pocket. 'What've you done to him?'

The Veil curled round the last Shadowmask and he turned his sack mask to Moll. 'Alfie's soul is past the point of no return now. He belongs to the Veil and together they will conjure the eternal darkness I have been waiting for.' Wormhook clasped his hands. 'He's nothing more than a ghost to you.'

Moll watched, her heart breaking, as Alfie picked himself up and walked silently away, past the fountain and across the courtyard, before disappearing into the monastery. She let the pain flood through her and when she raised her eyes to Wormhook she realised she was shaking – not with pain now but with anger – because Wormhook's words were full of lies. Moll *still* hadn't given up on her friend and, as she thought of the promise she had made to Alfie every night since he'd left, she knew that, whatever it took, she wouldn't let the last Shadowmask steal his soul.

'You may think that I've surrendered Alfie to you, but Domino's right—' Moll's voice grew to a shout, '—not even death can stop me hoping because the Alfie I know is still out there and his soul will *never* belong to you!'

Wormhook lifted his hands suddenly and the gargoyles

shuddered, as if waking from a very long sleep, before ripping away from the walls and beating upwards with jagged wings. Moll watched in horror as they flew over the cobbled ground towards the fountain, breathing flames from their gaping mouths.

'Attack!' Aira yelled, loosing a bolt from her crossbow.

The gargoyles screeched and flapped above them, raining down bursts of fire. Domino's dagger brought down one and Siddy's pistol another while Gryff and Aira wrestled two more to the ground and Frank tore at the stone remains. But Moll wasn't interested in the gargoyles. Ducking and dodging, she strode towards Wormhook, the Oracle Arrow poised against her bow. The witch doctor lifted his hands and the Veil rose higher, then he pointed a tattered finger at Moll.

> 'At last she is come, her quest doomed to fail,
>   Into the hands of the Shadowmask's Veil.'

Wormhook glanced up at the quilt of darkness and Moll felt his words gnawing at the small shreds of courage she had left, at the hope she clung to for a boy who no longer knew her. Then Gryff bounded to her side and, as the witch doctor's chant continued, the wildcat growled over every word and, together, Moll and Gryff advanced towards the last Shadowmask.

> 'Feed on their souls, both the girl and the beast's!
>   And I'll stand back to watch as the Veil feasts.'

Moll barely heard Wormhook's words; her ears were trained to Gryff's growl and all the fight that was buried inside it. The Veil carved a channel through the gargoyles towards her and for a moment the darkness above was so all-consuming that Moll sensed her arms slacken. Then she felt the wildcat weave through her legs and thought of the ghost of the boy inside the Rookery.

'This,' Moll said through gritted teeth. 'This is for *my* Alfie.'

The Veil plummeted towards Moll and Gryff, rippling with delight as it fell, and Moll let her arrow fly. It shot through the air before plunging into the middle of the quilt, but the Veil kept falling, bringing with it a clock-stopping blackness that surrounded Moll like the darkest of nights and plucked at the impossible dream locked inside her. Then, just before the Veil itself folded around her, there was a splitting, tearing sound and, where the arrow had pierced the quilt, it began to break apart in the air. Reels of glittering thread unwound on to the cobbles, the darkness crept back and Wormhook rushed forward, clawing at his mask.

He stopped abruptly as the last of the Veil uncoiled before him, then he spoke, his voice a twisted snarl. 'You want to finish this, don't you?'

Moll rose up with Gryff and, as the gargoyles shrieked and the others fought around her, she picked up her Oracle Arrow and turned to face Wormhook.

'I *will* finish this,' she muttered.

A gargoyle swooped down to the Shadowmask suddenly,

as if bidden to silent commands. 'Kill the boy,' Wormhook muttered, 'the one she calls Siddy.'

Moll's mouth turned dry and, as she watched the gargoyle bulleting towards her friend, Wormhook slipped from the courtyard back into the monastery.

'Sid!' Moll screamed, rushing towards him with Gryff.

The gargoyle had her friend pinned up against the wall now and Frank had been flung to the ground, but, as the gargoyle drew breath to release its flames, Gryff leapt on to the creature's back and hauled it away. Domino rammed it with his dagger and the gargoyle crumbled into a pile of rocks.

Siddy glanced at Moll as Frank hurtled back inside his pocket. 'You've got to go into the monastery,' he panted. 'We can hold the gargoyles, but your fight is inside. You have to stop Wormhook.'

Moll shook her head. 'I can't leave you.'

Domino jabbed his dagger into another gargoyle, then he spun round to them. 'You don't have a choice, Moll. If Wormhook gets away, then all of this was for nothing.'

Siddy glanced up at the moon. 'Go after him. You don't have much time.'

The gargoyles screeched above and, as Domino, Aira, Siddy and Frank flung themselves back into the fight, Moll and Gryff raced over the cobbles and darted into the monastery – into the heart of the last Shadowmask's lair.

Chapter 38
The Old Library

I t was quiet inside the monastery and the shrieks of the fighting were muffled by the thick stone walls that lined the passageway in front of them. Moll tiptoed down it with Gryff, the Oracle Arrow nocked loosely to her bow. Wax drooled from candles in iron brackets either side of them and Moll flinched at the clacking of her boots against the paving stones. Somewhere, in the shadows of this place, Wormhook was waiting for her. She crept on, and with every step she took she tried to draw courage from the wildcat padding faithfully by her side.

After a few minutes, they came to an arch made entirely of thorns. Perhaps once, in the times when monks had used the place as a sanctuary for prayer, there had been roses here, but now dark thorns twisted above them like a mouth of tangled wire.

Moll swallowed. 'We can do this.'

Gryff nuzzled her hand with his head, then together they stepped through the arch. But, whatever Moll had been expecting on the other side, it wasn't what lay before her. An enormous cavern carved into the rock stretched fifty metres above and below them. A large stone bridge ran through the middle of the cavern, its supporting pillars entwined with dead ivy and lichen, and as Moll took a step out on to it dozens of black feathered heads poked out from the nests perched on the crags of the walls. They croaked into the silence, knowing there was an intruder in their midst. Moll glanced over the edge of the bridge to see the hall at the bottom was lined with statues of monks, the stonework smeared with bird droppings, but Gryff tugged at Moll's coat sleeve with his teeth and urged her on.

Where the bridge met the far side of the cavern there was another arch of thorns. Moll and Gryff stole through it to find a lantern inside flickering over three passageways. Those to her left and right were draped in shadows – stairs, it looked like – perhaps up to the turrets they had seen when they first laid eyes on the Rookery with Wallop. But Moll knew it was the passageway ahead that she wanted because there was a path of light coming from it and the rustle of paper being turned. Gryff blinked up at Moll and they walked on.

The thorns opened into a large room and Moll blinked in disbelief as she took it in. Lining the stone walls were *trees*. Crooked trunks twisted upwards and thin grey branches, from which lanterns dangled, sprawled across the slabs of stone. A long time ago, they might have been rowans bursting with berries – the last of the trees to survive the mountains and the cold – but now bark flaked from their trunks, dead leaves lay scattered around their bases and twisted roots scarred the floor. It was like being in a pocket of the forest, where all of this had started. But along the branches that stretched across the walls, in among the lanterns, there were books – beautiful leather spines with gilt lettering – laid out as if the branches themselves were shelves. This was a *library* and standing behind a lectern in the middle of the room, facing them, was Wormhook.

An enormous leather-bound book, almost the size of Moll, with edges dusted gold, rested on the lectern in front of the last Shadowmask and as Moll entered he glanced up, a black quill feather poised in his hand.

'The Ancient Book that Wallop spoke about,' Moll said slowly, raising her bow, ready to fight. Gryff growled by her side and Moll felt her voice harden. 'What have you done to it?'

Wormhook heaved the book shut and a cloud of dust puffed upwards. 'Oh, you'll find out soon enough.'

Gryff sprang forward, but the Shadowmask lurched back from the lectern, his robes a ripple of black, and from the slit in his sack mask, where his mouth should have been, something dark and swirling seeped out. It floated into the library like a trail of ink.

'A Night Spinner's gifts extend beyond conjuring storms and snow,' Wormhook sneered. 'I can call upon nightmares too – the darkest thoughts from the Underworld. *They breathe fear* and they have the power to tear you and your wildcat apart.'

The ink spilled into a large shadow and the unmistakable shape of a wolf hung before Gryff, its body and head bent low, its ears pinned back. The wildcat edged away, hissing, but the shadow grew in size, its monstrous head thrashing from side to side. And then the wolf pounced.

'It's not real!' Moll yelled to Gryff. 'It's just a nightmare!'

Wormhook's sack mask tilted, as if half amused by Moll's words. 'Not real?' he muttered. 'Oh, it's real all right.'

Moll watched in horror as the shadow hurled Gryff across the room, smashing him into the trunk of a tree. The nightmare had a mind of its own and, as Moll got ready to fire her arrow, more ink poured from Wormhook's mouth. Moll strained her eyes through the pitch-blackness, searching for the witch doctor, but he was hidden now and the nightmares slid closer, morphing into the shapes of giant bats. Moll felt a coldness cling to her skin. The darkness was absolute and, as the swarm of bats opened their wings over her face, she felt her bow and arrow clatter to the ground.

'They're not real!' Moll whimpered. 'They're not real!'

She struck her arms out against the shadows and for a second the darkness broke apart and she saw Gryff backed up against the lectern, thrashing his paws towards the wolf. Then the nightmares closed round her again, pulsing into a throng of bats, and, though they looked to be only shadows, claws raked at her face and leathery wings smacked her body. Moll fell to her knees as the nightmares sucked at her soul.

'Your parents were too weak to fight us and they died as cowards, snivelling for the child they'd left behind,' Wormhook taunted. 'We expected more from *the child and the beast*, but look at you both now.'

The bats clamoured around Moll, scrabbling at her face, and she was dimly aware of a sack-like hand snatching at something by her feet.

'You may have destroyed the Veil and the other five Shadowmasks,' Wormhook jeered, 'but I am more powerful than those you faced before and I am close to finishing your miserable little life once and for all.' He laughed. 'And when that is done, Molly Pecksniff, the dark magic will rise and, thanks to you, I won't even need to share the power with the other witch doctors; it will be mine and mine alone!'

Moll's neck throbbed as a bat tightened its giant claws around her, strangling the air in her throat, and then she screamed as she felt the skin at her nape tear. She scrabbled for the Oracle Arrow on the ground, but it was gone, taken by Wormhook, and Moll's heart shook.

Give up, a voice inside her whispered. *In the end they'll win, whatever you do. Alfie's gone – you can't pull him back from what Wormhook has made him – and the others are outside fighting a losing battle. The Shadowmasks' darkness is too strong; you never really stood a chance.*

The voices inside Moll grew and her shoulders slumped. They'd made it this far – to the monastery tucked into the clouds – but Wormhook's nightmares were a darkness too strong for any soul to withstand. Moll wrapped her arms round her head and let the despair crawl all over her as the last Shadowmask made his way back to the lectern, the Oracle Arrow in one hand, his quill held high in the other.

Chapter 39
The Ancient Book

The bats shrieked, Moll's fear swelled and then into the darkness Gryff growled. The noise was raw and fierce and at the sound of it the nightmares shivered and withdrew a fraction. The wildcat made his way through the shadows and Moll reached a hand out until her palm met with soft, warm fur, then she drew him close. He growled again and Moll soaked in all the courage and hope locked inside it. The nightmares thinned a little more, but it was enough for Moll to see Gryff's green eyes burning before her.

Fight, he was saying. *Fight*.

Moll balled her hands into fists. It was her fear that gave the nightmares power. She had to be braver. Stronger. She forced herself up – without her bow, without the arrow, without even a clear plan – just with the strength of her wildcat's growl inside her. And, as if their thoughts were bound as one, Moll and Gryff charged through the swirling darkness towards Wormhook. Gryff wrenched him back from the lectern, claws and teeth set hard into the witch doctor's cloak, and the Oracle Arrow clanged to the floor.

The shadows of wolves and owls hung back and then dimmed still more and, as Gryff forced Wormhook to the ground, Moll knew what she had to do. Somehow she needed to save the story the giants had protected.

Standing before the lectern, she brought her hands up to the book. Inscribed on to the dark green leather in gold-swirled lettering were three words and they glittered beneath the lantern light: *The Ancient Book*. Moll's skin tingled. This was the story of the old magic passed down through the generations and guarded by giants. But as she went to open it she found she couldn't lift the cover. She clawed at it with her fingers and, from beneath Gryff's hold, Wormhook gave a wild laugh.

'You can do what you want with me,' he sniggered. 'But you cannot undo what *I've* done to your precious story.'

The nightmares lined the rowan trees, dark and brooding, as if waiting for a command to pounce. Gryff sank his claws into the witch doctor's shoulders, pinning him down, and Moll found herself thinking of Siddy's words when they were with the giants: *What use is an ancient story to the last Shadowmask?* Only now did she understand. It was *everything*. Stories stayed, after memories were erased and people were forgotten. And here she was, at the very end of her journey, before a book that held the most important story of all. Moll heaved at the cover again, but it held fast.

Wormhook laughed. 'Now you realise … There is no key – the damage I've done will remain locked inside that book for ever.'

The nightmares raced in towards the lectern – wolves pounding, bats flapping – and the witch doctor drew breath to unleash more curses from the Underworld. But Gryff slammed a paw across his mouth and Moll stood firm against the battering on all sides, her eyes now fixed on the padlock binding the book shut. Suddenly she remembered the gift Willow had given her and she ripped the bone key from her neck.

'Please,' she whispered. '*Please work.*'

There was a scrabbling behind her and Gryff growled, but Moll was already fumbling with the lock, her fingers white around the key as the nightmares bit and tore and scratched at her skin. The key slid in and with a click the padlock sprang open and Moll lifted the huge cover back. She blinked once, twice, three times.

'No,' she gasped, frantically flicking through the pages.

Her face paled. Even amid the nightmares she could see that every single page in the Ancient Book was *blank*. Wormhook had erased the story of the old magic completely.

'You understand now?' Wormhook's voice was a rasp as he twisted his mouth free from Gryff's paw. 'There is no old magic any more. It's gone, rubbed out, forgotten. And, when I raise the eternal night, no one will even remember it existed.' He smiled. 'The book is ready for a new story now, one built from the shadows of the Underworld, and, before you barged in, I was about to write it.'

Moll's shoulders sank and Gryff's hold slackened for a second – but Wormhook seized his chance, wrenching himself free before gliding upwards, and, as he hung in the air, the shadows of wolves and bats poured from his mouth. Moll tore towards the Oracle Arrow, but the nightmares throbbed around it, blotting it from sight and thrashing against her body.

She closed her eyes to keep her fear at bay. She needed a plan – something to undo what Wormhook had done, a way to bring the story of the old magic back. She felt again for Gryff beside her and the beginnings of an idea began to form. She let it breathe for a moment, small and quiet against Wormhook's laugh and the force of the nightmares, until the strength of it forced her eyes open.

Bruised and bloodied, she reached into her quiver and drew out the golden feather, then she rushed back to the lectern and dipped it into the inkwell. She held her quill between trembling fingers above the first blank page and glanced at Gryff beside her.

'I – I don't know what to write.' She sucked the words through her teeth to force the pain back. 'I can't even spell most words.'

Wormhook glided above the lectern, his mask thrown back as he laughed. 'You,' he spat. 'You think you can rewrite the story of the old magic?'

The nightmares shook around Moll as if they were laughing too.

Gryff snarled at the witch doctor, then he nosed Moll's hand.

I believe in you, he was saying. *I know you can do this.*

Moll gripped the quill tighter. She didn't know where to start. She didn't even understand a lot of the old magic. Then she found herself thinking of a story she did understand, a life she knew, a tale that perhaps only she could tell. And though her handwriting was a mess, though the words were misspelt and blotched with tears and she could barely see the paper through the nightmares, Moll wrote Alfie's story.

Of how the Shadowmasks had stolen him as a child and used his tears to make their Soul Splinter. Of how they had broken his 'real'. Of how she had met him in Tanglefern Forest and he'd helped her escape Skull's gang. Of how he'd become one of their Tribe and lived with them in Little Hollows. Of how he'd fought alongside her and Sid and Gryff – past smugglers, kelpies and giant eels – and how the Shadowmasks had taken him away and used him for their dark magic.

And, as Moll wrote, as she fought to create – to build – while everything around her was falling apart, Gryff climbed up on to the lectern beside the Ancient Book and leapt towards Wormhook. The wildcat dragged the witch doctor down, fighting with a new-found strength. His claws ripped at the sack mask and tore the straw to shreds and, as Wormhook weakened, his nightmares shuddered and then broke apart before dissolving into nothing.

All the while, Moll kept on writing, filling the Ancient Book with Alfie's story even though her eyes were blinded by tears. Her words spilled on to the pages and then a remarkable thing began to happen.

The roof above the library – the grey slabs of stone that looked as if they might have been there forever – began to fade. The colour drained away before vanishing completely until there was no longer a roof above the room, just the cold dark night. Clouds blocked the moon and stars from sight and the blackness sang of the eternal night to come, should Wormhook succeed in claiming Alfie after erasing the story of the old magic.

But from the darkness something began to fall and it was not the cool white flakes of snow. This was *gold* – flecks of gold drifting down into the library – and, though Wormhook cried out again and again, still it fell around Moll, scattering like gilded rain on to the page before her.

Moll gasped. The flecks of gold weren't meaningless shapes tumbling down from an everlasting night. They were *letters*, hundreds of different letters, floating around her. Wormhook twisted beneath Gryff and screeched, but still the letters fell, in increasing numbers, on to the Ancient Book.

These were the letters that *Moll* had written – they were *her* words falling from the sky – and, though her ink was smudged and almost unreadable, the gold letters were absolutely perfect and they settled above her own scribbles as if she had written them that way all along. Alfie's story was how it should be, bright and bold and beautiful, nothing like the dark stain the Shadowmasks had made it. Moll wrote faster and faster, great sobs choking her throat, as the letters continued to drop like falling stars, until she was blind to the pain of her battered body and numb to everything around her.

She didn't see Gryff and Wormhook fighting – or the ghost of a boy stirring within the arch of thorns.

Slowly, cautiously, the boy took a step into the library. His gaze was distant and his steps uncertain. Moll gripped the quill tighter as the letters danced around her, falling on to the page with her tears. The boy quickened his pace, as if he could sense something important, then he broke into a run, his old boots sprinting over the flagstones, his faded body becoming clearer and clearer with every stride.

A word escaped from his lips, quiet and unsure of itself, and to most it would have been lost in the noise of the Shadowmask and the wildcat wrestling on the ground. But Moll heard her name and she looked up. Her eyes, red with crying, met the boy's. Not a ghost now, not a wisp or a faded memory. He was *real* – with a pulse and a heart and a soul that could only ever mean good.

Alfie charged across the room, his voice built up into a shout. 'Moll!' he cried. 'Moll!'

The quill fell from Moll's hands. Then she staggered from the lectern and ran towards her friend, throwing her arms around him until they were clinging to one another beneath a sky that danced with gold.

'Not possible,' Wormhook gasped, breaking free from Gryff for a moment. 'The Underworld stole your memories and I darkened your soul. And yet the curse has been lifted?'

Alfie drew back from Moll, ignoring the witch doctor's words because they were not important to him now.

'You kept your promise,' he said quietly. 'You came for me.'

Moll looked at Alfie. 'No matter what the Shadowmasks had in store for us,' she said, 'me, Gryff and Sid – we crossed forests and moors and seas and mountains. Nothing could stop us from finding you again.'

Alfie bit his lip. 'The last thing I remember is us up on the eagle's back and me reaching for the Soul Splinter.' He looked down. 'But I heard Wormhook's words in the courtyard – all those people poisoned by the Veil, by *me*. How can we ever really be friends again knowing what I did?'

Moll gripped his hands though her own were cut and shaking. 'There's a goodness fastened to your soul, Alfie, no matter what the Shadowmasks did to you before. I broke their curse with my hope in you. You're real now and nothing in your past can undo that.'

Gryff pinned Wormhook to the ground and Moll blinked upwards into the flutter of golden letters. These were not the words she had written now – she could feel it – this was the story of the old magic finding its way home because her impossible dream had been stronger than Wormhook's nightmares, strong enough even to pave the way for the old magic to return. She stood with her arms outstretched and her eyes closed, and Alfie did the same, then they threw back their heads and laughed as the gold came tumbling down.

Chapter 40
The Last Amulet

Moll stooped to pick up her bow and the Oracle Arrow. The witch doctor's mask hung about his face in strips of sack and all that remained of his hair was a clump of matted straw, but a shiver crawled through Moll as she heard the battle pick up again outside. She took a step towards the arch of thorns as she thought of Domino, Aira, Siddy and Frank fighting against the gargoyles, then her eyes flicked back to Wormhook with a rising sense of dread: the look on the Shadowmask's face showed that he wasn't through with her and Gryff yet.

The shadow of a giant snake slithered from his mouth, forcing Gryff back before coiling round the wildcat's body. And then a trail of enormous spiders spurted from Wormhook's throat. Alfie flung an arm out at the shadows and Moll gripped the Oracle Arrow as a spider crawled towards her, its fangs sliding together beneath its enormous head, then Siddy burst into the library, his face smeared with blood and sweat and his coat scorched by the gargoyles' flames.

His eyes widened at the sight of Alfie. 'It's *you* – it's actually you!'

But there was no time for more. The last of the flecks of gold settled inside the Ancient Book and then it snapped shut. Nightmares swelled inside the library again and Wormhook rose into the air, his cloak fluttering around him as he climbed higher and higher into the night sky.

'Don't show you're afraid!' Alfie yelled, wrenching a huge spider back from Moll. 'They can't hurt us if we don't believe in them!'

But, as the spiders hissed and stamped and made to bite, they couldn't help but believe in the terrors before them.

Siddy fired his pistol into a bulging shadow and Frank leapt from his pocket to tear the remains to shreds. 'You have to kill Wormhook with the Oracle Arrow, Moll!' he shouted. 'Domino and Aira can't hold the gargoyles back much longer so they sent me to help you stop Wormhook. It's the only way all of this ends!'

There was a cackle from above them and Moll's body tensed as dozens of hideous gargoyles flew over the monastery and massed around the last Shadowmask. Moll swallowed. What did that mean for Domino and Aira? Were they fighting the rest of the gargoyles or was the fight over for them too?

Moll screamed suddenly as a bolt of fire plummeted into the library, followed by another which missed Gryff by a fraction as he burst free from the shadow snake's hold. In seconds, the library was ablaze with flames – branches fringed with fire and old books reduced to piles of ash. Moll glanced at the Ancient Book, the story she had worked so hard to restore, now moments away from being burned to a crisp. She raised the Oracle Arrow to her chin and Gryff snarled a circle around her, but as she went to fire, the spiders hurled themselves against her and she stumbled backwards, dislodging the arrow.

Alfie and Siddy rushed to her side, thrashing at any nightmares that dared come close, and Moll lifted the arrow again, a splice of silver with the power to rip the darkness apart. She pulled against the bow, imagined her parents holding her tight and then, as Alfie and Siddy roared into the flames and the howling nightmares, Moll fired the Oracle Arrow.

It sailed up through the library, smashing a path through the smoke and the shadows before sinking into Wormhook's heart. There was an almighty scream from the witch doctor and Moll stumbled to the ground. The nightmares swirled around her and great chunks of stone hurtled down into the library as the gargoyles, free from the Shadowmask's magic, broke apart. Siddy and Alfie dodged the falling stone and Gryff hauled Moll aside with his teeth, then the nightmares shrivelled into nothing, the flames fizzled out and Wormhook started to descend.

Moll huddled with her friends amid the crumbled stone and, as the mountain itself began to shake, the last Shadowmask let out another blood-curdling scream. Moll raised her hands to her ears and watched, open-mouthed, as spools of black thread began to unravel from Wormhook's cloak. He sank towards them and the mountain shook again and again, sending every book except the Ancient Book crashing to the ground. Then the stitching holding the witch doctor together began unpicking itself until all that remained on the library floor was a useless heap of rags.

The mountain stilled and for a moment all was quiet. No one dared speak. And then footsteps stumbled over the bridge and Domino and Aira limped into the room.

'You're OK,' Moll gasped, clambering over the rubble towards them, even though every muscle in her own body ached and her clothes had been ripped to shreds.

They nodded and, when they saw that Alfie was there, they let out a cheer. But Moll could see that Domino was resting nearly all of his weight on Aira's arm and every word that he spoke was a struggle.

He smiled at Moll as he sat down on an upturned stone. 'It's just a scratch – it'll heal.'

Gryff stalked towards the remains of the witch doctor. The wildcat's fur was burnt in places and speckled with blood, but he held his head high and growled.

'Wormhook's gone,' Siddy breathed. 'Does that mean it's over?'

Alfie looked up into the night and shook his head. 'Not yet. Wormhook spoke of an eternal darkness and, though he couldn't use me to conjure it after all, he'll have found another way. It should be dawn soon, but nothing about that sky looks as if the sunrise will come. Unless we find the last amulet and free the soul trapped inside it, the sun won't rise tomorrow. We'll be trapped in the shadows until all six witch doctors find a way to return . . .'

There was a loud crunch from the far end of the library and the group watched, open-mouthed, as the wall behind the burnt trees crumbled away. They heard the rocks smashing and tumbling down the mountainside, then the trees collapsed outwards, opening up a view across the Barbed Peaks. But the trees didn't fall off the edge of the cliff; instead, they creaked and groaned, their branches stretching out longer and longer before twisting together to form a staircase that led up into the night sky. And, at the end of the staircase, a golden door materialised in the dark.

The door opened, causing a blinding brightness to shine down, then it shut quietly, blocking out the light, and a handful of figures were left standing on the highest steps: men and women in glowing gowns and even from where Moll stood she could see the swishes of colour sparkling around their eyes and hair as white as snow.

'Oracle Spirits,' Moll whispered.

Siddy raised a hand to his mouth and from his pocket Frank squeaked. 'That's a door into the Otherworld, isn't it?'

A woman with blue and green markings around her eyes and a white fur cape draped over her shoulders broke away from the others and walked down the staircase.

'Willow,' Moll whispered.

The Oracle Spirit stepped off the branches into the library

and then stood, smiling, amid the rubble of broken stones and scorched books. 'You have done well, my friends.'

Moll looked up at the velvet night gathered above the Barbed Peaks. 'But the sun hasn't risen. We need to find the last amulet to save the old magic once and for all.'

Willow stepped forward until she was standing before the lectern that held the Ancient Book.

'The first amulet stood for courage,' she said, 'the second for friendship and the third – it stands for hope, for faith in what you cannot see.' She looked at Moll and Gryff standing side by side, then at Alfie and Siddy behind them, their clothes charred and torn. 'You kept hoping against all odds – when friends disappeared, when evil swarmed around you, when the darkness pushed you to the brink and you were forced to make unbearable decisions.' She glanced at Domino sitting on a rock with Aira and then smiled. 'The hope you clung to made Alfie real and it restored the story of the old magic.'

She lifted a hand and placed it on the Ancient Book. 'You will find the amulet on the last page, Moll. It is up to you to set the soul within it free.'

Moll frowned. 'It was there in the book all along?'

Willow nodded. 'But it was not ready to be set free until now.'

The Oracle Spirit drew back and Moll stood before the lectern with Gryff by her side, his paws raised up by the book so that he could see too. The key was still in the lock and Moll turned it before lifting the leather cover back. She flicked through the pages and pages of gold-letter script and then, finally, she turned to the last one.

Moll squinted at the book and then shook her head because there was no writing, just an image: a girl with an olive-skinned face, smeared with smoke and dirt, and, next to her, a striped fur head and two cocked ears. The last page of the Ancient Book was a mirror.

'I – I don't understand,' Moll stammered.

And then she gasped as her own reflection disappeared completely, even though she hadn't moved, leaving only the wildcat's head, gazing down with large green eyes.

'Gryff,' Moll murmured, looking up at Willow. 'Gryff is the last amulet?'

Willow's eyes grew sad. 'In Kittlerumpit's tunnels you struck a deal to save the old magic – *a feather from burning wings* for *the last page of your story*. The Ancient Book has been your story, Moll. It has been Gryff's too. But, when he drank from the raven's skull instead of you to seal the trade with the goblin, Gryff took the bargain in your place and gave the last page of *his* story, his soul, back to the old magic.' Willow put a hand on Moll's shoulder. 'Gryff was not born of this world, Moll.'

Moll wriggled free. 'He was. He's from the northern wilderness,' she whispered, staring at Gryff's reflection in the mirror. 'The Bone Murmur says so; it talks of a beast *from lands full wild.*'

Willow shook her head. 'It means the Otherworld, Moll. There the land is *fully* wild and every person has a spirit animal. Your spirit animal was Gryff and you would have met him when your time came to leave this world, but the old magic knew you would need him so it sent him to be by your side early – to protect you and to help you fight back against the Shadowmasks' magic. Now, though, it is time for Gryff to go home.'

Moll stared at the image of Gryff. She knew every marking on his face, the way his black stripes curved and then dipped around his eyes and how two more stripes ran up over his head before trailing past his ears. She blinked and a large tear splashed down on to the mirror. And then, because there were no words left to say, she held Gryff tight.

Chapter 41
A Soul That
Comes Freely

Moll crouched among the rubble with Gryff and, as she thought back to her time with him, she realised that the truth had been there all along – Moll just hadn't wanted to see it. Gryff had turned up in the forest the night her parents were killed and only the old magic could have sensed the exact moment she would need him. And then there was the day Moll had encountered Willow for the first time and Gryff had trusted her immediately, as if the wildcat shared a bond with the Oracle Spirit far beyond Moll's understanding. And the times Gryff had sensed the old magic arriving – Willow's letter back in Glendrummie and the ospreys who carried the raft – because they came from a world that he belonged to.

Moll looked down. This had been a journey to set things right for the sake of the old magic, but for Gryff it had also been a journey home. The wildcat burrowed into Moll's body, purring and pushing against her chest, and they stayed like that for a while, trying to say goodbye.

'You're free to live your life now, Moll,' Willow said. 'Free of the Shadowmasks and their dark magic, but you have to let Gryff go to stop the eternal night.'

'No,' Moll replied, her voice both frightened and fierce. 'I might be free, but I won't be happy. No matter what you say, I can't be without him. I can't give Gryff up.'

Alfie stepped forward. 'He belongs with Moll. With us.'

Siddy nodded. 'We're a Tribe and we stick together.'

Domino struggled to his feet, his body hunched in pain. 'Please, Willow. Leave Gryff with Moll. There must be another way.'

Moll could feel the wildcat's heart thudding against her own. Gryff might have had claws instead of fingers and fur instead of skin, but his heart beat to the same rhythm as hers, even though they were from two such different worlds. And Moll could read Gryff's heart now: it was filled with longing like her own. But not for golden doors perched up high or for worlds where the good went to rest. No. His heart was crying out for *her* world – for its broken beauty and for the girl who would go to the ends of the earth for the sake of her friends.

Moll clung tighter and let her tears fall as the hurt came crashing down. Then she stood up suddenly, her eyes burning, and stormed to the foot of the staircase leading into the sky.

'He won't come!' she shouted, tears streaming down her cheeks. 'You'll see. Even if the Otherworld is where he's from, Gryff won't leave me!' she sniffed. 'Because this was more than just a prophecy to him. And to me. This was *everything*.

The old magic might say he's the last amulet, but I've learnt something about stories since all this began. They don't start when you're ready! They don't go how they're meant to! And they don't finish where you'd expect!' She set her teeth. 'But, if you hope hard enough, they happen in ways you never thought possible.'

There was a long, drawn-out silence and then a chorus of voices came down from the door in the sky. 'There were three Amulets of Truth, three souls waiting to be freed.'

Moll thought of her beloved parents, somewhere beyond the golden door.

'The first two souls have arrived in the Otherworld,' the Oracle Spirits said, 'and a third soul must come to force the eternal night back and fulfil the Bone Murmur.' There was a pause. 'But the soul must come freely. The wildcat is not a tame beast and it is up to him to choose his path.'

Moll looked back at Gryff and dipped her head and he nodded back. Then she walked along the very edge of the room and sat down, her knees hugged up to her chin. She watched as Gryff picked his way through the rubble, pausing for a moment at the foot of the staircase, as if considering something. But Moll knew the wildcat's heart and she had no doubt that he would come.

Gryff padded softly across the edge of the library and sat down next to Moll. And, even though a great mountain of rock and ice slid away beneath them to nothing, Moll was not afraid – because she and her wildcat sat together, against the wind and the world and all the odds.

To Moll's surprise, it was not Willow or the Oracle Spirits who spoke next. It was Domino. Clutching his side, he limped over to Willow and whispered something in her ear. The Oracle Spirit nodded and smiled at Gryff, and Alfie and Siddy, with Frank still in his pocket, hurried over to Moll and threw their arms round her – because it was clear that Gryff was here to stay.

Willow walked towards them with Domino leaning up against her side and Aira holding his other arm, her head bowed low. The Oracle Spirit paused before the staircase and Moll stood up. She looked at Domino and saw the stain of red now streaked down his side.

'It's more than just a scratch, isn't it?' she said in a cracked whisper. Domino nodded, wincing as he took a breath, and Moll hastened over to him and clasped his hands.

'The deal I forged with Kittlerumpit . . .' Domino's voice was torn with pain and sadness. 'I traded *an early ending* for a cure to save those the Veil had poisoned. It bought me time to come after you, Moll, to show you that I'd never let you down. But it is time now. The Oracle Spirits have said a third soul must depart to force the eternal night back and that soul must come freely.'

Moll glanced at Gryff and shook her head. 'But—'

Domino smiled. 'Even if Gryff *had* gone back with Willow, I couldn't have stayed in this world, Moll.' He glanced down at his side. 'This is a wound too deep for earthly cures.' His eyes filled with tears. 'I fought as hard as I could – for the old magic, for you and for my ma and pa – to make them proud.'

He slumped down on to the staircase and Aira tried to prop him up, but he pressed her hand and then shook his head. 'Let me alone now. Just me and Moll.'

Moll leant into Domino as he wrapped his arms round her. 'You've always been a little sister to me, Moll. You know that, don't you?'

Moll swallowed again and again to fight her tears.

'Let them come,' Domino said. 'It's all right to be upset.' He kissed her forehead. 'But remember that at the end of these stairs there's a world without pain, a place where I am not afeared to go.'

'What – what will you do there?' Moll sobbed.

Domino's voice was breaking now. 'I will run with wild horses. I will stand tall on the highest mountains. And I will swim beneath thundering waterfalls.'

Moll closed her eyes and tried to think of Domino beyond the golden door – strong and smiling and full of life.

'Sometimes people leave us halfway through the journey,' Domino said and Moll sniffed as she remembered those had been Oak's words to her when Alfie vanished. 'But no one leaves for good.' He held her hand in his. 'Look after my ma and pa, Moll. They love you as fiercely as they would if you were their own blood.'

Moll's voice was nothing more than a whisper in his ear. 'I'll be seeing you,' she said. 'I know I will.'

And Domino nodded. Because Moll was someone who kept her promises. He looked up at Willow and dipped his head. 'I'm ready now.'

The Oracle Spirit dipped her head and then, very carefully, she helped Domino to his feet. Together, they walked slowly up the steps as Moll and her Tribe watched with Aira from the foot of the staircase, their faces wet with tears. Up and up they climbed, Domino's body stooped and weak, but, as they went, the sky around them began to change.

And, from behind the furthest mountain peaks, the sunrise pushed through the night, a wash of pink and orange and yellow burning through the dark. A dazzling sun burst over the horizon, scattering the mountains in light, and Moll watched as the Oracle Spirits opened the golden door to the world that held her parents. Then Domino walked inside and Moll stood with her friends, looking into the brightness of dawn.

Chapter 42
The Gathering

The giants arrived at the Rookery shortly after sunrise, whooping and cheering as they bounded over the mountains. Moll and her friends watched from the edge of the library as they gathered before the crumbled wall, then the Ancient Ones opened up their rocky palms to reveal a bundle of tartan kilts and ginger beards.

Wallop winked. 'Found some smidglings out on the Barbed Peaks who wanted to see you.'

'My Highland Watch!' Aira cried as the men stood up on the giants' fingers, raised their crossbows and roared. 'And – and Angus, Morag and the twins too! You all came after us!'

The twins held on to their parents' hands and grinned, then Petal stepped forward, the icicles in her hair jangling. She extended her enormous fingers and Moll and Siddy's faces broke into wide smiles – because inside Petal's palm was a boy with milk-white hair and jet-black eyes.

'Bruce!' Moll cried. 'What on earth are you doing here? You should be with your family!'

Bruce clung on to Petal's finger, then waved a shaky hand.

'I wanted to say swell bum to my friends!' He shook his head. 'I mean, **WELL DONE**!'

Siddy laughed. 'You are, without doubt, the best selkie we've ever met, Bruce – and now you get to meet Alfie too!'

Wallop cleared his throat. 'We'll have time for introductions later, but right now we have a journey ahead of us.'

Siddy's shoulders slumped. 'Not more Shadowmasks? Not another prophecy? Or maybe it's a second kraken or some leftover witches?'

'There's probably worse still to come,' an elderly voice from another giant's palm chirped. 'Trolls, warlocks, that kind of thing . . .'

'Murk!' Moll laughed. 'Even you've come!'

Wallop grinned. 'The dark magic is behind us now, but there's a celebration waiting to take place, down on the heath beside Tanglefern Forest, and, unless the wind spirits I sent have strayed, there are rather a lot of people hoping to welcome you all home.'

Petal huffed impatiently. 'Can I eat the selkie smidgling before we set off? I'm starving!'

'I will *not* have you munching on the guests, Petal,' Wallop growled. '*All* the smidglings here are invited to the celebration and we will carry, not devour, them to the heath. Then, when the celebrations are over, we will make our way north again, dropping loch monsters, selkies, Highland Watch and Glendrummie villagers at their homes along the way.'

Moments later, Moll and her Tribe were scooped up into Wallop's great hand and the Ancient Ones lumbered over

315

the Barbed Peaks, carrying their wards safely in their fists. And it was only then that Moll finally took it all in: they were going home – and they were going home with Alfie.

The Tribe had a lot to catch up on as they talked inside the giant's palm, but mostly they spoke of Domino and of what they would do back in their camp to remember him. On and on the giants ran and anyone who happened to stroll along the west coast of the land that day spoke of strange rumbles in the ground and enormous moving stones, but few believed these tales when they were shared, such is the way of magic glimpsed by those who do not properly understand. Even those who had witnessed the Veil's darkness wiped the events from their minds, but the people who believed in the old magic remembered and they knew that there was a deeper wonder buried in their land than what first met the eye.

Eventually the giants slowed and Moll peeked out between the cracks in Wallop's fingers to see a brilliant blue sky and a midday sun shining down on a wide expanse of gorse, heather and bracken. They had reached the heath and beyond it she could see the autumn leaves of the beeches, elms and oaks. Tanglefern Forest. They were home at last. And, when Wallop set Moll down, her feet barely touched the ground as she raced over the bracken, and rushed round the gorse bushes, into the arms of Oak and Mooshie.

All the gypsies from Oak's camp had come – Cinderella Bull wrapped in her gold-penny shawl, Hard-Times Bob with his pipe and accordion, Siddy's ma and all her purple petticoats – and there were others, too, friends whom Moll had not expected to see again. Willow, now bright and clear with a voice as strong as the wildest wind, was speaking with Puddle, the lighthouse keeper who had sheltered them from the smugglers! And little Scrap, Barbarous Grudge's daughter who had led the Tribe to the second amulet and who now lived with Puddle, was rushing between the giants' legs to see her friends again! Even Hermit, as terrified as ever, and Porridge the Second, as miserable as ever, had been brought along for the occasion.

There were tears in the hours that followed, but there was laughter, too, and those who passed the heath that afternoon would have seen eleven large plinths of stone rising up in a circle and might have assumed that the rocks were an ancient landmark that they had missed before, but inside the ring of giants there was a celebration going on.

It was only when the sun set that the giants called for quiet. The gypsies and all the friends the Tribe had made along their journey sat on the ground and in the middle of the circle, on top of a tree stump, lay the Ancient Book, its golden story glittering in the light of candles that the gypsies held. Nobody spoke. Only a nightjar cried, somewhere out on the heath, then, into this stillness, the Ancient Ones began to sing – a low, lilting tune that Moll imagined rivers might make if they could speak.

'Arise young girl and close the book
The story is told and victory took.
Fire the arrow and the key
Into the night as we bow to thee.'

317

Wallop looked across at Moll and nodded. And, with the giants' song still ringing in her ears, Moll stood up from her place between Alfie and Siddy and, together with Gryff, she walked towards the Ancient Book. As Wallop had instructed her, she reached over and heaved the book shut before looking down at Gryff who dipped his head towards the key hanging on a string around her neck. Moll slotted the key into the padlock and turned it until it clicked, then Alfie stood up with the Oracle Arrow in his hands and Siddy came forward, clutching Moll's bow. The boys walked out quietly into the clearing, then they helped Moll bind the key to the side of the arrow by winding the piano string round and round it and then tying it in a knot. Then Moll set the arrow to her bow and pulled back.

She thought of all the other times she had fired this arrow: to scale the Stone Necklace, to strike her own friend, to kill Wormhook – and then, putting everything out of her mind, Moll closed one eye and looked up into the sky. There were no stars yet – just a sheet of black arching over the heath – but now the night didn't frighten her because she knew that the sun would rise the next day and the day after that and all the days that followed. She looked at her Tribe, at the wildcat and the two boys who had fought alongside her every step of the way, then she pulled back on her bow and fired.

The arrow soared out – fast and sure – but this time Moll knew it would not fall down again. Because the Ancient Book was closed, the story was safe inside it and the old magic had, at last, been restored. The arrow sailed on and, as it vanished into the darkness, thousands of stars pricked through the night sky, burning like a maze of golden footprints. And when Moll, Gryff, Siddy and Alfie turned to face the giants they saw that they, and all the people gathered around them, had stooped to one knee. They were bowing to the Tribe – and, as the stars glimmered above them, Moll, Gryff, Siddy and Alfie looked at one another and smiled.

'We did it,' Moll whispered, running a hand over Gryff's head. 'We beat the dark magic.'

Frank did a somersault from Siddy's pocket and Alfie grinned. Then the giants rose up to their full height and, as the gathering broke into cheers and clapping, Moll and her Tribe laughed.

Amid the applause, Willow stepped forward and clasped Moll's hands. 'Some day – many years from now – I will see you again, Moll. And when you and Gryff set foot in the Otherland there will be family and friends waiting for you with open arms.'

Moll felt her heart quicken at the thought of seeing her parents and Domino again.

'But, until that day, remember your journey,' Willow said. 'Remember the amulets that stood for courage, friendship and hope so that when you feel like the world is against you and you cannot find your way, you can dig down to that quiet grit buried in your soul. You have a fight that is unconquerable, Moll, and you will always have the old magic on your side, no matter what may happen.'

Willow withdrew her hands and raised her arms to the

sky, twisting her fingers and wrists. A large golden shape floated down from the darkness and dropped into the circle of giants before changing into a table the length of the gathering, surrounded by chairs. On it sat goblets filled with sparkling liquids and platters laden with meats, vegetables and exotic fruits. There were bowls of chocolates, too, and plates and cutlery that glittered gold. Even Murk looked impressed. Then the whole gathering rushed to take a seat at the magical banquet, and Willow smiled one last time before floating upwards and disappearing into the night.

The festivities went on for hours, with Scrap at the end of the table teaching Bruce how to use a knife and fork, then Moll next to them, one arm slung round Alfie's shoulders, the other hanging down to slip food to Gryff beneath the table. Then there was Siddy on Alfie's other side trying to muscle in with the Highland Watch and Puddle demanding dance after dance with Aira while Hard-Times Bob played tunes on his accordion.

The gathering ate, drank, sang and danced together until, eventually, the giants broke their circle and scooped up those whose homes lay beyond the knotted branches of Tanglefern Forest. Moll watched, tucked beneath Oak's and Mooshie's arms, as the Ancient Ones bounded off into the dawn, their hands clasped tightly around Puddle, Scrap, Bruce, Murk, the Highland Watch and Angus' family. Then she turned towards the forest and, hand in hand with Oak and Mooshie, Moll walked through the trees towards her wagon in the woods.

Epilogue
Tanglefern Forest

Deep within Tanglefern Forest there is a clearing framed by ancient oaks. Snow lies plump and fresh on the branches, almost completely covering the balls of mistletoe in the upmost boughs and the dreamcatchers that hang below. Small children wrapped in duffle coats and scarves busy themselves inside the ring of colourful wagons: a girl with a red headscarf stands on tiptoe on the steps of her home to hang a stocking from the bowtop roof; a young boy places good luck omens – lemon peel, horseshoe nails and fragments of mirror – along the ledges of a green wagon; others scoop up handfuls of snow and hurl them across the fire.

It is a cold, crisp afternoon, but these are not people who need to huddle inside. They are men, women and children of the forest – their skin stained by campfire smoke and dirt, their faces lined and pitted from a lifetime of meals eaten out in the open air and nights slept tucked beneath trees.

Cinderella Bull sits on her wagon steps, bundled in blankets and holding her crystal ball with ringed fingers before Siddy's ma. Mooshie, a dozen tea towels tucked into her pinafore, perches on the steps of the wagon next door, twisting holly leaves and berries into a wreath. Beside her, in a battered old armchair he's hauled out into the snow, is Hard-Times Bob. Bent double like a hairpin, he tries to squeeze his wizened body through the hole of another wreath to entertain the camp's youngest children while Oak lays a small plate of gingerbread behind his wagon, a gift for the soul of the son he lost.

There will be lanterns glowing from the branches of the trees later and music – fiddles, accordions, pan flutes – round the fire. It is Christmas Eve in the forest and the camp is getting ready to celebrate. But beyond the ring of Sacred Oaks, past the cobs grazing on the piles of hay and down the path that winds through the elms and beeches, there is a glade filled with yew trees. And halfway up the oldest yew, notoriously hard to get to but there all the same, are slats of wood hammered into gnarled branches. A wildcat is curled on a bough beneath the tree fort, its striped fur dusted with snow, and up inside the hideout three people have gathered.

Moll lets her eyes wander over the shelves lined with jam jars. Inside those are the Tribe's Forest Secrets – including unusual fir cones, giant nettles, owl pellets and woodpecker feathers. Looking at them now, Moll can't help thinking of all the other treasures they found on their journey: amulets, golden feathers, arrows at the bottom of lochs and ancient books guarded by giants ... She glances at Alfie who is carving something into the slats of wood above the door, then at Siddy who is trying to get Frank to meet his earthworm, Porridge the Second.

'Do you think any of this will seem normal after what we've seen?' Moll asks.

The others look up. Only a few weeks before they had been standing at the very edge of a monastery perched between peaks and clouds. Moll listens to the high-pitched cry of a kestrel outside and for a moment thinks it strange that ears that have picked up the sounds of a witch's song and a kraken's roar are now tuned to the calls of woodland birds.

Siddy cuddles Frank to his chest. 'It all seems smaller, doesn't it?'

Moll nods, then she runs a thumb down the carving of a seal pup on the handle of her catapult. 'Like we've lived our lives already.'

Alfie picks up the steaming mug of tea Mooshie has made for them: spiced cinnamon with rosehips and blackberry leaves. He takes a sip and smiles. 'But there's Christmas,' he says quietly. 'And stockings and snowmen and feasts inside the clearing.' He looks from Moll to Siddy. 'I've never had a Christmas before.' He pauses. 'I've never had friends or a proper family before. So, even though we've fought marsh spirits and gargoyles, I think our greatest adventures are still to be had.'

Siddy smiles. 'We could go sledging down the hill on the heath.'

Moll grins. 'And have snowball fights down in the glade.'

'Ice skating on the lake in the Deepwood?' Alfie asks.

'There's a lot we've still to see and do,' Siddy says. He plops his earthworm into a cardboard box he's filled with soil, then moves towards the door with Frank perched on his shoulder. 'Come on. If we go now, we'll get first grab at Mooshie's cranberry muffins.'

Alfie and Siddy clamber out of the tree fort until it is just Moll left inside and for a moment she stays where she is, her eyes fixed on the word Alfie has carved into the slat above the door. *Domino*. It's only a name and yet that person sacrificed himself freely so that Gryff could stay in her world.

'Run with wild horses,' Moll whispers. 'Stand tall on the highest mountains. Swim beneath thundering waterfalls.'

She climbs out into the yew tree. Alfie and Siddy are already down in the glade, but Gryff is still there, waiting for her, his green eyes wide against the snowy boughs. He stands up, claws gripping hard into the bark, then he dips his head and together the girl and the wildcat weave through the branches to join their friends below.

Acknowledgements

When I was little I used to have a list of my favourite words. Among them were: *goblin, whisper, bubble, silver*. And now I would like to add another word to that list: *trilogy*. Because I had thought that that word belonged exclusively to people like Philip Pullman and Cornelia Funke but with *The Night Spinner* out in the world, I get to have a little trilogy behind my name now, too. And that wouldn't have happened if hadn't been for the support of many brilliant people.

Writing this book was like going back and becoming twelve years old again. I was lucky enough to grow up in the wilds of Scotland where weekends were spent scrambling over the moors, jumping into icy rivers and building dens in the woods and I want to thank my incredible parents – Lucy and Charles – for giving me this childhood. You allowed me the space and freedom to play outside and the memories I found there not only built the foundations for this book but they stamped a sense of wonder on my soul. Thank you also to my siblings – Will, Tom and Charis, and my Angus Girls – for all the adventures we had together up north. So much of the world in this book has been drawn from my childhood in Angus: Glendrummie is based on Edzell, the nearest village to the house I grew up in; The North Door is really The Blue Door which marks the start of one of my favourite walks beside the North Esk River, which became The Clattering Gorge in my book; the folly Moll, Sid and Gryff find there is actually the based on Doulie Tower that sits above the North Esk River. And so it goes on.

Thank you to the talented team at Simon & Schuster for all their hard work and in particular to my wonderful editor, Jane Griffiths, and PR and Marketing gurus, Hannah Cooper and Liz Binks. Thomas Flintham and Jenny Richards have done another superb job on the cover and the map – thank you – and Jane Tait, your copy edit was hugely helpful. Thank you also to my fantastic agent, Hannah Sheppard, for your continued support and wise advice along the way.

My friends have been an unbelievable support and I want to thank one or two of them, in particular, for their direct help in shaping the book. Thank you, Rebecca Fletcher, for naming Wallop, thank you, James Jardine Paterson, for naming Spud (and swimming across Loch Duich with me, which later became Loch Murk), thank you, Rowena and Jules Osborne, for the amazing week up at Druidaig which saw my Lost Isles come to life, thank you, Paddy Stanton, for letting me write a big chunk of this book at your house in Norfolk and thank you, Humphrey Aird, for telling me what noises ferrets make (Frank was really grateful for that).

Thank you to the amazing teachers, librarians and

booksellers who have championed my writing from the start, and to the awesome children who have read and loved the books. Lena Hadley, thank you for the idea of using mirrors and cages down in Kittlerumpit's tunnels, Flossie Forbes, thank you for allowing me to pinch your brilliant shop, Bel's Butchers in Edzell, and pop it into my book and Catherine Arecco, I know one day you will become an author, too.

My last thank you goes to my husband, Edo, who I met on a hay bale when I was twelve – and while Moll, Sid, Alfie and Gryff started their Tribe at that age, Edo and I took a few more years to kick our adventures off. But we made up for lost time with plenty of escapades in northern wildernesses, all of them worthy of the Tribe's antics in this book: climbing mountains in Aberdeenshire, swimming in fairy pools on Skye, watching killer whales off the Lofoten Islands and dog-sledding across the Arctic. Thank you for being such an exciting, positive and kind person to live alongside. As I always say, Edo, you are a very wonderful human being.

Get ready for an adventure in the polar north.

In the kingdom of Erkenwald, whales glide between icebergs, wolves hunt on the tundra and polar bears roam the glaciers. But the people of the north aren't so easy to find. Because this is a land ruled by the Ice Queen.

Summoned from deep inside the ice, she has imprisoned every man and every woman in the towers at Winterfang Palace. She wants the children, too, but they are in hiding. And even when they hear the voices of their parents singing from the palace at night, they do not emerge. Because they know about the Ice Queen's anthem. They know that she is collecting voices and when she owns every single one in Erkenwald, her song will be complete and the rest of the dark spirits locked inside the ice will rise up.

Join Eska, a girl who breaks free from a cursed music box, and Flint, a boy whose inventions could change the fate of Erkenwald forever, as they journey to the Never Cliffs and beyond in search of a long lost voice with the power to force the Ice Queen back. This is a story about an eagle huntress, an inventor and an organ made of icicles. But it is also a story about belonging, even at the very edges of our world . . .

I start every story I write with an adventure. *The DreamSnatcher* trilogy saw me carving catapults in the forest, abseiling into jungle caves and scaling mountains in Scotland. But for this book, I went further afield to find my story. I went to the Arctic and up to the Lofoten islands. I watched killer whales dive for herring and I glimpsed the northern lights rippling across the sky. This was a land shrouded in silence and locked in darkness – the sun doesn't rise at all in the winter months – but if I really listened, I could hear the place whispering: the crack and pop of ice, the underwater clicks of the killer whales and the whir of ptarmigan wings over mountain peaks. And eventually, the idea of a kingdom ruled by an enchanted anthem wandered into my head.

Finding a heroine for this story was easy. When I was trawling through photos of remote tribes on the internet, I came across the Kazakh Eagle Hunters, a formidable group of people out in the wilds of Mongolia who tame golden eagles and use them to hunt foxes, wolves and marmots. It is an ancient tradition handed down through generations but what struck me most was that almost every single person in the tribe was male. Then I read about twelve-year-old Aisholpan, one of the only eagle huntresses, and I knew then that I had my heroine. Many emails and months later, I found myself trekking through Mongolia's snow-capped mountains to find her. I learnt about sheep's ankle bones used in children's games, I discovered wolf fangs decorated with silver and I learnt to hunt with Balapan, Aisholpan's golden eagle. All of this has found its way into the book, along with an inventor boy who keeps an Arctic fox pup in the hood of his jacket, because as I say when I visit schools and speak at literary festivals, authors aren't necessarily the cleverest people in the class; they're the most curious, the ones who say yes to adventures and go after the stories no one else has stumbled across yet.

About the author

Abi Elphinstone grew up in Scotland where she spent most of her childhood building dens, hiding in tree houses and running wild across highland glens. After being coaxed out of her tree house, she studied English at Bristol University and then worked as a teacher in Africa, Berkshire and London. She is the author of *The Unmapped Chronicles*, *Sky Song* and *The Dreamsnatcher Trilogy*. When she's not writing, Abi volunteers for Beanstalk charity, speaks in schools and travels the world – from the Arctic Circle to the mountains of Mongolia – looking for her next story.

You can find more about Abi at www.abielphinstone.com or follow her on social media:

Facebook: www.facebook.com/abi.elphinstone;
Twitter: @moontrug;
Instagram: @moontrugger